Forbidden
Desires

MADHURI
Banerjee

RUPA

Published by
Rupa Publications India Pvt. Ltd 2016
7/16, Ansari Road, Daryaganj
New Delhi 110002

Sales centres:
Allahabad Bengaluru Chennai
Hyderabad Jaipur Kathmandu
Kolkata Mumbai

ISBN: 978-81-291-3730-2

10 9 8 7 6 5 4 3 2 1

First impression 2016

The moral right of the author has been asserted.

Typeset by SÜRYA, New Delhi
Printed in India by Nutech Print Services

Ariaana—For being the only Princess in the world for me. You make me so proud every day. Never change who you are. You are perfect for me.

Bala—For choosing to be in my life every day with all my 'nakhras'. Love you forever.

Kiran—For showing me new perspectives and giving me strength every day. Grateful.

Prerna—For thinking beyond and loving me no matter what. Humbled.

Tanveer—For your creative ideas and everlasting dramatic scenes. Truly thankful.

Mom—For 'Like'-ing everything I post on Facebook and trying to understand me better. You are my backbone. Xoxo.

NAINA

1

Naina: Born and brought up in London to Punjabi parents. Smart as paint with an Honours degree in English Literature. Uber cool. Supremely sexy. High exotic cheek bones over her porcelain white skin. Sparkling brown eyes. Long, dark brown hair. Model features but more sophisticated, with curves. 34 DD chest. Takes oomph to another level. Excellent cook.

Met Kaushik, her husband, in London. In a bus. They both went for the same seat. 'Ladies first,' he had said. She was playful that day, 'No no, it's reserved for the elderly.' It was instant attraction. They decided not to sit. Chatted for hours in a coffee shop. Till the rains came and went. It was love at first sight. A well-meaning friend would later try to warn Naina, 'Men who fall in love so quickly fall out of it just as quickly.' By then the advice had come too late; Naina was in love, she didn't care: the chemistry was electrifying. The first thing she noticed about him was his hands ('love those fingers in my hair…pulling me back hard…') He was captivated by her no-nonsense attitude. Her drive to succeed. Her gorgeous breasts.

'Ask me a dirty question,' she had brushed her foot against his leg at the coffee shop on their first date. That had immediately given him a hard on. He'd never met an Indian woman like this. *She was different from most Indian women he had ever met*. Probably because they were all so homely. This one? This one was challenging.

'How long does a shag last?'

Without blinking she had answered as if it was most natural for two strangers to talk this way, '10 to 20 minutes. You?'

'About 40 minutes.'

'Liar.'

An hour later he would prove he wasn't a liar. They went to his place and she didn't leave till the next morning. He was right. Forty minutes.

Six months later, they were married.

Naina's parents loved Kaushik. They couldn't have arranged it better if they had put an ad in the matrimonial papers. Tall, good-looking, cultured, studying to become a lawyer. Enamored by their daughter. Born of cultured Bengali parents who lived in Chittranjan Park. Soft spoken. A family man. Perfect.

But Kaushik's parents were apprehensive about her Punjabi background. 'Too much rowdiness don't you think, Kaushik?'

'Oh yes,' Kaushik had replied. 'But I like it like that.' They gave in. He was their only son and they wanted him to be happy.

Kaushik and Naina couldn't keep their hands off each other. They would find ways to meet up in the middle of the day for a quick shag. They worked round the clock at their jobs. Both were passionate about their careers. He loved that about her: a woman as driven as him made him wild with pleasure.

They would drink at bars and dance the night away only to go back to work in the morning. London allowed them to do that. The city demanded more out of you. Their love gave them that stamina.

As soon as they got married she moved into his apartment in Soho, giving up the rented place which she shared with a roommate. She wasn't homely at all except for the cooking. She made elaborate dinners for Kaushik, fattening him up with her food and her love.

After six months of marital bliss, she was pregnant. She held the pregnancy stick, leaning against the bathroom sink, staring at the clear, two lines, 'Fuck! How could this be?' They were so sure they were doing the withdrawal method properly! It was too soon for them to have a child.

They discussed if they should keep the baby. 'I'd like to spend more time with you,' Kaushik had said. But what else could he say? It was her body, after all. And he did want to be a father at some point. He was hoping, though, that it didn't happen now.

'I still want to work,' Naina had disclosed, unsure, a train of thoughts trailing behind what she spoke.

But then they went for their first sonography, and they heard the baby's heartbeat. So fast! And alive! That's when they knew they were ready to have a baby.

They moved back to Delhi. Both their parents were there; it would be easier to take care of a child. He got a job with an international law firm in New Delhi. At first Naina was hesitant to leave London and her career. But with a little convincing from her parents that she could soon find a job in India and manage a child, she was eager to come back home.

Her parents were happy. They didn't like her working in London anyway. They always said she didn't come down to visit often enough. She would always say she couldn't afford to take leave from work, getting only two weeks off in a year. 'I'm a chef at Four Seasons, Ma,' Naina would remind them. 'Someday I'll bring you here and you'll see for yourself how packed we are and how busy I am all the time.'

Her parents didn't have to worry once they were in Delhi. They saw her all the time. A little too much for Kaushik's liking, though. 'Please don't make me go to their house again,' he would plead ever so often. She had her complaints too: she was tired of all the Bengali food at his parents' place, to start with. 'I want to stay at home and have pizza, Kaushik,' she would whine. 'I can't have fish curry-rice again for Sunday lunch!'

Soon their daughter, whom they would name Shonali, was born. A year later Shiuli came. Naina cursed herself for being so fertile. Things began to change between Naina and Kaushik; their new life unraveled. Dirty nappies replaced dirty talk. Sleeping replaced shagging. Love replaced lust. Conversation dwindled, caring increased.

Naina slowly lost her friends from London and the old ones from Delhi—who were still single, clueless and intolerant about conversations of cracked nipples and postpartum depression. It was too much for them. 'Babe, where's the Naina who used to dance on bar counters and rub against strange men?'

But Naina liked being a mother. Sleepless nights and body changes notwithstanding, she wanted to be the best mother she could be to her two girls. She used to think she didn't have it in her to be nurturing; yet here she was, turning into a fierce, protective caretaker of her children. A biological instinct was evoked and Naina became more soft, caring and gentle. She listened more, read more. She even started doing laundry!

The wild Naina was tamed. Sex took a back seat. Who had the time? And her body changed. Her moods affected her. As her friend had warned, Kaushik's love faded and they grew apart. It took only five years but it happened. Couples stay together for the sake of their children. Never for the sake of the love that brought them together. Too often even the memories of the love fade away. Or the demand for it to return brings with it a burden. Couples easily move into new roles as parents, or some 'in-law' to someone in the family. People flood their lives. It pushes the love towards the back.

Naina tried to get Kaushik to love her again. But he was so busy with work that he forgot what it meant to be passionate for her at all. She tried every trick in the book but often enough she was tired. Motherhood was too damn tiring. Two small children who constantly needed her attention and her milk. It left her body depleted. And when a woman stops giving her body to her husband, the husband finds a way to stop giving his time to his wife.

After five years of looking after two children, Naina started working again. She gave cooking classes to batches of four people every alternate weekday, for six weeks at a stretch. It gave her the opportunity to pursue her passion and still be able to have the time to fulfill her other duties, like picking up her children from school. She eventually found a group of mothers with whom she was comfortable, and they met every Monday for lunch that lasted several hours. They kept in touch often and formed a WhatsApp group. All this gave her some relief, though sometimes she found their lifestyle to be very alien to hers.

These new friends of Naina's organized parties that were so elaborate. Their clothes were always designer. They travelled abroad for vacations and called celebrities to their homes for musical evenings. As much as she wanted to fit in with the South Delhi crowd, Naina couldn't. Sure, they loved her British accent, but there were things about her they didn't relate to: she was cautious with her money, she didn't flaunt her possessions like they did. She knew the value of money, having worked hard all her professional life in London and having the sense to save. She couldn't join them for all their outings to eat out or shop for new bags as often as she liked. Still she made an effort, as these shallow activities stopped her loneliness. Sometimes.

She devoted herself to her cooking classes. In one of the batches, she met a producer of a TV channel who encouraged her to audition for the Masterchef competition. She did, and she got in, and eventually she won the title. It was grueling but she proved to herself and to Kaushik that the fire within her had not died. Everyone was so proud of her Masterchef stint. Kaushik threw her a party the evening that she won the title. Everyone said she should just cater her party herself. She had fun that night. It would be the last time Kaushik did anything nice for her.

She soon realized that he did nice things only when people were around to see what a good husband he was and how lucky she was to have him. It made her blood boil sometimes when he refused to lift a finger when she asked him for help but would do the same thing when her parents were visiting. They couldn't understand why she complained about him; soon she stopped.

'You've had a love marriage, Naina. Now make it work!' her mother had told her. They were conservative Punjabi parents who lived in Karol Bagh. They had a mundane existence and barely understood their daughter. Her need to cook for a competition, her need to live abroad, her supposed wild ways were alien to them. They loved her but never understood her.

For sure, though, they were proud when she became famous. Since that day, life became hectic. The kids needed to go to school and she had work to do. Her WhatsApp group helped her whenever they could. But they missed her being around to gossip with them. Her parents came more often to look after the children. She began to work on a cookbook and started her own cookery show on a channel.

In the midst of all this madness, Kaushik and Naina's marriage took even more of a back seat. Their conversations dwindled to, 'Will you be home for dinner?' While he encouraged her to live out her dreams, his actions did not back his rhetoric; he wasn't supportive enough to look after their small kids in her absence. A part of her resented him for not taking a step back from his own work when her career was taking off. Why did she always have to make the sacrifices? It was fine for Kaushik to imply, 'I will love you as you earn a handsome income while I sit at home and look after the kids.' But when the time came to live up to his words, Kaushik had always felt that this was nothing more than a temporary arrangement in Naina's life and therefore he shouldn't give up his own career. What would society say, after all? His ego would take a huge blow.

Eventually, Naina took a step back. Even though she was outstanding—less than seven years of working in Delhi since she moved from London, and she had already reached the heights where she was—and she was being given more offers, she stepped back. She went back to giving cooking classes at home. And even though her parents told her to continue with her TV shows and travelling around the world to cook with renowned chefs, she wanted to be there with her children. She needed them to know their parents hadn't abandoned them.

'They're in good hands, Naina,' Kaushik told her once, impatiently. 'They are your parents, for God's sake. And I take them to my parents' house on the weekends when I'm free and they visit here when they're free. We can focus on our careers. That's what we wanted in life anyway. That's why we moved from London, wasn't it?'

Yes! That was what she had wanted once upon a time. But she had changed. And Kaushik hadn't. Could that be the reason why marriages fall apart? Naina didn't want her small girls not to have their parents around. She appreciated having help from both sets of grandparents but, like all grandmothers and grandfathers do, they tended to give the girls everything that they want. She didn't want her girls to end up spoiled.

So she gave up a flourishing career. Because Kaushik wouldn't. 'I'm going to be made a partner in the firm soon,' he said to her. 'I need to put in the hours.' He worked with Mukherjee & Partners, an extremely prestigious law firm with an international base and high-profile clients. 'This was my dream. Please don't expect me to be there for the kids. There are enough people looking after them. That's why we're in Delhi and not in the U.S.A. or London, where my work is better. I've made the sacrifice. Don't expect more.' He was matter of fact and clear. He had no time for his family right now; he would spend time with his daughters when he needed a break. Not when they needed him.

Naina needed to be there for them. And so she pulled herself away from Kaushik. And he plunged himself deeper into work. More than mutual respect, marriages are about sharing your daily life, understanding each other's dreams and supporting them. Naina knew they had stopped doing that. If marriage was about surrendering your desires to make the other person happy and then loving the person for what they become, rather than hoping they'll change back to what they were—then sadly, Naina and Kaushik did the exact opposite.

Kaushik stopped speaking about his work and Naina stopped asking him. If he wanted to speak about his projects, he should have when she made time for him every evening. But he was always late from work. Kaushik was unlike other Bengali men, Naina knew. He was driven. Motivated. She loved that about him. And suddenly she didn't when she wanted him to be as motivated to spend time with his children. He missed concerts, ballet recitals, parent teacher associations. She had to make up. Her children were too small to really miss their father. They had enough people in their life. But she missed them being a family.

The last two years had been tough on their marriage. With his constant travelling and her career taking off, they barely had time together.

'Do you feel we had a better life in London, Kaushik?' she asked one night when he was at home and they had some free time.

'Yes. But we were younger then. Without kids. Broke.'

'Do you regret me getting pregnant so fast?'

He was quiet. 'I love our daughters. I just wish I had more time with you before they came.'

'I didn't think I was so fertile, you know!' She didn't mention it was his fault. His not using the condom the first time, and again the second time. 'Can't feel you,' was his stupid excuse.

'I know. It's okay. We have money.' He went to sleep. Was that the solution to everything? Money? She looked at the clock on her bed side table. It read 12:15.

She whispered to Kaushik, 'Happy anniversary.'

He didn't hear it. He was fast asleep. Naina stared at the ceiling and crossed her hands under her head. Eight years. Where did they go? Eight years ago they would have been making out in a bathroom of the restaurant where they would have celebrated their anniversary, their hands all over each other, not wanting to wait to get home to make love. And now they sleep on opposite corners of the bed.

She turned to him and held him while he lightly snored. She whispered light enough to wake him but not enough to disturb him, 'Forty minutes. Liar.'

He mumbled back, 'Go to sleep, Naina.'

Yes, things change. No matter how much Naina wanted to hold on to the past, the future had come at her with such force that it threw her present into disarray.

2

'Bhaiya, yeh kya hai?'

'Madam, this is chicken fricassee.'

'Isme gravy shavy toh hai nahin?'

'No madam, this is a French dish. It's lightly steamed with herbs.'

'Herbs ki aisi taisi. I don't want to eat this. How bland yaar! Naina! Usko bol yaar, isko theek karne ke liye.'

Naina was out at her kitty party lunch in a new French restaurant that all the girls wanted to try out. Once a week she met a group of women who were fellow mothers in her daughter's school and had become friends from the time their firstborns went to play school. Since then they were in a WhatsApp group together and they met once a week to go to new restaurants, eat and chat. Naina thought this was a good way to catch up with her friends and get to see what kind of cuisine was working in Delhi. Clearly French was not a favourite with Punjabi women who wanted 'gravy shavy'.

'Simran, this is going to be bland. You ordered it.'

'Main nahin kha rahi hoon. You tell them to make your French chicken. I like it just the way you make it.'

Naina laughed. She had had her friends over a few weeks earlier at her place where she had cooked all the recipes from her new book. She wanted to test her recipes out to see if they would make the cut in the book. However, she had added an

Indian touch to all the international recipes so that Indian families could enjoy them given their spicy palate.

'Arrey that was my own recipe. Ab kya boloon usko?'

'Usko bata na!' Simran said with a grumpy face. 'Bhaiyaji tabasco sauce le ao.'

'Madam,' the waiter, speaking in perfect English, replied, 'We don't stock tabasco in our pantry. The chefs would like you to try the authentic French cuisine here and not add anything extra to it. Otherwise you won't get the flavour.'

'Yeh leh! Tabasco bhi nahi rakhta. Kitni mehngi dish mein koi flavour hi nahin hai. How am I supposed to get the flavour, dear, if there is no flavour in it?' Simran said to the waiter, trying to keep calm as her blood boiled.

Naina immediately came to the rescue. 'Tu meri dish kha le. Take this. It's better than that.' Naina didn't know when she had become a Delhi-ite. It was a state of being, she guessed. She had successfully moulded herself from being a Londoner to a total Dilliwala. It crept in, slowly but surely. In the way she spoke to the servants, the autowalas, the vegetable vendors. The culture of Delhi was completely different from any other part of the world. It was unique, interesting and completely entertaining. And only a woman knew how it was different from any other part of the world. Because when you were with other friends from Delhi, you became exactly like them!

They switched their plates. Simran took a bite out of Naina's order and was happy with the food. 'Chal theek hai. You're so sweet yaar. Waiterji please keep some chilli flakes at least. What is this? Aapki restaurant nahin chalne wali hai!'

'Madam, our waiting list is full until November,' the waiter said in reply. 'For every evening.'

Simran dismissed him. 'Haan haan. Bada big shot ho gaya restaurant. We are not coming back here. Pandara Road food is better than this bland nonsense!'

The other women giggled when the waiter left.

'Simran, tu bhi na. Kaisey flirt kar rahi thi waiter ke saath!' Ishita said.

Simran blushed, 'No yaar! What are you saying! Please, that's not flirting. You come to my son's birthday party next week na. I'll show you what flirting is. There is this handsome father jo aata hai apni patni ke bina. I like him a lot! Main toh uske saath chipak jaati hoon.'

'Hai rabba! Simran!' Ishita said, 'Naina, please explain to her not to do these things. I love my husband. I can't imagine having an affair.'

'Yeah me neither,' Simran clarified. 'But flirt karne mein kya jaata hai. Keeps the spark alive. My husband sees me flirting and he gets so jealous. Main bata nahin sakti hoon. He goes home and...,' Simran dissolved into giggles and said, 'Chal chodh!' All the girls had a unison of 'Ai hai!' And then they dissolved into their own stories of what aroused their husbands. All except Naina. She hadn't been able to arouse Kaushik for quite some time now. For a man who couldn't keep his hands off her not too many years back, he now refused to touch her even once a week.

But Naina smiled and asked for details from her friends who were only too happy to give her some. She felt important with her friends. As much as she felt she wasn't needed by Kaushik, she felt that much more relevant in her friends' lives. Even though she had been busy with her career for some time, they had always called to check on her. These friends had been her support system when the crazy days of Masterchef had given her no time with family.

They had picked up her children and taken them on play dates and dropped them back. They had taken them to birthday parties when her parents weren't around or when Kaushik was busy. They had called her to ask if she was doing well on the days she was tired and posted on her WhatsApp group that her body was hurting from too much work. They supported her decision to work and supported it even more when she decided to take a little break and not start her own restaurant or do too much. They were happy when she conducted cooking classes because then they got to come over and eat the leftovers in the evening. They were loving and supportive and Naina knew they were her best friends. They didn't pry into her life too much. They knew she did her own thing.

But they weren't like her. Naina was different. She was wild and ambitious and motivated. She wanted to be more than a mother and wife. She wanted to be perfect. And she wanted to find the balance between both. And because she wanted to be perfect, she faltered. She only had that much time in the day to either be with her children or be a world-class chef. She was an extremist. She could not find the balance in her life. She couldn't have it all. She needed to choose and every day the choices she took killed her. Because she felt she should have made the other choice instead.

These women were simpler. They loved being housewives. They loved their husbands to death. Yes, they complained about them bitterly but they were proud of their husbands. They didn't need them to do more than what they were doing. And they were happy spending their husbands' money. Naina wanted to earn and support her children and herself. She felt proud if she could buy things for herself with her own money. There was a sense of accomplishment in that.

Once Naina had asked, 'Don't you want some emotional support from your husband? Some loving? Some conversation?'

And they had answered to the effect, 'Why? We get sex once a week at least. And they give us money for our vacations and house renovations and whatever we need to buy. For conversations, we have all of you!'

Simran had clarified it to her, 'Dekh simple si baat hai. I don't want to slog. My parents wanted me to get married and have kids and I've done that. Aur Gurmeet aur main bohat khush hain. We do talk. He tells me about his business and I listen to him. And when he wants me to be home, I'm at home. When he wants food, I make sure it's there. And when he wants sex, I spread my legs. Haan haan. You will say it's gross. But that's the role of a wife. And that's what makes a happy marriage. This is what is bonding. Iss sey zyada aur kya chahiye?'

And that's the way it was. Girls were meant to have conversations with. Husbands were meant to be an anchor. So they wouldn't have to work. They could live a good life and look after the children. Their roles were set.

Naina was confused. A part of her wanted what she and Kaushik had in the old days. And a part wanted him to take a step back from work so she could take a step forward in her career. She had thought that she was at peace with her decision to take a step back in her own career, but lately she had been feeling that she still wanted to pursue her career. This not finding a balance in her life was eating her up inside. She took out her phone and made a call to Kaushik and stepped away from the table when he picked up.

'Hello. Kaushik. Hi. What time will you be coming home?'

'Late. Why?' he answered tersely.

'It's our anniversary.'

There was silence at the other end. 'Okay. I'll come home by seven.'

Naina wanted to scream back at the receiver, 'Don't do me any favours!' Instead she replied, 'Mummy Papa have organized a celebration at Def Col. There's a new place that's opened there. Punjab Grill.'

'Ooff Naina. I hate those Punjabi places!'

Naina bit her lip before responding in a softer tone, 'They've already called a lot of people, Kaushik. Your parents are also coming. I'll send you the details.'

She could hear the exasperation in his voice, 'Okay fine.' And he hung up. Naina blinked back the tears. He hadn't asked who would take the girls, how she would go, if he wanted him to pick her up, what present she wanted for their anniversary. He hadn't even wished her that morning. She was glad this lunch had been there to ease her mind from the stress of this marriage and their anniversary. But she could no longer keep up the pretence. While all her friends spoke about their perfect marriages, Naina didn't feel like sharing or participating in the conversation anymore.

'Suno main ja rahi hoon,' Naina said as she came back to the table.

'Kyon,' a chorus rose up from all the ten women who were sitting and chatting.

'Because it's been three hours since we got here and mujhe bohat kaam hai.' Naina said as she took out money from her wallet.

'Kya kaam hai!' the chorus started again.

Simran said to everyone, 'Arrey uski anniversary hai. She probably wants to go back home before the children come. Her husband must be waiting in bed for her. Hai na?' She winked at Naina as if she had shared a secret with her.

Naina just smiled and didn't confirm anything while she came around the table to give each of them an air kiss on the cheek before she left. 'I'll see you guys next week. Love you, babes!'

She knew she couldn't give too many explanations otherwise they would all come up with more excuses for her to stay. She needed to get away. She needed a different perspective.

As soon as she went outside she called her driver, 'Guptaji aap kahan ho? What? Oh no. Achcha theek hai. Wahin pe rahiye.' The driver had forgotten to come back after dropping her and was still at Kaushik's office. Naina decided to take an auto.

'Bhaiyaji aap Vasant Vihar jayenge? Kitna?! Rehene dijiye!'

The fight with the auto walas in Delhi would continue perpetually. They asked for an exorbitant amount and women never wanted to pay that much. Never mind that she was carrying a Prada purse. She refused to pay an extra hundred rupees for an auto. It was a matter of principle. If one woman gave in to the demands of the auto guy, he would do the same with other women. The auto walas charged extra because the women of Delhi were always dressed so well. She needed to haggle for women all over Delhi. And finally she sat in an auto to head back home.

'Bhaiyaji left lijeye yahaan se. Left!' She didn't want to take the lonely gullies that led up to her house. She was always on guard. It was something she had learnt from her single days in London.

Why couldn't any politician do anything about the safety of women? Almost 84 per cent of Delhi women felt unsafe in public transport. This should be the main concern of every politician, she thought. And yet they were arguing about the economy. If they couldn't make women feel safe, half their work force would go into a revolution. Hadn't anyone learned from all the rape cases in court that what Delhi needed was safety for women! Naina felt disgruntled every time she needed to travel in an auto.

'Thoda jaldi chaliye,' she told the auto wala. She couldn't get home fast enough. She was already in a foul mood.

3

Why do romantic relationships fade away? Does the magic slowly die? Or do lovers simply wake up one morning realizing they are done? Is it a trick that time plays on happy couples or is it something more profound, an evolution perhaps of our feelings and our needs?

The anniversary party went off extremely well according to everyone else and horribly wrong according to Naina. Kaushik arrived late, at 8:30, and left in an hour. He said he was in the middle of a big deal and he couldn't get away for too long. In that one hour he spoke to his in-laws, met all of Naina's family, carried Shiuli around in his arms and played with Shonali as well. He gave Naina a kiss on the cheek before he left (making sure everyone saw that he did). Later her mother told her, 'You're very lucky to have him, Naina.'

Naina's cousin, Nidhi, chimed in, 'You're so lucky, Didi. You must tell me how you keep your marriage so alive.'

Naina's marriage wasn't alive; if only they knew. It was all a show so they could live out their lives like actors for an audience. Only the actors themselves knew they had given their best performance for the evening.

Still, Naina was determined to be a good wife. The next day after the girls had left and the house had been cleaned, she walked around her large, flawless drawing room, admiring how she had put every piece together over the years. Italian marble flooring. Large French windows with mahogany coloured monotone drapes. Satish Gujral paintings on the white brick walls. Large off-white and dark rust sofas with a centre table in ebony wood and glass in one corner and a large dining table at the other end. A mantelpiece with the family photographs on one side and a bar arrangement in the remaining corner of the large drawing area. Carpets from Turkey were rolled up to one side because the kids had been playing with their mini cars on the floor the last few days.

Naina walked around slowly with a cup of coffee in her hand. She picked up a photo of Kaushik and her in London before they got married. She remembered a conversation they had had.

'You're Bengali, right?' she had asked him on their second date. They had gone to a club. A place where you could get lost in the music, and each other. She was in a tight black dress with a neckline that plunged a little too much for a regular Indian girl. She wanted to give him the signal that she was different.

He nodded. 'Yeah full-blooded.' He got it. He got her. He wanted her.

'So you think about sex a lot?'

He had thrown his head back and laughed. 'Yes. But it's probably the same thing with every man. We think of sex a lot.'

'How much?'

He had put his face close to her ear so she could hear him over the din, 'All the time.'

'Really?' Lightly she fingered a loose strand of hair across her face, her eyes wide with feigned innocence.

He wrapped his arms around her waist and moved her closer to him. She could feel him getting hard underneath his clothes. He whispered in her ear, 'Really.' He slowly moved away but held her close. She swivelled around and started to dance. Slowly. Exotically. Swaying her hips slowly against his groin. Moving to the beat. Her eyes closed. Her hands moving slowly down her body. Her straight, dark hair caressing his face. The smell of her strong Lancome perfume soaking into his skin. The music pumping in the club. Warm sweat trickled down her back. His pulse raced. She wriggled her breasts inches away from him. Teasing. Her eyes open. Smiling. Bright, beautiful. Touching her trembling lips with one finger.

'God, Naina,' he whispered. She looked ethereal, unreal in the dim light. A lustful goddess.

She said nothing. Languorously placing her arms across his shoulders. Leaning in her breath was warm and moist against his face. She arched away. Taunting him. He couldn't take it anymore. Heat emanated from his body. He swallowed hard, his body screaming to give in. He was burning inside. He never liked any public displays of affection. No, he was a Bengali and Bengalis didn't do these things. And yet this woman! This woman made him feel these things. Things he couldn't wait to do. He leaned over and held her face before he claimed her lips, crushing her into his body, feeling every pore satiated with her in his arms, giving himself freely to passion. Right there in the middle of a club, with people watching, without caring about what anyone thought. For the first time. His first public display of affection. The kiss seared his mind. It was in that moment he knew he couldn't live without her. She had felt it long before that.

Naina woke herself up from her daydream. She had changed. She wasn't that person anymore. He couldn't expect her to be that same woman. She was a mother now. She had responsibilities. She was working hard to be stable, normal, strong. She was no longer that reckless young woman he met almost a decade ago. He couldn't begrudge her that, could he? People grow up. They change. They need to!

'You can't move away from me because I've changed,' she whispered to the man in the photograph. 'You've changed too.'

She needed to stop worrying about her husband. Naina always knew that he had dreamt of becoming a partner with Mukherjee. It would take many hours and a long struggle.

She had thought that once it happened he would be a little more relaxed. But the last two years, with her own career taking off, he had been home even less. There was politics in the workplace to take care of. It wasn't easy. He needed to bring in clients. He was always working. He got home tired. The Bengali man who used to have sex on his mind all the time, now could not even think of having sex once a week with his sexy wife.

His parents spent more time at home than Kaushik did. They looked after the children when she was busy. Naina wondered when was the last time just the two of them were together. Then she had an idea. She would plan a holiday just for Kaushik and her. Maybe even surprise him. She was sure it would bring back the romance. She called Kaushik's PA, Tara.

'Hey Tara, it's Naina. Can you please tell me when Kaushik has a lean period anytime soon?…Yes I know there are no lean periods but when will something get over or when can he take a long break?…Maybe three or four days, not too long…?' They spoke for a while and finally Naina hung up with a few dates in her hand.

She went online, quickly found her dates and booked tickets and a hotel in Bora Bora. She couldn't be more thankful for the income she had earned from her cooking shows and her cookbook; she had saved up enough money to plan a surprise for Kaushik. It was the only way they could save their marriage. Her parents would manage the children for those days and Kaushik only needed to take three days off. Combined with a weekend, it would make for a long glorious vacation where they could reconnect. Maybe she would show him that dance again, let him know that her wild side had never really died. It had taken just a break because of two small kids. They needed time away to rekindle their romance. Naina was feeling very excited about her plans and she couldn't wait to tell him.

But Kaushik didn't come home early enough, and by the time he did she had already fallen asleep. He crashed in the guest room. It was a habit that Naina didn't like. She believed that whatever happened, couples needed to sleep in the same room because the more you slept apart, the more distance you'd create. She had told him it didn't matter how late he came in, he needed to sleep in the same bed with her. But many nights he had crashed in the guest bedroom and would come in later in the morning before the children woke them up. He would shower before he fell asleep and he would say that having the whole bed to himself helped him sleep better; exactly what he needed after an 18-hour day. But Naina resented it.

This morning, though, she didn't want to make a big deal out of it.

'Kaushik, I have a surprise for you,' she beamed brightly as she brought him his morning cup of coffee.

They were in their bedroom and Kaushik was reading the papers. Dark-rimmed glasses perched on his nose. Grey around his temples. A few lines slowly showing around his eyes, signs of maturity, experience, life. Light falling on his olive skin that made it gleam. He sat casually, legs crossed on the bright rust coloured sofa Naina had bought in London. He was still so handsome, Naina thought.

'I've booked us tickets for Bora Bora for two weeks from

now. It's all done. You don't need to do anything. And I checked with Tara. She said you had an easy period coming. She checked with Kalinda, your boss' secretary. He'll also be travelling so it's going to be an easy period. We're going to stay in this beautiful place…maybe we could…'

'You *what*?!' Kaushik snapped. He almost jumped out of the sofa, the papers flying out of his hands and landing in a heap on the ground. Suddenly he was wide awake, fuming mad.

'I…booked…us to go…just the two of us…,' Naina couldn't speak straight; she was instantly flooded with guilt.

'How could you do that!' his voice was hard, ruthless. 'I have no time. What do you mean Tara told you? I've not told her all my plans.'

'But…'

'You'll have to cancel it, Naina.' There was an edge of panic in his voice. 'This is not the right time.'

Naina didn't speak, too stunned by his bluntness. She knew she would lose money on the air tickets but thankfully, she had not spent on the hotels yet. She still couldn't figure out why they couldn't go.

'Kaushik, we need this. It would be nice to spend some alone time…remember how we were in London?' She moved closer to him and tried to touch him on the chest but he moved her hand away, as if it was a hot iron scalding his torso.

'Now is not a good time, Naina. Please. Just check with me before you do any of this stupid stuff again.' He gave her a sideways glance of utter disbelief before he went into the bathroom. She heard the lock click. He turned the shower on.

She was puzzled. The shock caused the words to wedge in her throat. 'I thought you wanted me to take initiative,' she thought she was speaking loud enough but could Kaushik hear her through the door? 'I thought it would be good for our marriage.' She held back her tears. Why was he behaving like this? She had given him everything in their marriage. She loved him tremendously. But maybe he wasn't seeing that. Like last year on his 35th birthday when she and the girls had worked so hard to pack 35 presents for him, all he had said to them was, 'What was the need for all this?'

'Don't you like them?' Naina had asked after putting the girls to bed.

'Sure. But it's such a waste of time.' And with that he went off to sleep, leaving Naina disappointed that he hadn't seen her effort. Expectation and disappointment; a roller coaster ride of marriage that leads to depression and distance.

After this incident Naina could only come to the conclusion that he had stopped loving her. Why did he want to stay in this marriage? But she didn't want to be unhappy any longer. She would plunge herself in her work and make something of her life. She would prove people wrong and show them that even if your personal life is not set, your professional life can still be successful. She no longer had any idea how to fix her personal life.

4

Naina got to work on her new cookbook, her second one since winning the television cookery competition. She already had a few recipes and had a few more to go. But after the debacle of her anniversary and her failed attempts at bringing romance back into her marriage, Naina felt emotionally drained. She wanted some advice, some relief. She needed someone she could open up to who would not judge her. While her mom's group was great, they all seemed to have blissful marriages and liked gossiping about those who didn't. She needed to talk to someone who would not tell on her secrets.

It was one of the mornings when she was lacking female company that she decided to go visit her friend, Pinky. Pinky ran a beauty parlour in Naina's colony. She was an entrepreneur and they got along famously.

'Well hello, sexy,' Pinky said as soon as Naina walked through the door. She got up from her corner-table and met her. They gave each other a peck on the cheek.

Pinky: 40. Born and raised in Delhi. Short. Plump. Boisterous. Punjabi. Exquisite clear honey-kissed skin. Dark green eyes. Coloured blonde hair. Bore a strange resemblance to Kareena Kapoor but claimed they weren't related. Wore loud clothes. Extremely warm and friendly. Queen bee. Had three children.

'You look terrible,' Pinky said as soon as they settled on

their chairs. 'I think we need to do the whole package for you today.'

'Nice try madam, but I have no money for the entire package. You looted me last time. I'll stick with a head massage today. Or maybe I'll just sit and chat with you. By the way what a lovely suit you're wearing.'

'Hai na? I got it at that exhibition at Hotel Ashoka that I told you about but you couldn't come. They had beautiful stuff. You should have come with me!' Pinky spoke with a heavy accent.

'I know!' Naina loved going for exhibitions with Pinky. Pinky had a great eye for designer ripoffs. She would make Naina buy an outfit that she had spied in Fashion Week but which was made by a tailor at an exhibition for half the price.

'You toh were busy with your child's birthday party na?' Pinky called the maid and asked her to make two cups of tea, 'Do chai dena. Achchi adrak wali.'

'Yeah, Pinks,' Naina replied. 'I took three months to prepare for that.'

'Why do you do so much? Pizza Hut mein le chalo. Sabko khilao aur bhaga do,' Pinky said with a wave of her hands.

Naina laughed merrily. 'I wish I could. The other mothers I know all throw parties at farm houses and hotels. They have theme parties with magicians flown in from Paris and all yaar. If I send my children to those parties then I have to throw a party on the same level right?'

'It's all your fault for sending your children to high flying schools. DPS, Modern, all these fancy schools na.'

Naina shook her head. 'But they don't go to these schools. They go to a private international school.'

'Leh!' Pinky said dramatically. 'Aur bhi mushkil. Aur lakhon ke party karte raho phir. By the way what did you do for your kid's party this year?'

'Circus theme.'

'Baap re. Where?'

'I rented a large ground near Mehrauli. And I invited a big circus to put up tents so kids could do acrobatics and play. There were bouncy rooms for the smaller kids and bungee jumping for the bigger ones. There was a small area for petting animals also like a mini zoo.'

'Were you one of the animals? Because you're an ass for spending so much!' Pinky laughed. She wouldn't take so much liberty with Naina if the two of them weren't so close. They had known each other for years now. Naina was very fond of her.

'You should have come,' Naina said, taking a sip of her tea. 'The kids would have loved it.'

Pinky smiled and said, 'It was good we were away for our holiday then. Otherwise my kids would also want such parties. But Switzerland was amazing. Thank God all of us like the cold weather. Varna hum kabhi bhi kahin nahin ja paate.'

Naina nodded. 'Ab chod na. I have to do these things. It's a vicious cycle. If I send out an invitation to go to Pizza Hut, none of my kids' friends will land up. And then they will feel bad. And they will be ostracized from their group. All because I want to save money. And then they won't be invited for their friends' lavish parties. Maine toh kuch nahin kiya. Last year there was a mother who did an entire Princess theme where she flew down all the "Frozen" princess lookalikes for the girls to take photos with. And she did an entire make up and costume party with real costumes of Disney princesses for everyone to dress up in. Then there was a performance by some singer also. I think it was Sunidhi Chauhan. That was for the adults who attended the party.'

'Baap re. How old was this child? 18?'

'Seven.'

'Seven?!' Pinky almost fell off her chair. 'My three kids know nothing about these princesses. Chota Bheem and one cake that everyone cuts. Samosas and chips as snacks.'

'Seriously, Pinky? And your children are happy with that?'

'Ab what to do? Sunny lost a lot of money in the last IPL na. And I need my annual vacation with the whole family. So whatever money is saved goes in that. Not birthday parties.'

'How did Sunny lose money?'

'Betting!'

'He bets?' Naina was horrified.

'No no.' Pinky shook her head vehemently. 'He takes money from people and puts it in teams.'

'You mean he's a bookie?' Naina had gotten more curious.

'You could say that. But everything is legal nowadays.'

'No baba it's not,' Naina said quickly. 'Be careful.'

'If it's not then how come all these politicians and film stars are doing it? Won't they also get caught?'

'Which film stars?'

Pinky started telling her what she knew from her husband's stories. Naina couldn't believe what she was hearing. Then suddenly Pinky's mobile phone rang and as she picked it up her voice turned lower. 'I'll have to take this. Pati. One minute.'

She stepped outside and Naina could only hear snippets of what she was saying to the person on the line. 'Baby. I'm not in the mood to party today. You go alone na. But why? Okay I'll come. But this time we're not doing what we did last time. Kyonki bruises ho gaye! Haha. Chal theek hai!'

As Pinky came back in Naina thought she was looking a little flustered. 'Are you alright?' she asked Pinky. 'Is everything okay?'

'Chod na.' Pinky shook her head. '*You* tell me. What's happening with you? Writing a new cookbook? Flying off to new places?'

Naina knew that Pinky would tell her what the problem was when it was time. She didn't want to pry into her friend's life. She said, 'I am so bored. I can't think of any new recipes to write. I have no new batch of cooking students. And as usual my kids find me tedious.'

'Where is the husband? Shouldn't he be taking care of you?'

Naina shrugged her shoulders. 'Nahin. Apparently if he doesn't put in a certain number of hours at the law firm, they'll get very upset.'

Pinky threw up her hands. 'Men and their jobs. It's as if we need all their money. Maybe if they worked less and spent more time with us, we'd be happier housewives huh?'

'Maybe we wouldn't need to work.'

'I think we work because we love it. I love my parlour. I've made so many friends since I opened this parlour five years ago. It kept me sane through my post-partum depression. I could come here to get away from the children, get away from my in-laws.'

Naina laughed out loud. 'They're that much of a pain?'

Pinky laughed too, 'No I didn't mean it like that. It's great living with my in-laws. They help with the children. But sometimes I need my own space. I love being a mother. Chintu, Bittoo and Guddi are growing up so fast. I think I want another one now.'

Naina almost choked on her tea. Pinky laughed. 'I'm kidding! I already have three. And since the twins were born I never lost any of that weight. Though Sunny doesn't seem to be complaining,' she winked. It was so easy talking to Pinky. She could go on about her life, her opinions and chat away without boring you.

'Tell me about your new cookbook or class?' she asked Naina.

'Oh I have nothing right now. It's a vicious cycle. When I have a batch of people, it motivates me to try new things and then I come up with new recipes and then I feel like writing and cooking more. And when I don't, I don't feel like cooking new dishes. I can't eat all that. I'll have to run a marathon every morning to burn it off.'

'Well I know one person who wanted to get private classes. He can't join a group because he has limited time. But he's a bachelor and head of this big event management company. He wanted to learn how to cook.'

Naina looked mildly interested. 'Will he come to my house?'

Pinky shrugged her shoulders. 'I don't know. You can ask him. I can give him your number if you like.'

Naina was uncertain. 'Okay I guess there's no harm in calling.'

'Of course. And he will pay you well. You can buy yourself a new car!'

'That much he'll pay or what?' Naina asked with a smile.

'Pooch toh lo. Ultimately everything in life is about having fun. Pushing your boundaries. Discovering more from life. Maybe he could be that new aspect that could help with your cookbook na?'

'Yes but where does he stay? Is it safe?' Naina asked.

Pinky put a hand to her heart and let her jaw drop open. 'Would I even recommend it if it wasn't safe? What kind of a question is that? He's the sweetest, most innocent man you'll meet. He has a lovely, large farmhouse in Mehrauli and another place here close by somewhere. His name is Arjun.'

'Doesn't he have a cook?'

'You'll have to ask him. All I know is he's been wanting to learn how to cook.'

Naina pondered while Pinky attended to her customers.

Naina could see she was going to get busy. She picked up her bag and whispered to Pinky, 'I'm going.'

Pinky raised her eyebrows as if to ask what Naina had concluded about their conversation.

'Okay, give him my number.'

Pinky smiled, 'And you can charge him vada vada paisa. Bohat loaded hai.'

Naina smiled. The thought of earning always cheered her up. Maybe she needed that drive again. It was time to start feeling independent. She needed to find the balance between home and career. Maybe this could help her.

5

'Hi, I'm Naina. I'm here to see Arjun.'

Naina had reached her new client, Arjun's home. The maid allowed her to enter and led her to the living room from where she could see most of the house. It was a large apartment in Hauz Khas. It had large paintings on the walls, dark wooden floors, soft comfortable white couches in the living room, a gigantic TV on a clean wall in the drawing room and a brick wall effect around a bar that was in a corner in the balcony, which overlooked a vast expanse of greenery all around. It had beautiful modern floor lamps and an open kitchen with an island. Similar to the one that they showed in magazines with a marble counter in the middle of the kitchen which was open on all sides to walk around, with bar stool chairs on one side. The kitchen had white wooden cabinets with light wooden flooring and black and white paintings around. Clearly this man was into art. He had refined taste. He was rich and unmarried. On one of the cabinet counters she saw photos of him with a young girl. His daughter?

Naina walked around the open living, dining and drawing room areas. The space was huge and breathtaking. A maid came and gave her a glass of water and asked her if she wanted some coffee or tea to which she replied, no.

A tall, dark figure stepped out from the shadows. Arjun came out from a corridor, wearing a designer yellow shirt and dark navy-blue jeans. His salt–and–pepper hair was wet as if he had just stepped out of the shower. Drops of moisture clung to his damp forehead. He was well built, with mahogany skin and dark piercing brown eyes. He was devilishly handsome with an innately captivating presence.

'I'm sorry to have kept you waiting, Naina,' Arjun said as he extended his hand towards her, keeping a safe distance and not making her feel uncomfortable. The magnetism of his smile captivated Naina. His hands were beautiful, long fingered, and strong; his voice, deep and raspy. His Gio Armani aftershave settled around his aura as he showed her to a couch. 'Thank you so much for coming over. I didn't want to take classes in someone else's house. I wanted to get more familiar with my own kitchen.'

'No problem,' Naina replied. 'Tell me what you know? So that I can gauge where we should start from.' He told her about how little he cooked and since his doctor had told him to start eating a more healthy diet, perhaps with a sprinkling of Mediterranean cuisine here and there, he had decided to start making his food himself. All his Indian cooks apparently put too much oil in their food and could cook only Indian food. He had tried ordering in from restaurants and hiring a foreign chef but eventually all the food that was made got wasted as he didn't eat that much in a day. He could make rice and boil eggs, he said, almost too proudly. She laughed. He smiled at Naina. She was bewitching. Such natural beauty.

She got up and kept her bag on her shoulders. She wanted to get to work and not be distracted by this handsome gentleman whose smile alone was captivating.

'If you're not in a hurry, can I offer you a cup of coffee? I make great coffee. And only coffee. No food!' He laughed as he moved towards the kitchen and showed her the way with his hand.

'I wouldn't mind a cup of coffee, Sir.'

'Oh God now you are making me feel really old. You know I'm only 40-something. I know you're 18 but please don't call me Sir. Just Arjun.'

'You're a flatterer. I couldn't be 18.' She gave him a smile.

Arjun reached for the coffee pot that had been brewing for some time and poured two cups for them. He took out some milk from the fridge and put it in the microwave to warm. 'I know I'm not supposed to ask a woman her age. So let me ask you how many years have you been cooking. And giving classes?'

Naina sat down on the bench opposite the kitchen island, placing her bag next to her. 'I've been cooking since I was a little girl but taking classes only for the last few years. Before that I was a chef at the Four Seasons in London.'

'Oh amazing. I can't wait to learn all those dishes from you, Madam.'

'Oh please! Call me Naina. I'm not 45!' She felt at ease.

Arjun gave her a cup of coffee as he leaned in with his own. 'Cheers to that!'

'I love your kitchen. Did your wife design it?' Naina asked, fishing for Arjun to tell him he was unmarried, just as Pinky had told her. She looked around at the quality of the wooden flooring, white cupboards and red tulips sitting on a glass vase at the counter. Dark black marble on counters gives an edgy, modern contrast and still a wonderful feel.

'Oh God don't I look happy to you?' he said. 'I'm not married. Was. Got out. Went into another relationship. Almost got married again. Ran away! She got married to someone she found on the internet. I chose to work instead. I'm marriage-phobic, I guess. That's my life story.' He spoke with an easy and charming demeanour.

'Pinky told me you were into event management.' Naina sipped on her single origin Brazilian coffee; it was exquisite.

'Yes. I was in a TV channel as their head of Programming for a long time. Then I wanted to do something more dramatic with my life.' He laughed at his own joke. 'Now I want to learn how to cook and maybe start a chain of restaurants.'

'Really? I've always wanted to run a restaurant.' Naina realized she had just revealed her biggest dream to a complete stranger. If she had the support of her husband she would have done more. But her kids had been too small and she couldn't leave them alone. It had been a huge conflict. She didn't want to relive the past anymore.

'How amazing!' Arjun was completely taken in by this woman. She was gorgeous, warm, obviously smart and motivated. Yet something was missing and he couldn't quite put his finger on it. He felt he needed to protect her. A tiny voice inside him was exasperated with his presumptuousness. 'Let it go, Arjun. Remember what happened with K? Just let her teach you how to cook, at least for now?'

'Shall we get started?' Arjun asked as he tidied up his cup in the sink.

Naina took out two aprons from her bag. 'Put this on first. We don't want our clothes getting dirty.'

She washed her hands and started asking him questions to familiarize herself with the kitchen setup, the pantry, and the utensils. 'So you have someone who can prepare ingredients for you,' she began. 'But what I'm going to do is set a menu each day for us to learn. So you can cook a variety of dishes by the end of our six weeks. This will include a starter or a soup, a main course and a dessert. I'll also teach you how to chop ingredients properly, and how to cook the vegetables so that the flavours and nutrients remain.' She paused. 'Does that sound fine?'

'Yes, certainly.'

'Can you show me your fridge and what you've got in there?'

They started walking to the fridge.

'I'll make a list of things you will need to purchase for our next sessions as well. Ordinarily I have all this at home but since you wanted the lessons in your own kitchen, I'll need all these condiments here.'

Arjun nodded in agreement. 'I'm quite anti-social, you can say. And since I'll be cooking in my own house, I wanted to get familiar with my own kitchen instead of leaving it like a beautiful museum piece that everyone admires but never uses. That's why I wanted you to come here instead. I'll pay you double your normal rate.'

They discussed money and settled on an amount that made Naina's heart do a little jump. Maybe she could take a vacation on her own to London. She would have enough money saved from this gig alone to take a break and visit her old friends.

The first session was Italian, as Arjun claimed to be a huge fan. Naina decided she would begin with the simplest penne arrabiatta.

'No, no don't chop up the tomatoes just yet. First blanch them.' She moved around the kitchen with flair. He watched her, admiring her confidence, her body moving gracefully as if she was dancing. Her fingers fluttering around chopping, stirring, pouring. He realized he was finding it all erotic. He watched, he learned, he made notes in a diary she gave him. She forced him to take notes. She laughed when he dropped an entire batch of prepped ingredients on the floor and they had to start all over again. It would take longer for this student to learn, she reckoned, but she wasn't upset. She stopped once to call her mother to check if her kids were okay. He noticed her from the corner of his eye. She seemed like a concerned mother besides being a good chef.

Only when they finally sat down to eat the meal they had just prepared did he realize how astonishing it was that he could have made it. Above all else, Naina was a great teacher, he thought.

'This is amazing!' He took mouthfuls from his plate. 'You are such an amazing cook.'

'No, you are. You did the work.'

'I don't think I'm paying you enough!'

She laughed. 'It's more than enough. Let's dig in? Bon appetit!'

'Would you like some wine? This meal would be great with a bottle of fine red wine.'

Naina looked at her watch. 'I have to go back to my kids so I don't want to drink. I'm driving.'

Arjun nodded, acutely reminded that this wasn't a date. It was a business transaction. He was so glad that Pinky had recommended these classes to him. Naina hadn't asked how he knew Pinky yet and he hadn't offered to tell. Some things were better left unsaid.

He asked Naina about her Masterchef experience and though he was pleased to hear her describe her life with ease, he also felt that there was something she wasn't saying. There was meaning between her lines.

She spoke fondly of her husband, told him that Kaushik was a lawyer and even said, 'You must go to him if you need any legal advice.' She wanted to make Arjun believe that she was in a stable marriage.

She loved her children, the mixture of Bengali and Punjabi roots they had. Her eyes brightened as she spoke about food and her face fell when she told him about how she now had to keep a personal trainer to keep the kilos away. She was vibrant and beautiful. Arjun was smitten. He made her some more coffee and asked her some more questions.

That afternoon, Naina talked and talked some more. It was as if a dam had burst and she had got a friendly, non-judgemental, male ear to listen to her stories. Sometimes a woman just needs to talk about her life, gloat about her accomplishments, have someone appreciate the mundane-ness in her choices and regale in her beauty. She felt like Arjun did all that, making the appropriate gestures to make her feel comfortable, asking her apt questions to let her talk freely and yet not being creepy or too probing.

When Arjun saw her to the door, he said, 'Can you wait for a minute?' He ran to his room.

He came back with a cheque for the entire amount of the classes. She saw what it was and said, 'But you need to give this to me at the end of the course. You only need to give me the signing amount right now.'

He shook his head. 'What difference does it make? Now or later? I'll forget later. Better now.'

Naina paused. 'What if I run away with all this money?'

Arjun smiled impishly. 'Then I would have learned how to make an amazing penne and clear soup and it would have been well worth all that money.'

Naina smiled. She liked him. There was something about him that was nice. He wasn't lecherous like some men with lots of money and power. He was warm and comforting, like her 'paasher baalish', the pillow she held on to at night near her chest.

'Our next class is on Saturday,' Naina said as she left. Arjun showed her to the door and made sure that she was inside her car before he closed his door.

Naina looked at the cheque when she got home. This was far more than what she earned with four people in her class for six weeks. And it was easy. He was willing to learn and didn't do such a bad job either. She was feeling excited again about cooking and teaching.

6

Women always give their husbands a warning before they engage in extramarital affairs.

It's the small signs that they do or say to give the man one last chance at saving his marriage. Naina gave Kaushik not one, not two, but three chances to save their marriage.

First, she booked them on a solo vacation where they could spend time alone. She ended up getting ridiculed; he simply said he could not go.

Then she cooked him his favourite meal. After all, people say the way to a man's heart is through his stomach. She put on her best negligee to remind him she still had her moves. But he ate so much that later when they were alone in the room he said, 'Naina, you're too heavy now for me. Maybe you should not be eating everything you're cooking for your clients, huh?'

She felt so humiliated after that, that she didn't care anymore if they slept together again. She started giving him space, letting him sleep in the other room so he wouldn't be so tired. She was nicer to his mother, and she stopped complaining about him coming home so late. She didn't mention that the foreplay wasn't enough for her during their monthly sexual ritual. She tried to initiate sex but he was always tired and even when they made love, it was all over within minutes, leaving Naina very dissatisfied. Usually she would have told him what she wanted and how she liked it and he would have given in. But she stopped complaining and was ready whenever he was or not so as the matter demanded over the last one year.

Kaushik didn't understand any of her hints. One night they were sleeping in the same room when Kaushik started kissing her. She responded and ran her fingers through his hair. Then suddenly he opened his eyes and saw her in the dim light of the room. He held her shoulders, pushed her back and turned to fall asleep again. She was so shaken up by that event that she confronted him the next morning. But he denied anything had happened saying she had imagined it and was going crazy.

Naina even went to Kaushik's office to have lunch with him once. She wanted to see if there were other women in his office who were flirting with him. But he had been in his office, talking on the phone when she walked in. He scolded her for not calling to tell him she was coming.

The last thing that Naina did to try and save their marriage was to talk to him about it. Communication could save all relationships. That's what Naina believed.

'What's going on, Kaushik? Why aren't you in this marriage with me?'

'You're talking rubbish, Naina. I'm here every night.'

'That's not what I meant. I meant that you're not interested in this marriage. You're not interested in me anymore.'

'Don't talk stupidly, Naina. You've been busy with your classes and I've been busy at work.'

'So busy that you don't have time to ask me how I'm doing? How my classes are going? You know, it's a very sexy man I'm tutoring nowadays. I can easily sleep with him.'

Kaushik looked surprised. 'Well I wouldn't like that.'

Naina thought that it was the most horrible answer a

husband could ever give his wife. 'What would you like then, Kaushik?'

Kaushik remained quiet. Oh how she hated his silence. She knew he was a damn good lawyer. Sometimes he remained silent just so that the other person would make a mistake and it wouldn't be his fault. Then he wouldn't have to take the blame for the failure of his choices and in this case their marriage. But that was the court and this was their life! Why was he using the same stunt!

'Kaushik, we're not having sex anymore! We barely go out. We've not taken a vacation for a year or two now.'

'Naina, bakwaas band karo. Just because your friends go on vacations doesn't mean we have to. And we do have sex. Just not that often. And you're to blame equally, Naina. So many times in the middle of sex, you want to go check if the door is locked or you suddenly want to switch on the AC because you're feeling hot. Or you want to close the curtains. It makes me lose my concentration.'

'But I just don't want the girls to walk in or the neighbours to see. What's wrong with that? We live in a conservative society.'

'I hate this society. I hate being in India. We were so free in London. And now you're always doing what your friends are doing. Wanting to become like them. Talking like them. Wearing clothes like them. Look at you. In suits. You would never wear salwar kameezes! How terribly boring you've become. I'm not attracted to you anymore! It's difficult to have sex.'

Naina was shocked. She couldn't move a muscle. She wore suits because they were comfortable. Because the Delhi heat only allowed women to wear loose cotton clothing. And whenever she wore a dress to go out, people would stare at her. If she was running around to do chores, she couldn't be in tight jeans and uncomfortable clothes. She didn't have the body to carry it off anymore.

Kaushik closed his book and mumbled, 'I'm tired.'

She snapped at him, 'You're always tired.'

Kaushik's tone was acerbic, 'Because I'm always working.'

Naina was now in tears. He had humiliated her. 'No one asked you to.'

'Oh God, Naina. This is what I like to do. I'm on the verge of something really big. Do we need to have this talk today? Let me sleep, please.'

'I'm telling you I'm planning to have an affair and you don't want to talk about it? You call me unattractive?' Naina felt slighted.

Kaushik turned off his bedside lamp and lay in his bed. 'That's not what I meant. Please. Now let it be. You're just throwing a tantrum for no reason. Are you having your period? No? Then let this go. I'm dropping the kids to school tomorrow morning. I need some rest.' And he turned around and went to sleep, completely dismissing her feelings and her need to communicate.

What was Naina supposed to do when she wanted to talk but Kaushik was unwilling to listen? What could Naina do when she wanted to save the marriage but Kaushik thought there's nothing to save? What could Naina do when she's being horribly belittled?

Maybe Naina should show Kaushik she was right about her threat.

AYESHA

7

Ayesha: Slim. Petite and flower-like. Oval face. Almond eyes. Exquisitely dainty nose adorned with a diamond nose ring that sparkled like her dark eyes. Long, rich, glowing auburn hair. Sharp as a knife. Soft-spoken. Demure. Loving. Caring. Perfect housewife. Had had an arranged marriage. Never loved her husband, simply believed in the idea of marriage and giving something back to her parents.

'Chaal!' Sanjay said as he put in a chip in the teen patti game.

'That's a lakh, Sanjay,' Ayesha squealed partly in horror and partly in admiration for her friend's lawyer husband who could afford such a high-stake table. Everyone from the party slowly gathered around the table as only two players remained. Sanjay, the lawyer who made a few lakhs every month, and Ayesha's husband Varun, the IAS officer who made only fifty grand a month.

'You're afraid your husband is going to lose, Ayesha?' Sanjay said with a cocky smile.

Ayesha clutched her heart. 'Honestly I don't like such high-stakes games. But you boys do whatever gives you happiness.' Ayesha only partly meant it. If Varun lost this hand, they would lose three months of savings. Savings that were hard to come by.

'Show!' Varun said as he put in another chip and Ayesha's

heart fluttered again. Someone held her hand and she looked around to see that it was her friend Tarini from her school days. Tarini had fallen in love and married Sanjay, the lawyer, while Ayesha had had an arranged marriage a year later to Varun, an IAS officer. They had been best friends since they were five years old but their destinies had made one rich and the other struggle to keep up with expenses all the time. That's when they had moved apart. Until they rekindled their friendship and began calling each other over for parties.

That's why it was so important that Ayesha's husband win this game. Sanjay could just take on a new client and earn the money back in a month. Varun, well there was no alternative. All he had was power. Several industrialists came to him for consent on their ventures. His peers had tremendous respect for his skills. And his powers also extended to other departments where he could just make a phone call and ask a colleague to get something done for friends who weren't in the government. But power didn't pay for fancy vacations or food. That Ayesha had to manage on his salary.

'Ace!' someone shouted as Varun put down his first card, slowly revealing his hand one card at a time. There was joy all around. Obviously many people were hoping Varun would win. It was his house. And he was also the underdog.

Ayesha looked around and saw the entire party gather around the table. It was her annual Diwali party and she had thrown a grand affair inviting all the IAS officers Varun and she knew, and some friends from the corporate circle. She had arranged seating in small circles all around her expansive living room so many people could move around and sit wherever they chose. Some groups wanted high stakes and sat around on a white gadda while some wanted lower stakes and sat on red round tables or on the floor seating arrangements strewn all around. There were diya stands with small burning lights in every corner. Large bunches of sweet-smelling flowers sat in bright coloured vases at different places across the room. The low lamps and the bright rugs gave the place a warm and cozy atmosphere. A bartender had set up a drinks counter at the far end of the patio that overlooked their large lawn which was covered with hanging twinkling lights and large lamps from FabIndia that swayed in the cool November breeze. Women were at their blingiest best. Rich hand woven, designer saris, Amrapalli jewellery, gold sandals, nail art on their hands, dark lipstick, perfectly blow dried hair and smoky eyes completed their looks. Diwali was a grand time in Delhi. It was a time for people to show off their houses, their marriages and their achievements and come together in a great camaraderie of friendship and fun.

The alcohol flowed and the snacks were warm and delicious. Ayesha had made sure the party was a huge success and everyone spoke about it for months as they always looked forward to being invited next year. It wasn't only for the great hospitality. It was also a way for corporate clients to speak to IAS officers about their new businesses since each knew one needed the other for starting something new and finding out the inside gossip of the workings of the government or corporate sector. So the guests ranged from government servants to lawyers, businessmen to industrialists and bankers to entrepreneurs. People always made new friends at Ayesha's parties and she was happy to contribute to her husband being at the centre of this growing network of people.

It would be the last party she was to throw in Delhi for a while. Varun's posting in the capital was over and he needed to move back to his cadre, Lucknow. Every IAS officer had to spend a few years in the home cadre that was allotted to him after he came out of the Academy and then he would be posted to Delhi to be in the thick of things before his time was up. Then he would return to his state and that was mandatory. They were going to be shifting in January or February. Ayesha wasn't looking forward to it at all.

Despite the dipping temperatures at eleven in the night, the table was hot with the two men slowly revealing their cards while everyone stopped playing, drinking or wondering if the kids had gone to sleep with the maids in the rooms inside. Ayesha had made every arrangement for everyone so they would think she was the perfect hostess and Varun and her marriage was perfect.

The truth was far from it.

The Truth was, as an IAS officer's wife, one had to keep up with the pretences. The marriage, the job, the life, the kids, were supposed to be picture-perfect for the husband to succeed at work.

'On the count of three,' Varun said as he and Sanjay put their final card on the table. This was it. Ayesha was nervous.

'Colour. Both have colour but Sanjay has King high. Varun loses!'

'Awwwww!' a chorus of voices let out a sigh at Varun's loss. A wave of emotions swept over Ayesha. She let go of Tarini's hand and said, 'It's alright. It's just a game. Let me get dinner started.' Then she smiled and tossed her long, warm chestnut hair back, gathered her lovely red silk sari and walked to the kitchen where she started giving orders for dinner arrangements.

While the entire party contemplated how unfair teen patti really was, Varun said loudly, 'Let me get some more alcohol, guys. We'll have one more game.'

Ayesha took a moment and went into her bedroom. It was large with high ceilings and a king-size bed in the centre. On the opposite wall was a television with a rack at the bottom. On one side of the room was a floor-to-ceiling bookshelf where Ayesha kept all her books. On the other side was her dressing table and a door attached to the master bathroom. She noticed there was some paint chipping off from the walls and wondered if they would ever have money to buy anything new in their house. The dressing table, the bookshelf and the bed they had had for the last eleven years of their married life. They moved with them whenever Varun got transferred and she was now sick. Sick of the furniture, of the moving, and sick of her husband playing high stakes with their finances.

Even though a housewife didn't earn any money, her husband's money was hers as well, wasn't it? She kept house for him. Looked after his interests and raised a child whom he could be proud of. Should she have sacrificed all that for her own career and maybe had her own savings? She shook her head. It was too late to think about that. She had devoted the last eleven years of her life to this man. And now that she was in her mid-30s, she couldn't think of what had gone by.

She looked at the mirror adjacent to her bed and saw a reflection of a very beautiful woman. A woman with luscious cream-coloured skin perfect blow-dried hair that was pinned back with a clip with a few strands around her face, large almond eyes and a tiny waist that didn't show she had a ten-year old son. She had small breasts that were just perfect for her petite and flower-like build. She wore a gorgeous dark red sari with a golden border that her mother had given her last year. She wore silver jewelry that she had bought from their trip to Jaipur a few years ago. The last of their trips. Ayesha was the epitome of a gentle yet strong housewife anyone would be proud to have.

Just then, Varun walked into the room and went to his cabinet where he stashed the extra whiskey that he used on special occasions to impress people. He saw Ayesha standing in front of the mirror calmly reapplying her lipstick without as much as a hint of annoyance.

'You know I had no option Ayesha, don't you?'

Ayesha stayed quiet. They had this argument every Diwali. Every time Varun said he wanted a party to show all his friends how accomplished he was with his big house and his beautiful wife and every time he promised he wouldn't gamble with his friends but simply play the bartender and conversationalist. And almost every year he lost some money. He was terrible at keeping his promises and even more pathetic at playing high-stake cards. But Ayesha had indulged him. Somehow, she felt guilty that she would be letting her father down if she ever spoke back to her husband. And so she stayed silent. Year after year. Sacrificing her needs for his. That's what a loving wife does.

'Don't be upset. I gamble only during Diwali. You know that,' Varun said. And that's when Ayesha stiffened as though he had struck her.

'Yes but it's enough to set us back for an entire year. What happens to our vacation now? We were planning to take Adi to Switzerland to ski.'

'We can still go, I suppose. We'll figure something out, right? You always do.'

Ayesha cleared her throat and spoke, 'It'll be too tight.'

Varun held the two bottles of whiskey in his hand and said, 'Why do you make a big deal out of everything? It's just one vacation. We can go somewhere cheaper in India. Like Manali, for a few days. There's skiing there, right? Can I not have one fun evening?'

He stormed off and left Ayesha almost in tears. She wasn't making a big deal. She never did. But she had been looking forward to this vacation for a long time. Varun hadn't taken her anywhere. And with her birthday coming up as well, he had said it would be a combined birthday and Christmas present since he hadn't given her any gifts for the last few years. He hadn't even bought her flowers. She was so used to him forgetting every year that it had been pleasantly surprising when he had mentioned he was getting a good deal to go skiing in the Swiss Alps and maybe they could go before the family headed back to Lucknow for five years.

Adi had turned ten a few months back and had told everyone in school about this vacation. Suddenly his confidence had also gone up and his social circle had expanded. Like it or not, these days the travel and power a family had mattered to children as well. Not that it bothered Ayesha because she was raising him to be a fine child. Except with everything he did right, there was never any reward until now. And even that would be taken away from him. What would his peers think of Adi?

Last year when Varun had lost fifty grand at the Diwali party he had told her, 'I need to play these stakes, Ayesha. It's more about the way people perceive me. You know a man's prestige and dignity lie in how his peers look at him. If they see me as poor they won't respect me.'

'Being in the IAS is respectful enough,' Ayesha had muttered under her breath. Varun heard only what he needed to and he continued to do exactly as he pleased every year.

As soon as Ayesha went out again to the kitchen she saw that her staff of maids, cooks and cleaners had heated up the dinner and were ready to serve it. She was thankful that even if they didn't have money, they always had a battalion of people who helped in the house. That was the greatest benefit of being in the IAS.

Tarini came into the kitchen, took Ayesha aside and spoke with a soft whisper, 'Ayesha, Sanjay is not going to take the money from Varun.'

Ayesha shook her head proudly, 'No, a game is a game. He won fair and square.'

Tarini leaned against the large fridge as Ayesha told the kitchen staff, 'Bring everything out please.' She walked outside to the dining area where she had arranged a large flat platter with floating candles and small white jasmine flowers with food all around. Tarini followed her and spoke softly, 'Listen to me, Ayesha. These guys are mad. They play this game but we don't need to comply with all the rules.'

Ayesha suddenly felt like she didn't need the sympathy. She was a proud, independent woman who had managed her family and her life perfectly without any support for the last ten years. Her parents lived in Allahabad and only came for a few days at a stretch to meet their grandchild. They offered to give money to Varun once but he felt slighted and they left the same day. She had never taken anything from them for the house. Her mother occasionally gave her only daughter saris and jewellery to keep her happy.

She held Tarini by her hand and said, 'I'm sure Varun will win it back next year. Now don't worry about it. You know what would really piss me off? If all this food doesn't finish. I have no place in the fridge to put it!' She laughed and Tarini smiled as well as she took a plate.

'It all looks delicious. But Ayu, please don't let this game affect our friendship,' Tarini suggested hesitantly.

'Does it ever? You buy me lunch next week okay? At Habitat? That will be your way of making it up to me,' Ayesha said. She would never let her husband's stupidity get in the way of her childhood friendship. It wasn't Tarini's fault that she was rich even though it pinched Ayesha sometimes to see her friend shop for whatever she wanted whenever she felt like and go on vacations twice a year.

Ayesha called everyone for dinner and laughed and joked with all her guests till they had finished dinner. With food ranging from Mughlai cuisine to Italian pasta, Ayesha had put out a lavish spread. She remembered once when she had just served a few items and Varun had scolded her for not managing the house correctly. She never made the same mistake again. If they had to spend their money on one party a year, it would be a fabulous one. She served everyone a choice of hot gulab jamuns, warm chocolate brownies and a crème brulee for dessert. All made at home by her. She had slaved in the kitchen for the past few days and stored everything for tonight. And after a few guests had left, she served the remaining people hot chamomile tea and freshly brewed coffee at two in the morning with coconut macaroons she had had flown down from Hyderabad.

Throughout the party, not once did she show an iota of her true feelings. Ayesha was tired of this facade. Somewhere she had lost her willingness, her dignity and her ego to a marriage she hardly cared about anymore. She was forever devoted to a man who had a gambling problem and who had stopped loving her a long time ago.

After all the guests had left and she cleared up everything since the servants had also turned in for the night, she took a long bath and applied lotion on her arms and legs. She curled up into the bed next to her husband, who as far as she could tell from his snoring was already in a deep slumber. She looked up at the ceiling and said a little prayer to give herself more strength to be a better housewife. Sometimes it's hard to love your husband in spite of all his vices. Sometimes it's hard to be happy with the life you've chosen. Sometimes it's impossible to think of an alternative. And that's when you need a little prayer to help you understand that things are going to be okay. She could suddenly feel a ripple go through her body telling her that maybe this was the last time she would ever do anything for someone else. Soon she would be doing things just for herself.

8

Delhi is always a mess the day after Diwali. A thick fog envelops the city, smog that lays low as people sleep in till mid-morning. The smell of burnt firecrackers lingers heavily in the air. The streets are littered with debris from crackers and unexploded Diwali bombs. Scared dogs that had hid the previous night start to crawl out from under the cars to find food. And the regular rumble of vegetable vendors with their thelas and broomstick sellers on their bicycles, snake their way through the small lanes as they call out for customers.

Honestly, Ayesha hated Diwali. Adi insisted on buying firecrackers every year and starting three days before Diwali would start bursting them as soon as he came home. His father indulged him, of course, buying thousands of rupees worth of crackers. On Diwali night Adi and his father would be bursting bombs, anars and chakras outside their house while Ayesha would sit and hope the agony of the day and the festival would end soon. Her headaches on these nights were always bad. 'Wasn't Diwali about celebrating lights, being with friends and family and eating good food?' Ayesha thought. It's not supposed to be about gambling, and bursting crackers or getting stuck in traffic when you go to the market. Why was Delhi all about the show? Two weeks before Diwali, all the markets would be packed. Women would be buying decorations from Dilli Haat till Karol Bagh, spending all their time and money on gifts for people who hardly cared about them and buying clothes and jewellery for their families so they could look and feel good. Diwali was a big farce, Ayesha thought. It was nothing more than a huge marketing scheme for people to spend their hard-earned money on things they would never use again.

She herself, only because of the pressures of everyone around her, had gone to G. K. M Block market a week before Diwali. She was incredulous at the amount of money people were spending: table runners were selling at five thousand rupees and people were actually buying them! 'Madam, yeh exclusive piece hai. Kisi ko dikhaya nahin hai abhi tak. Jaldi le lijeye varna chala jayega!' She was sure these shops made lakhs of rupees in one day, experts as they were in the art of marketing that no MBA institute could possibly match. And now after two weeks of the dust and smoke settling, Ayesha was still cleaning up and putting away the Diwali presents an IAS officer received.

'I'm going for golf,' Varun said, disturbing her thoughts. He was wearing his shoes as he spoke. It was Sunday and Ayesha was exhausted from all the parties they had attended the days before leading up to her very own Diwali bash. She could tell she was suffering from a kaju katri hangover. From farmhouses to outdoor gardens, Delhi had really outdone itself this Diwali.

'Are you going all the way to Noida?' Ayesha asked as she walked to Varun. The best part about being an IAS officer was the houses and apartments they were allotted. As you moved higher in rank, the number of rooms in your house rose as well. From DII to CI, Ayesha had shifted from colony to colony and trudged her old furniture to new houses and had changed the upholestery to give it a new look without wasting too much money.

'Yes. Why?'

'I need to send the driver to give this gift to Mrs Verma in Sector 36.'

Varun shook his head. 'I don't know why you keep giving these gifts.'

'Arrey, she gave me a lovely tray and tea set for Diwali. If I don't give something back, I'll look so greedy.'

'You need to stop this lena dena stuff. It never ends. You women spend more money in giving to each other than actually making any money.'

Ayesha bit her lip and wanted to say it was all much cheaper than what he had spent gambling but quietly handed over a gift-wrapped package. 'The address is on this. Please send Gokulji as soon as you reach Noida Golf Course.' Varun's weekly ritual was to go to the golf course to meet his colleagues and friends to tee off and after a round of walking and playing to have a few beers and a heavy lunch and head back home in the evening. A few times Ayesha had gone and chatted with the wives who accompanied their husbands but soon she got bored of the conversations with the women who only spoke about who was transferred where and who travelled where during their holidays or as usual, their children. The food was the same in all the clubs, whether it was the Gymkhana or golf course—chicken tikkas, some cold snacks, an oily buffet and two varieties of desserts. She hated it. Varun loved it.

Once Varun left, Ayesha went back to her room to survey the mess. She had put off the inevitable for too long. She needed to pack up the house. All their summer clothes were lying in the cupboards. Adi's books and toys were scattered in his room. The carpets needed to be cleaned and put away.

It was two weeks after the party. After she had broken the news to Adi that they couldn't go on their vacation he had thrown a huge tantrum and stormed off, giving her the silent treatment because she was the one who broke the news to him. Adi was fine with his father, as usual. He didn't blame his father, who had lost the money. He blamed his mother because she hadn't saved enough and was not working! Ayesha had felt like she had been slapped in the face that day. She wanted to tell him that she had sacrificed her life for him. So that he could grow up with at least one parent around who would always go to his soccer and cricket games and school plays. A parent who was proud of her son and knew every detail about his life. And he was taking his father's side? Ayesha had no words. That's when she had borrowed money from her father and told Adi that they would go because she had managed it.

So she had delayed the packing.

She had gone to meet Tarini as she promised and had a wonderful lunch at Habitat, her favourite place for hearty Italian food that felt more from Chandigarh than Rome. Tarini had just bought a new Dior bag for four and a half lakh rupees. Ayesha would never spend so much on a bag. She was a practical woman. She had studied and passed in the first class in her Master's program in sociology. She was planning to study more before she was married off. She had a keen interest in physics as well and often wanted to speak to someone about the topics that interested her and not just about the house and Adi. But with Tarini, Ayesha was the listener and Tarini the talker. As much as she and Tarini were friends, she was never into fashion and brands. Her elegant saris and statement jewellery were all that she needed to make a mark in any social outing. And now she had to pack it all up for another move.

She sat in front of her cupboard and sighed. How many times had she done this? Four, maybe five since Varun had shifted houses within Lucknow and Delhi a few times as well.

She was tired. She wanted a stable house with a walk-in closet where she could just hang her winter clothes and not worry about the whole, tedious process of airing each and every one and putting them away in trunks. But being the wife of an IAS officer meant that one would constantly be travelling, shifting houses and putting away woolens in trunks, suitcases and box beds every spring.

'Savitri,' Ayesha called out to Savitri, her trusted maid who had been with her for over ten years. 'Shall we put moth balls with the clothes?'

Moth balls. The world had progressed in many ways but no one had solved the problem of keeping warm clothes away without silverfish insects eating into them. Ayesha sighed. She knew she didn't have enough trunks for the new winter wear they had bought this year. Adi had grown so tall that none of his old sweaters fit and she had had to buy a whole new wardrobe for him. But she didn't have the heart to throw away his old clothes. They were reminders of a simpler time. Clothes sometimes become memories more than photo albums ever do.

Savitri walked into the room, surveyed the mess and asked, 'What about your kanjeevaram saris? Do you want to keep them out in case there are any more parties?'

Ayesha sighed. She was done with parties. Her grand Diwali party had left her mentally and physically exhausted. She hadn't even gone for her yoga class since then.

Adi would finish his semester in DPS R. K. Puram this term and then they would move. Since all their friends were travelling during the winter holidays, she knew there were no more parties happening in the next few days. And in Lucknow they would need to settle in before they could re-connect with their old friends there, people she had never got along with but socialized with for Varun's sake. They were all superficial and shallow. Something she believed she could never be.

'Let's pack up as much as we can. Later on we can see if I need anything.'

'Do you want to keep your western clothes out?' Savitri asked, picking up a pair of jeans from the stack.

'Just a few. I'll wear it with a coat if I need to step out casually.' Ayesha had very few jeans and blouses but she mixed and matched them so wonderfully that she never needed to buy anything new to add to her western collection. She rarely wore jeans anyway, always preferring salwar kameezes or saris even if it was to go out with friends or to shop.

Ayesha loved Delhi, its cultural vibrancy. From plays and book launches, to gallery openings and cocktail parties, the conversations, the art, the music, the academic richness— there was always something happening in Delhi. And even though she was from a small community in Allahabad she was at heart a big-city girl and hated the close-mindedness of small town India and the vacuousness of its intellectualism. She was sent to north campus Delhi after completing her schooling in Allahabad. She stayed in hostel and had an aunt who she visited on the weekends who was her local guardian. She watched plays in Kamani and ate at Pandara Road. She shopped at Khan market and G. K. and even went to Chandni Chowk one Sunday with Tarini to get the experience of old Delhi. She loved every bit of it. The shops were beautiful. The people were warm and friendly. There was rich culture all around her. History emanated from every corner. Tarini had lent her a camera for a month and Ayesha spent all her free time wandering around monuments and taking photographs: Purana Quila, Jantar Mantar, Delhi gate, Ajmeri Gate, Red Fort, Lal Darwaza, Sunheri Masjid, Safdarjung's tomb. By the time she had to give back the camera, she had hundreds of

photographs, a suitcase of memories and a passion for Delhi
that she had never felt for any other city before. She was
heartbroken when her college days ended and her parents
called her back to Allahabad. They wouldn't let their only
child stay alone in the big bad city, after all.

So when her father found an IAS officer who was based in
Delhi, she jumped at the chance to get married.

Varun was tall and handsome and had studied economics
to enter the IAS. Intellectual enough, she had thought initially.
And pleasing to the eye. They used to have conversations in
the beginning but Ayesha soon realized that Varun only knew
economics. He had no other interests, never wanted to discuss
anything new. Adi was born in their second year of marriage
and suddenly all her plans of becoming a sociologist were put
on hold after a difficult pregnancy and birth. Her family
became her world. Her photography was left behind. Before
she knew it, they had to shift away from Delhi.

She turned to walk out of the room before she remembered,
'Oh Savitri, Adi's summer clothes have become small. So
we'll give some of them to the Blind Shelter. But all of Sahib's
and my clothes I want packed in the large trunks. Bahadur will
help move the suitcases. We might as well put away as much
as we can in one go, na? No point in working again later.'

Savitri nodded and went about her job. She was accustomed
to her mistress' needs. She had come with her from Allahabad
and looked after Ayesha and Adi as her own family. In the last
ten years, the family had shifted five times. From a small D-1
quarter to a C-2 apartment (the types that government servants
were given according to their rank and entry into the system),
a bungalow in Lucknow to a flat in Moti Bagh, Delhi, and
finally to a lovely, posh three-bedroom large corner plot in
Vasant Vihar with a garden, where they had their last two
Diwali parties. Savitri had helped Ayesha pack, shift and set up

home repeatedly. She could see her mistress didn't want to move but such was the life of an IAS officer. She was just glad that Ayesha relied on her far more than she did on anyone else.

Ayesha went into the kitchen to supervise Hari Prasad, their long-time cook, for the evening meal. She tasted the soup.

'A little more salt. Oh and Sahib likes his casserole with cheese and since I'm just having soup, put it into the oven just before he comes so it'll be nice and crisp.'

Ayesha had a large staff, something that most IAS officers were entitled to. These were the few perks they had. No money of course, because the stipend was meagre. Working for your country should be an honour. Being a bureaucrat meant that you were admired, revered and respected in circles that went beyond Delhi. It meant that you would have a driver, a cook, a gardener and a few maids to clean and manage your children if you needed them but you would hardly have money to buy an expensive car, fancy clothes or luxurious jewellery.

Ayesha touched her solitaire earrings, her favourites. Ten years she had worn the one-carat diamond earrings that her father had given her on her wedding day. As a gesture of gratitude. Her husband's side had given her two gold sets. One for the sangeet and one for the reception. They were kept away in a locker. She only wore these earrings. And her wedding ring. She would have loved for her husband to gift her something special on their tenth anniversary but he had just given her cash to buy whatever she wanted. How thoughtful, Ayesha thought, with a bitter taste in her mouth.

It wasn't as if she wasn't grateful. She was happy that she had a loving husband and a happy home. It was just that sometimes she wished there was more to her life than being a housewife.

9

There are three things a Delhi woman loves to do: Go to the parlour, shopping, and meeting friends.

The top of the list was always the parlour. Delhi women go to the parlour for every reason they can find: a manicure, pedicure, hair spa, a blow dry, a facial treatment. And every Delhi woman had a favourite parlour. Ayesha's was Pinky's Parlour. It was her favourite place to relax in her neighbourhood. Pinky pampered her and always gave her lovely adrak wali chai. Pinky had a staff of a few women and two men who gave the most delicious pedicures and hair spas. They knew just the places on a woman's feet to press to give immense pleasure. At any given time women were getting pedicures or head massages at Pinky's parlour.

For Ayesha it wasn't the massage but the constant gossip and chat with Pinky that made her day interesting.

'Ayesha! Kaisi hai?' Pinky asked as soon as Ayesha entered the door.

'I'm fine! How are you? Have you lost weight? You're looking so thin!'

Pinky, who was five feet two inches tall, weighing some eighty-two kilos, blushed. 'Haan yaar. I have lost two kilos. I have been starving myself for the last one week.'

'Starving? Why? How?' Ayesha sat down on the soft, bright red sofa next to Pinky.

'All the Diwali mithai I ate. Made me put on three kilos. So for the last week I only ate fruits and dahi. Have you heard of this GM diet? By God maine do din kiya aur mein mar gayi. Then I ate all the calories I lost and from then I went to a new dietician and started a new diet. It's been three days and I've lost two kilos.'

'So you mean you actually put on one kilo.' Ayesha reasoned.

'No no. This is a cleanse diet. You must try it. Only juices and fruits. It's quite healthy. In any case. Tu toh iti slim hai. You don't need to diet. I hate you!'

Ayesha laughed out loud. That was Pinky's way of saying she was jealous but she said it with love and a smile. 'It's just genes. My mother is thin.'

Pinky scrutinized Ayesha from top to bottom. 'True. That's why you don't have breasts only. Small little nimbus you have.'

Ayesha blushed. But Pinky quickly said, 'What difference does it make? Men still love any breasts. Stupid creatures. Women have made whole careers of flaunting their breasts. No brains, nothing. So you should always be proud of yours!'

Ayesha thought Pinky was too abrasive since she spoke about taboo topics but didn't say anything.

'Chal are you getting a pedicure done? Anything else? Chalo change kar hi lo. Pata nahin baad mein aur kya karwaogi.'

Ayesha nodded and Pinky shouted to the room where some clients were already sitting and a few men in Pinky's Parlour uniform were standing around, 'Manoj! Pedicure le leh Madam ki. Sunita, gown de de.'

Ayesha changed into a thin, strappy gown, put a towel over her shoulders and sat down on a warm, cushy leather chair. She then dipped her feet in hot, bubbly water.

'Paani theek hai?' Manoj asked as his fingers caressed her toes lightly under the bubbles.

Over the next 45 minutes or so, Manoj cleaned, buffed, scraped, pulled, tugged and pressed her legs, knees and ankles and slapped all the fat of her calves back into shape. It was his way of giving her a strong pedicure and Ayesha loved it. He dropped cream on to her legs in small drops all the way from her ankle to her thighs. The cold drops hit her skin and made it tingle. Then he began to slowly make circular movements around each drop, moving his hands up her legs to gently caress her thighs. Ayesha rolled her head back and closed her eyes. It felt warm and fuzzy. She could feel herself getting moist as her legs were being massaged by a complete stranger. Then he wrapped a hot towel around her legs and slowly moved his thumbs from the base of her feet, up towards her calves and thighs. Ayesha gulped. A simple pedicure could feel so good.

'Hair spa, hair oil nahin karengi, Madam?' Manoj asked as he lay his full palms on her legs and thighs. Ayesha rolled her head back and said, 'Karwa hi lo!'

Then Manoj called for some hot oil and started rubbing it on Ayesha's head and slowly moved down to her shoulders and back. He moved his hands over the towel down her back, slowly kneading his fingers into her spine. Then he moved in front and caressed her collar bone, moving gently over the top part of her breasts over her gown, never going lower.

'Pressure theek hai?'

That was the signal if you wanted him to do more. And Ayesha, whose only kink in her otherwise staid life was this weekly hair oil massage, replied, 'Thoda aur pressure chahiye.'

He moved his hands magically over her clothes, down her back and her sides till all her erogenous zones were aroused and she could feel a moistness between her thighs. She gave him an extra tip when he finished.

She looked amazing with soft hair that was neatly blow dried and nails that sparkled for an evening on the town.

Pinky asked, 'Service kaisa tha?'

Ayesha smiled. 'As usual, amazing.' She handed Pinky her payment.

Pinky smiled a knowing look, 'But why all this sajna dhajna?'

'The new HRD minister, Harshvardhan Singhania, has called us to his place for dinner. I must look my best.'

'Of course,' Pinky smiled. 'And you're looking lovely. I'm sure he'll be impressed!'

'Oh I don't know about that. I don't even know if I'll get to meet him.'

'Well, all the best.' They said their goodbyes.

Ayesha was looking forward to the last dinner of the season. She would make a dazzling impression at this politician's place. Even if she was a housewife, she would be the only housewife anyone ever noticed in that party!

10

Ayesha dressed carefully for the evening. A gorgeous black chikan sari with mukaish work all over it that made her sparkle like a diamond. She accessorized with a chunky red stone Amrapalli necklace and stuck to her small diamond earrings. With bright red nail polish on her fingers and toes and her gorgeous hair blow-dried to perfection around her face, she looked the epitome of the perfect bureaucrat's wife. A trophy wife, if one could say so.

As they walked into a large bungalow, Ayesha felt a little nervous. She had never been to a politician's house. And what if she said something wrong, would it affect her husband's career?

They entered straight into the lawns of the politician's bungalow from the side entrance. It was lit up with twinkling lights hanging from trees and several round tables with crisp, white table cloths that had a bowl of flowers on each. There were waiters in uniforms who were serving people drinks and snacks. A buffet counter was placed at one end. The host, Harshvardhan Singhania, was greeting people casually, sitting with everyone and chatting with the bodyguards around him.

'Arrey Mika aane waalla hai.'

She heard snippets of a conversation that some ladies were having while sitting at a table.

'Arrey nahin Sunny Leone aa rahi hai.'

'Sach?!' one woman gasped, catching her neck as if the thought had choked her.

'Yeah. Apparently she will perform also.'

'My husband will toh die only!' another woman said as she giggled. 'He loves that song Pink Lips!'

'Nahin nahin Baby Doll hai woh gaana.'

Ayesha smiled as she kept walking. She knew she wouldn't get along well with these women and she wanted to have a drink. She moved towards the bar when Varun brought over a colleague of his, 'Ayesha, I want you to meet Sanjay. He has just come to town with his wife.' Varun added a few more sentences to Sanjay's introduction and said, 'He needs my help with a new project. Hopefully hum saath mein kaam karenge ab.'

Sanjay smiled. 'Inshallah! Namaste, Ayeshaji.'

Ayesha folded her hands. 'Namaste. Kabhi aayie humarey yahan.'

Varun felt proud of his wife. 'Yeh bohat achcha biryani banati hain.'

'Achcha? That's remarkable. Ab toh aana hi padega.'

Ayesha excused herself, saying she needed to find a restroom. She was instantly bored and the night had not even started yet. Varun introduced her to the same type of people with the same dialogue. And all Varun could convey about her was her cooking. She had more skills than that! She was an intelligent and talented human being. And here she was, being demoted to a cook whose only task was to make sure her family was well-fed. As a housewife she should have been happy with just that, she presumed, but she wasn't. She felt restless and upset.

Maybe it was the cold air that was giving her a headache or the dullness of the conversations but she started walking towards the house to get away from the party and the cold air.

She entered the house from a side entrance and started looking for a restroom. But curiosity got the better of her and she decided to have a look around this politician's house. She always liked seeing how people decorated their homes and she especially wondered how a bachelor politician like Harshvardhan would do it up. He had only been in his position for a month but he was already being groomed to be the possible next Prime Minister in the next elections. She knew one could tell a lot about a man by the way he kept his house.

She had a quick look to check if any one was following her as she walked into the drawing room. It was a two-storey house in the most posh locality of Delhi. The drawing room was simple, with a plain beige sofa at one end and a TV at the other. A large Turkish carpet sat in the middle. As she walked further, she entered an office. There was a large L-shaped mahogany table in the front with a red swivel chair at the back. There were a few photos of Mahatma Gandhi and Mother Teresa hanging on the walls and a set of black-and-white pictures of a couple on the desk facing him. There was a computer on one side of the table and a stack of files. To one side there was a wall-to-wall bookshelf. Ayesha walked up to the bookshelf to see the kind of books this politician kept. They ranged from economics to Stephen King, from maps to motorcycles, and from history books to Nobel Prize winners on different shelves.

'What do you like to read?'

Ayesha jumped up, startled by the voice behind her. She turned around and saw Harshvardhan standing there, smiling with his hands folded behind his back.

She asked another question in reply. 'Have you read all these books? Or are they just for show?'

Harshvardhan laughed. His voice was deep, melodious. 'Who would I show them to?'

Ayesha was quickly embarrassed at being tactless. 'I'm

sorry if I offended you. I didn't mean to. And sorry for barging into your study, I didn't mean to do that either. Before I could stop myself I was wandering around.'

'No it's perfectly fine. I'm Harshvardhan.'

Ayesha smiled. 'Ayesha.'

'It's lovely to meet you, Ayesha.'

'You truly have a lovely place.'

'Thank you. Most of the stuff a designer handles but there are a few things I love. Like this bookshelf. Do you like reading?'

'Oh, immensely. I don't get enough time to, though.'

'What do you read?'

'A lot of fiction. But I feel liked I'm moving away from it. Tired of the same old stories discussing relationships. I've recently discovered Osho.' Ayesha surprised herself by discussing her reading habits with this stranger/politician. This was the most random conversation she had ever had in her life and yet it made sense.

'I've just been reading my files. Inundated with them actually. I would really just like to sit in peace somewhere and read some Thich Nhat Hanh. Have you heard of him?'

Ayesha shook her head. Harshvardhan continued, 'He writes about mindfulness. Better than Osho.' He walked to the bookshelves and ran a finger over the spines, looking for a title. He picked one out. 'Why don't you borrow this,' he said as he handed the book over to Ayesha. 'Tell me what you think of it.'

'You want my opinion on it?' Ayesha was a little stunned.

'Sure. If you get a chance to read it.'

'Of course.' She smiled as she took the book from his hand. 'I would love to get back to you on that.'

Harshvardhan walked over to his desk and that's when Ayesha noticed him properly. He was in his late 40s, maybe early 50s at the most, probably the youngest HRD minister in the cabinet. His hair was black and showing a few strands of grey at the temples. His eyes were dark green brown and he walked with nonchalant grace. He towered at maybe over six feet tall. Ayesha at just five feet two inches felt even smaller.

His profile as he looked down at his desk suggested a stubbornness that came with great power and struggle. His square jaw thrust forward as he picked up a piece of paper and turned around to address her.

'I want to help the girl child in India,' he said. His skin taut over his elegant cheekbones, he spoke loudly and clearly with authority, demanding attention. 'My speech tonight is going to be about that. What do you think of this idea?' He looked down to read as he flicked his glasses out from a case and perched them on his nose. 'If I suggest empowerment of women through education of every girl child from the villages to the towns because each and every daughter is important to India. And that's why we need to educate them to build a stronger nation.'

He paused, looked at her intently as if asking for her approval. Ayesha would have immediately said yes. Sure, it was a great idea. But she had another one. 'While the idea is wonderful and noble,' she began with a bit of hesitation, 'the media unfortunately won't lap it up. Every act of a politician's life and his success is based on the perception the media gives to the people.'

'Yes I know that,' he said. 'And?'

'It's been done before. While everyone thinks education of the girl child is important the burning question today is safety for women. That should be your agenda. Then feeding every girl child. Because if they're hungry, then they won't learn anything anyway. That is a very complicated process if you ask me.'

Harshvardhan's eyes were instantly alive. 'Go ahead, tell me more.'

Ayesha walked around slowly, thinking as she spoke and gesticulating with her hands as she explained, 'Well the infrastructure of many places has improved but the safety of women in towns and in villages has not. You need a simple solution.'

Then he noticed how beautiful she was. She had a petite and taut body with luscious long auburn hair, a small diamond nose ring that offset her smoky, chocolate-coloured eyes and a sun-kissed complexion. She wrinkled her nose as she spoke and he immediately found this extremely endearing. He had never been with a woman who could carry off a sari so elegantly or someone who could challenge him with such clarity.

'Employ more police?' Harshvardhan found himself engaging in a thoughtful discussion with this charming young woman. 'That will need more funds and further talk.'

'No,' Ayesha said, surprising him and herself, too. But she continued, 'You need to have well-lit areas in every metro and train station in your district. Even within the compartments. Tube lights at every corner and maybe even CCTV cameras. Safety for women on public transport. Autos that will go after dark for a woman passenger, no matter how short the distance is or else they will be hauled to jail. Emergency phones that if picked up, call the police station immediately, at strategic points near bus stops. There needs to be a fear that people can't get away with the rape and assault or harassment of women. The judiciary can't do that much. They need to know that they can get caught!'

Harshvardhan nodded. 'So if I start with the metros in urban areas beginning with Delhi, besides well-lit areas, maybe I can enforce a separate metro for women late in the nights where there will be cameras in every bogey so they can feel safe.'

'Yes, maybe.'

He walked grandly towards the door, 'I'll need to get a few more ministers involved with this. Great. So can we go now so that I can give this speech?'

'What about the speech that you were making?'

'I'll figure it out,' he said with a smile. He was known for his great extempore speeches and his ability to charm a crowd. He had completely floored Ayesha with his magnetic personality and humility.

He gestured for her to leave his office. He stopped her for a moment as she passed him and she could feel his breath upon her face as he spoke softly, 'Thank you. Thank you...' He waited for her to say her name and with a mere whisper she replied, 'Ayesha.' Later she would find out that he already knew her name.

'Thank you, Ayesha.' He smelt like a combination of fresh cologne and Ariel detergent.

'You have a beautiful house,' she said with a smile.

'Thank you. Someday I hope to show you the rest of it,' and he meant it. This was an association that he knew would not end that night.

As they walked outside, bodyguards immediately surrounded Harshvardhan as Ayesha walked in another direction to find Varun. She stopped suddenly and realized that she hadn't even told the politician who her husband was. How would he know? Harshvardhan spent a few minutes in a corner speaking on his mobile phone. She noticed how he seemed enthusiastic with her idea and was nodding his head patiently as he heard the person on the phone.

Soon enough, an emcee announced that Harshvardhan was now going to give his speech. Ayesha looked around and saw that there was a small stage at the front of the lawn which had just lit up with diyas. She saw Harshvardhan ascend the stage in a stately manner. He greeted the crowd, 'Namaste.'

He began his speech. 'Thank you everyone for joining me on this wonderful evening. I hope you have enough drinks and food. I hope you're happy and well looked after. I don't have a wife but I'm sure that my boys will be more than willing to help all of you. I have spoken to many of you and am glad I've gotten to know you better.'

As he spoke, Ayesha noticed that he kept searching in the crowds for someone and she felt she needed to be in the light. She moved slightly towards a more prominent, sharper focus light coming from a lamp and he suddenly caught her eye before he continued.

'As you know I am planning to make several changes for women. The first thing I want to start out with is safety.'

There was loud applause from several women in the audience and he seemed pleased that they approved of his idea.

'I believe that all women are strong and independent and can make this nation great. They not only need freedom to do as they please, but also the support of the government to give them the safety to do so. And with this I propose a new scheme. A special metro train that will run at specific times only for women. It will have a special police force to keep the women safe even if they choose to travel late in the night to their destinations. Along with this we will install many more lights at the stations for them to walk freely. I will also ensure autos have a 'call the police' facility if the auto wala refuses to take a woman passenger after sunset. I want to assure you that these are just a few of my plans to keep all of you safe, to keep this city safe and to work towards a government that is for you,' he paused and looked straight at Ayesha before he concluded his speech with a sentence, 'Be safe. Be happy. I'm with you, for you, always.' The crowd applauded as he bowed his head and said, 'Please enjoy your evening. Dinner is served. I hope to meet more of you later this evening.' And then he looked around and Ayesha knew that part was also directed at her.

Through the rest of the evening, Varun stuck next to her as they moved from one couple to another making polite conversation. They finished their dinner and Ayesha said she was feeling tired. They decided to leave. It had become quite cold and despite the Pashmina shawl that Ayesha wrapped around herself, the biting wind was giving her another headache.

As they were leaving they found the politician and Varun said politely as Ayesha stood a step away from him, 'Thank you so much, Sir for having us. We truly had a wonderful time.'

Harshvardhan nodded his head. 'Glad you could come.' And then to Ayesha, 'I hope you didn't get too bored?'

Ayesha shook her head. 'No. The whole evening was magical. You have wonderful plans.'

'I got a little help with my idea,' he said with a twinkle in his eye.

As Varun walked towards his car, she looked back towards the gate and saw Harshvardhan's gaze linger on her a little more. Her heart skipped a beat and she wondered why. The man was almost a decade older than her and she was a married woman. Then why did she feel this peculiar attraction to this stranger? Maybe it was because for the first time in her life, a man of power had asked her for her opinion? A man who was learned and knowledgeable had taken her suggestion into consideration. Or maybe it was because of the way he looked at her that felt all wrong and yet so right.

11

'Zor se bolo!'

'Jai Mata Di!'

Ayesha looked around the room where there were women who were swaying to loud bhajans and singing with their eyes closed. She couldn't believe she had let her mother-in-law drag her to another Mata Ki Chowki.

'You have to do these things, Ayesha. Even if you're an atheist, you need to do things for your in-laws,' her mother had told her back when she had gotten married and refused to go for any religious function.

More than once she had argued with Varun, 'I don't believe in God. I believe in science. Why do I have to sit at these events? I don't believe in them and they're too loud.'

'It's not loud,' Varun had replied. 'It's a calling to God. To Mata. It's important to me.'

Ayesha had relented again and again, joining her husband and in-laws at religious gatherings. And again here she was, eleven years after getting married, still trying to please her in-laws, her own parents, and her husband. Everyone, it seemed, except herself.

'Jai, Jai Santoshi Ma, Jai,' Ayesha's mother-in-law chanted with the crowd as she swayed to the music and covered her head with a beautiful, blue-with-zardozi-chiffon dupatta that matched her gawdy blue and gold salwar kameez. Ayesha covered her head with her pallu. She wore a lovely silk sari with a string of pearls.

Her in-laws had dropped in unannounced two days ago. They stayed in Ghaziabad. They came often and stayed with Ayesha and Varun to spend time with their grandson and meet their friends. Sometimes Ayesha's mother-in-law, Suman Mathur's, social life was so exhausting that she stayed an entire week or two before she went back to her own house. Ayesha was at the parlour when they had dropped in. They were furious that their bahu wasn't at home and Varun had called to tell her to rush back immediately.

'Mummyji, Papa, what a pleasant surprise!' Ayesha exclaimed as she entered the door. 'If you had told me, I would have stayed at home. I had to do some emergency grocery shopping. You know how the servants are, they can never pick the correct vegetables for Adi.' Ayesha rattled off her words so her in-laws would not have a chance to scold her or complain.

See, marriage makes you smart. You learn to better understand the nuances of making your in-laws happy. One, you play the grandchild card: If anything that you did was for their grandchild's benefit, they wouldn't be as harsh on you as they normally were. With in-laws visiting, the equations always changed in the family. You no longer have a right to speak against your husband in front of them. You no longer have the free will to just leave things untidy or not bother about your children and the rules if you're too tired. When the in-laws visit, a housewife always needs to be on her toes from morning to night to prove to her in-laws that they chose correctly for their son, who probably will not do any work around the house anyway while they praise him for being such a great son.

'Where are you roaming about, bahu?' her mother-in-law

demanded an answer. 'Why weren't you looking after the house? And you don't seem to be teaching Adi here any of our sanskriti! Where are this boy's manners!'

Ayesha nudged Adi to his grandparents. The boy touched his grandmother's feet and she pulled him up to a warm embrace. He was old enough to understand that he had nothing to speak to his grandparents about and he could sense they didn't like his mother very much. It affected his relationship with them even though they bought him presents when they came and took him to eat at all the favourite junk food restaurants that were forbidden by his mother.

'Mummyji, have you had lunch?' Ayesha asked her mother-in-law. 'There is some fresh food made in the morning. Bahadur would have laid out the table if you had asked him.'

Mrs Mathur looked at her disdainfully. 'There was just chicken. Since when do you not keep any other vegetables or dal made for lunch? I've told Bahadur to make some aloo rassa, some bhindi ki sabzi and some fresh phulkas for us.'

Ayesha groaned inwardly. Varun and Adi wouldn't eat any of the vegetables her in-laws had asked the servant to make who would grumble later to her about how his workload had increased. Their family always had some non-vegetarian dish for practically every meal and since she only ate one roti with whatever was made for the men in her life, they were used to eating only one dish.

'Let me get the table ready then,' Ayesha said as she walked to the kitchen to assist Bahadur. It was Savitri's day off as well and she couldn't believe her luck since her in-laws had come on the one weekend that she had given her help some leave. She thought it was going to be an easy day, as Varun had gone to play golf and would be back only by six in the evening and would be so tired that he would go to bed as soon as he had some pakoras and chai.

It was an unsaid rule that daughters-in-law should always have to work hard when the in-laws came because their constant approval would mean a stable marriage with her husband.

'This is a great lunch,' her father-in-law said, as he finished his meal. 'Make something fresh for dinner, Bahu. Now that we've eaten this, it can be given to the servants.'

'And at least for the next three weeks that we are here, get fresh vegetables. None of the frozen packets that you keep serving Adi for his tifffin,' Suman said, as she wrinkled her nose and gave herself a sterner look.

Ayesha knew that not only her wine, but non-vegetarian food too would be banned in her own household for three weeks. As it had always been every time her in-laws came to visit. This is going to be a long month ahead, she sighed to herself. It is their son's house, she reminded herself; not mine. They had more of a right than she did, as they presumed.

'Bahu!' Ayesha's mother-in-law was calling out. 'Where are you? Bina aunty ko hello bolo.' And Ayesha came out of her reverie to quickly saunter over to her.

'Hello, Bina aunty.'

'Kaisi ho beta? Yeh nayi sari hai? Aaj kal dikhai nehi deti ho.'

Ayesha's mother-in-law piped in, 'Haan beta you must go visit Bina aunty.'

'Next week,' Bina spoke with great gusto. 'I am having a havan at home. You must come.'

'Of course we'll be there,' Suman Mathur replied for both herself and Ayesha.

Ayesha smiled while secretly wishing she could run away from the entire episode.

She said, 'Actually Aunty, we're taking a vacation so we might not be here at that time.'

'Oh where are you going?' Bina asked, impressed that the Mathurs had money to travel.

'To Switzerland, Aunty.'

Bina looked at Suman with raised eyebrows. 'Bade achche din aa gaye!'

'Main nahin ja rahi hoon,' Mrs Mathur said. 'Sirf Varun, Ayesha aur Adi ko leke ja raha hai.' She let out a deep sigh before continuing, 'Ab no one wants us old people around at all. My son would have taken me alone. But he spent all his money on this vacation na. Ab honest IAS officers don't make enough to take two vacations.'

Ayesha didn't say a word though inwardly she wanted to scream that Varun had almost blown the entire vacation and it was Adi's idea not hers to take a family vacation. But she continued with the small talk with the other aunties to whom her mother-in-law introduced her. She had met them before but since they all looked alike she never remembered their names. 'Ji Aditya bilkul theek hai. Aur Varun bhi. Ji, khush hai. Ji aayie kabhi ghar pe.'

Soon the ceremony was over and Ayesha stood around while her mother-in-law spoke to her friends. Her mother-in-law and her were like chalk and cheese. While Suman Mathur had a vast social circle, Ayesha only had a handful of friends whom she liked to meet. While Suman was religious and loved going for satsangs and jagrans, Ayesha was an atheist who didn't even talk about God to her child. And while Suman Mathur loved spending money on new clothes, Ayesha wore the same saris repeatedly to every function because she thought she should save money if her husband ever ended up gambling away all his earnings.

On the way home Suman noticed with a touch of sarcasm, 'At least you could have worn a new sari. I would have lent you one.'

Ayesha didn't say anything. Mrs Mathur continued, 'Oh by the way I asked Savitri where your suits were. I've taken a few for Leela.'

Ayesha turned her head toward her mother-in-law. This was the umpteenth time she had taken her clothes without asking her for her daughter, Varun's sister. 'Leela won't fit into my clothes. She's broader.'

'Koi baat nahin. Alter kar lenge. Hope you don't mind.' It wasn't as much a request as it was a statement.

Ayesha couldn't say anything. The tradition the whatever the daughter-in-law had in the house went to the unmarried sister, remained forever. She had been giving her clothes since the day she entered her in-laws' house. And even now when she was not staying with them, her mother-in-law took her clothes to give to Varun's sister.

Ayesha knew she had only two options. Either she could shout and tell everyone that they could not touch her things anymore and she refused to give any of her clothes. Or she could just give in and let harmony remain in the family. Her father would buy her new stuff anyway. But if her in-laws got upset by her not giving her clothes, they would think she was selfish. Her father wouldn't approve and there would be chaos at home.

'No I don't mind,' she said as she looked out of the car window. She didn't want to go home.

She had slowly been feeling it recently but she was always unsure; now she wouldn't deny it anymore: she felt trapped. She couldn't breathe. She needed a release. She was tired of playing the role of a dutiful wife and daughter-in-law when all she wanted to do was to be free and happy.

12

'Happy birthday, Mama,' Adi said as he opened the door to the master bedroom. He went to give Ayesha a tight hug. 'Thank you, baby,' Ayesha replied. Adi was getting himself ready for school that morning; he told Ayesha that was his birthday present to her.

Suddenly reminded, Varun mumbled in his sleep from his side of the bed, 'Happy Birthday, Ayesha.'

Ayesha said politely, 'Thank you.'

She got out of bed and stepped outside the room to find her in-laws just emerging from the guest room. She touched their feet and received their blessings for the New Year. She then went into the kitchen where Savitri was preparing breakfast. Without saying anything Savitri gave her a big hug and the widest smile. It was probably the kindest gesture Ayesha received from anyone. Soon her parents called and wished her and when she wanted to take the phone to her room to speak privately her mother-in-law said rudely, 'Why do you need privacy? You can talk in here.'

And so Ayesha spoke courteously and cautiously and then kept the phone down. A few friends wished her as well. She felt good, almost able to forget all the negative feelings she was having just last night.

In the middle of the afternoon, she got a most surprising phone call from the office of the politician, Harshvardhan Singhania, in whose house they had attended a party a few weeks earlier. Luckily her in-laws were sleeping and she was alone in her room with the TV on when she got the call.

The politician's secretary put him on the line after a few moments of waiting and Ayesha could feel her heart racing in the few seconds before she heard his voice. 'Hello? Ayesha?'

'Yes.'

'Hi. How are you?'

'I'm fine.' This conversation is strange, she thought. Clearly she hadn't told him when her birthday was so what was this call about?

'Listen, I took your suggestion and I'm starting a metro train only for women. I wanted a woman's perspective on it. And since it was your idea, I thought it would be good to get your opinion.'

'Okay?' she said, tentatively. She still had no idea what he wanted from her but she was extremely flattered that within a few weeks he had been able to take her suggestion into consideration.

'Would you like to go for a ride with me on the new metro tonight?'

Was this a joke? Ayesha thought. But he didn't seem the type who would make light-hearted remarks.

'Okay, I guess.'

'It will have to be late in the night since the regular metro will be running through the day. Will you be able to come out then? I'll have a car pick you up at ten o' clock?'

Ayesha had never gone out that late in the night without Varun. She knew they would probably be home by then. Her in-laws had dinner early and she would be able to slip out later. She would have to make some excuse to her in-laws and Varun to be able to do so.

But this Harshvardhan was a stranger! Ayesha reminded herself. What was she getting herself into? But her mind told her to do it anyway. She imagined it would be something like being sucked in a black hole: where every light and happiness was sucked up. She hadn't done anything exciting her entire life. Maybe she could go for a metro ride at ten in the night with a stranger she had exchanged a few words with some time ago. What could happen in a public place anyway, and with his bodyguards surrounding them?

'Sure,' she said, this time more confidently.

'Superb. See you tonight.' And with that he hung up the phone. Ayesha wondered again if a friend had just made a prank call. Was it a birthday present from someone? But he hadn't wished her and he wouldn't know. The rest of the afternoon was spent in thinking and re-thinking the scenarios of what she was about to do.

That evening Varun came home early and plonked himself in front of the TV. Ayesha asked him when they would leave for dinner. 'In a bit,' he said. 'Let me unwind. There's no hurry. It's just seven thirty.'

But a full hour later he still wasn't ready while the entire family had bathed and dressed and were ready to go. Finally they left at nine, and there weren't many choices to discover as they couldn't travel too far. Adi was hungry and so were Ayesha's in-laws.

'Let's go to Sagar,' Varun suggested. 'Everyone likes south Indian food.'

Ayesha looked down at her clothes. She had worn a lovely new sari that her mother had sent. A beautiful choker and silver sandals. If they had to go to Sagar she would have worn jeans. Thankfully her mother-in-law said, 'It's Ayesha's birthday. We can go someplace nicer. Where do you want to go, Ayesha?'

Ayesha was tempted to say the new French restaurant on Lodhi Road but she found herself saying, as usual, 'Any place you would like. I'm not fussy.' Why didn't she open her mouth when she was asked, she wondered. Why did she so easily give in to the demands of the family? Her unhappiness was partly her own fault. Just because she went along with what everyone said, they expected her not to have an opinion on anything. And soon they were taking her for granted.

'I want sizzlers,' Adi said.

Sizzlers were Ayesha's least favourite food. A slab of meat on some burning plate that always left your tongue scarred and your dress dirty from the flecks of sauce flying in all directions was something she just didn't want.

'We could have Thai food,' her reply lacked a ring of finality.

'Um…do you *really* want to have Thai? Ma and Papa don't really like it too much.' Varun was firm and didn't even look in her direction.

'Chinese?' she offered.

Adi jumped up and down, 'I love Chinese food!'

Varun seemed perplexed. 'There aren't enough options for vegetarian plates in Chinese food. What will Dadu and Dadi have, Adi? Let's think about them as well. And I'm tired of driving now. We've reached South Extension. Let's go to the Indian place here. It's nice with good seating.'

With that he turned into the parking lot and everyone got out. Adi didn't seem to mind as long as he had ice cream after dinner. Ayesha got out and straightened her sari. Varun walked ahead with his parents, talking to them about something while she trailed slightly behind. Then Varun turned and waited for her to catch up while his parents walked ahead to the restaurant.

'Why do you always have to wear a sari, Ayesha? Can't you keep it casual sometimes?'

She swallowed before answering, 'I thought you liked me in saris.'

'Yes sometimes. But just try to be your age. Why must you always be older than who you are? Here we are,' he said as he reached the entrance and were seated by their host.

Ayesha felt upset. Her appetite was gone. She didn't want to eat Indian food again. She had it at home. She needed a drink. She wanted a present. It was her goddamn 35th birthday. The least Varun could have done was appreciate her for what she had worn. Suddenly she remembered she needed to go out later that night, 'Varun,' she said, leaning towards him after they had ordered, 'Pinky has arranged a little birthday party for me after dinner. She'll send a car. Is it okay if I go?'

Varun didn't look happy with the idea. 'Will you be gone the entire night?'

'No. Just after Adi sleeps. For a few hours.' Her voice was shakier than she would have liked.

'I didn't know you were that close to Pinky?' Varun was sceptical.

'You know how you're always telling me to get more friends. Now I've made one.' She was annoyed that Varun was asking so many questions about a female friend.

Ayesha breathed a sigh of relief. As she nibbled at her food she reasoned with herself that if she hadn't told a lie, she wouldn't have been able to go. Varun wouldn't allow her to go for a train ride with a politician. He hated them. They had made his life miserable by moving him from one department to another; even though it was a profession he had chosen.

Ayesha pledged that this would be the last time she would lie to Varun. That phone call had come completely out of the blue, as if the universe was giving her an adventure for one evening. It was to be the birthday present that no one thought of giving her. She would experience that and get back to her life as a devoted mother and faithful wife.

She would meet up with Harshvardhan Singhania, take the metro ride, tell him what she thought, and then the car would drop her back home. It shouldn't take longer than two hours. She'd be curled up in bed before anyone even woke up.

13

It took more than two hours she took for the ride she would never forget.

At ten o' clock sharp a black Mercedes arrived at her place. But the family only got home by 10:30 and in her rush she didn't bother to change. Her in-laws both gave her a look that said they didn't approve; she ignored them.

She reached the station and a man whom she presumed to be Harshvardhan's bodyguard was waiting for her at the entrance. She hesitated. What if this was all a ruse to kidnap her and harm her?

Just then Harshvardhan emerged from another car that she didn't notice was already parked opposite hers. Harshvardhan was wearing a dark blue kurta and jeans. For a man in his late 40s, he looked better than most men half his age.

'You made it,' he said, his mouth curving into an unconscious broad smile as he took long, bold steps towards her. He gently touched her elbow, guiding her towards the platform as his bodyguards walked behind them

He didn't waste any time. 'So when we spoke about safety,' he said to her, 'you had mentioned lighting. I have had these emergency lights placed all over the stations. This one is just a reference point. I've also got cameras installed. See there?' He didn't try to hide his excitement. Indeed the platform was well lit and CCTV cameras were in place. As a train approached she quickly noted the pink streak running along the coaches. She was impressed. He had actually taken steps to make a women-only train a reality. The train was clean, the AC was working well, and it even had a plug point for phone chargers. There were CCTV cameras on both sides of the bogey.

'This is all good,' she said as she looked around. There was space for ad hoardings on the tilted ceilings. And there was even an emergency phone on one side.

'Any passenger who needs help can just pick up the phone and without dialing it connects to the station master at the next platform. Immediately police officers reach the next platform.'

She was amazed. It was well thought out and her suggestions had been taken into account.

'Shall we take a ride?' he smiled as he sat down on the bench and the two bodyguards went to the other end of the coach and stood there.

'We're going to move?'

He nodded and raised his hand and the train came to life as if by magic. Ayesha sat opposite him as the train began to leave the platform. *I'm truly on this crazy ride now*, she thought. No one knew where she was.

'So what do you think, Ayesha?' he looked at her intently.

'It's impressive. Where will we stop?'

'Wherever you want it to. Otherwise it will go to the end of the line and come right back here.' He was gauging her lack of ease. 'Are you feeling alright?'

'Yes.' She looked out the window, the twinkling lights of Delhi flying past her, looking pretty across the skyline.

'Thank you for coming,' he said. 'I wanted to get a woman's point of view and all the women I know are in my family. They never give me an honest opinion about things. It sometimes feels as if they agree with me only because I do favours for them.'

Ayesha wondered if he was opening up to her because she also felt like she could tell him anything. 'This really is such a wonderful birthday present.'

'Oh! When is your birthday?'

'Today.'

'Happy Birthday, Ayesha. I wish I could have given you flowers.' The warmth of his smile echoed in his voice.

'That's alright. This is the most wonderful gift I've received.'

'You look beautiful, if I may be so forward as to say so. Stunning in a sari.'

'Thank you.'

'So I'm planning to make a statement about this scheme next week. I've written down some thoughts and I'd like you to tell me what you think. Will that be alright?'

'Sure.'

He smiled and took his phone out to read his notes. 'May I sit with you?' he asked.

She nodded. He sat next to her and began scrolling down his notes. Overall they were good but she had a few suggestions; he took them graciously.

Once she accidentally brushed her hand against his and immediately felt electricity. He nodded his head, laughed, spoke, hesitated, spoke again and she became more and more sure of herself around him.

'Thank you so much, Ayesha,' he said when they finished.

'You're welcome.'

They kept sitting next to each other. 'So tell me about yourself,' she said.

So he did. From his childhood to his political career, his taste in single malts and history books. He gave her a little glimpse of the highs and lows of living the life of a bachelor.

'Why did you never get married?' as soon as the words escaped her lips she realized she may have overstepped.

He didn't seem to mind. 'I never found an intelligent woman who could challenge me,' he said while looking deep into her eyes. 'And what about you, why did you get married so young? You must have been, what, twelve?'

Ayesha laughed. 'No no, I had already finished college. Well, the short of it is that my father found the right man for me.'

'Is any man ever right? I've heard women say there is no such thing as "the right man", only the right time.'

'Oh yes that's true.'

'And I've also heard people say that all men need to be moulded anyway so how does it matter who you marry? All you need is a whip and a stern look and the man is just mush in your hands.'

Ayesha found him charming. 'That's hardly the case here. But is that why you never succumbed to any woman? You didn't want to be moulded?'

'Oh no. I'm happy to be moulded. I would love to listen to a woman's suggestions about my career and life. They're far more intelligent than men anyway. Why do we keep them at home and waste their lives away by making them cook food and raise children? In fact, men should do that and let the women lead the country. They would do a far better job. Look at the women entrepreneurs and women managing CEO positions everywhere. They are the backbone of growth. Not the men who fight wars because of their egos.'

'You really think women can do all that?'

'Of course! Look at how they multitask at home. Imagine if they had to do that in a workplace without worrying about children or what's cooking for dinner. The world would be a much happier, calmer and thriving place.'

Ayesha studied her hands. 'Have you read Stephen Hawking?'

'Yes I have. A Brief History of Time. Have you?'

Ayesha felt alive. Why did a woman need an intellectual connection with a man to feel attracted to him? No matter how good-looking a man was, if he liked things that she was not interested in, a woman would never feel compelled to spend time with him. That was the simple truth of any relationship.

The conversation was easy. They spoke about books, theories, the country and their lives. He questioned and listened and she in turn questioned and listened. He didn't know why he felt so attracted to this woman who was already married. He knew it could not lead to anything and yet he wanted her approval, her appreciation, and wanted to protect her, too. It was very unusual for him.

Ayesha didn't know how the time passed. Who was this stranger she was speaking to? Why was he asking so many questions and why was she replying? When he spoke about his family and his life as a politician, she felt a wave of emotion of wanting to nurture him.

As the train came to a halt, he instinctively moved to prevent her from falling and stopped himself a few inches short so as not to touch her. How he longed to hold her. Maybe this was the last time they would meet. He had no more excuses. She was a married woman. He needed to leave her alone.

The train stopped and Ayesha got up, suddenly aware that the bubble had burst. She now needed to go home. To her family.

'Well it was lovely meeting you,' she said, a pensive shimmer in the shadow of her eyes. 'All the best for this. I think it's a wonderful idea and women will love it.'

They slowly walked back to their cars as he said, 'Thank you for taking out time for me and giving me your valuable feedback. The same car will drop you home safely. I've given you my number in case you need anything. Please just call me. For anything. *I'm with you, for you, always.*' His dark eyes locked with hers for an instant.

She nodded and shook his hand. 'Thank you so much.' She turned before her voice could choke.

He watched the car leave as he stood in the cold winter morning, wondering whether his life would ever be the same again. His heart ached.

14

Ayesha had barely a week to prepare for their Switzerland trip. It was mid-December and they were going to leave as soon as Adi's school days ended. She had postponed packing to the last minute not knowing if Varun would gamble away the tickets again.

It had been a week since that train ride. The very next day she received a huge, beautiful bouquet of flowers from Harshvardhan. There was no card but she knew. She had sent him a text message saying thank you for the flowers and he had replied, 'You're most welcome.' Ayesha dissected that SMS for a few days. What did 'most' mean? She felt like she was in high school all over again, with a crush on a boy. *I must shake this off quickly.* The best way to do it would be to plunge into their Switzerland holiday.

A few days later she got another SMS from him: watch the news at nine. Promptly after Adi went to bed she turned on the TV and said she needed to see the news. Just at that moment Varun walked away to his room to take a call. She watched as Harshvardhan was telling journalists about the new metro line for women.

The press asked questions and he answered them confidently. He also gave the brief speech that he and Ayesha had written together. She couldn't help but smile as she watched him. She felt proud of his achievements and at the same time felt humbled that he had taken her advice.

Just as he was nearing the end of his speech he paused and looked directly into the camera. Ayesha leaned forward as he did too from where he was. The camera zoomed in on his face, which to Ayesha looked like he was waiting for someone. Ayesha whispered to herself, 'Go on.'

At the same time he spoke, '*Be safe. Be happy. I'm with you, for you, always.*'

He smiled into the camera. Ayesha knew those last words were for her. He had said them the night of the party when he had looked directly at her, and then again after the metro ride. Those words were for her.

Now Ayesha wasn't sure if this was just a high school crush. It could be deeper and it scared her.

Later that evening he sent her an SMS: Did you watch it?

She sent a reply: Yes. Well said. Congrats. She wanted to appear collected. If she showed too much emotion he may get the wrong idea. What did she know about politicians, anyway? He could ruin her husband's career and her father's business and worst of all, her reputation with her children and society.

Will you meet me for dinner to celebrate? he replied.

I'm leaving for Switzerland for a vacation with my family in a few days. Have a lot to finish before that.

Okay. Take care. Enjoy yourself.

That was the end of the SMS-exchange. Curt. She knew she had put him in his place by reminding him that she had other duties and a husband with whom she was now going on a vacation.

Her heart felt heavy though. Her thoughts pained her.

Marriage is the ultimate chastity belt. You could have feelings only for one man for the rest of your life. Marriage made you loyal to one person. You were not allowed to lust after anyone else. You weren't allowed to think of another man in your life. There were no 'what ifs'. You had to make the best of your life and be happy with the man you had.

Ayesha wanted to make her marriage work. She needed to end whatever it is she is having with Harshvardhan. At least that's what she tried to convince herself.

She texted him: Maybe a quick coffee?

They met a few hours later. Far from being closure, it heralded a beginning.

15

'Why would you ever give up photography?'

Harshvardhan and Ayesha were having dinner at the Oberoi in a quiet, reserved corner of a restaurant and he was regaling her with tales of other politicians he refused to name. Ayesha was enjoying his company and he also listened to stories from her life, her childhood and her own child, Adi.

'I had to give the camera back to Tarini. I could never ask for a new one because you know, those are not things middle-class girls ask for anyway. It was over ten years ago. I was leaving Delhi and I really didn't want to photograph Allahabad!'

Harshvardhan could tell that Ayesha had made sacrifices for her husband and child. A family that took her for granted and didn't value her at all. Parents who didn't understand the bright woman they had raised. 'Well it's easy to start again.'

Ayesha shook her head, 'Now there's no time. All the money also goes to the house and making ends meet. It's not as if it's such a problem. It's just that I really have no time either…' Her voice trailed off as her mind flooded with thoughts about the house. He noticed her zoning out.

Suddenly Ayesha felt sad. This would be the last time she met him. She needed to finish packing and they would be leaving soon.

As if he had read her thoughts he asked, 'What's wrong?'

Ayesha shook her head, choked up. 'Nothing.'

Harshvardhan looked around to check that no one was looking and gently reached out across the table to lay his hand on hers. 'Ayesha,' he whispered. 'Everything will be okay. I'll make it okay. Just don't worry. Let's just enjoy this time here today.'

Ayesha nodded her head, holding back her tears and raising her head to smile at him. She needed to stay in the moment. If she thought about her future she would feel bleak and empty again. But she needed more time with him. Her coffee was over and so was dinner. He would send her home with his driver soon. He was that kind of a gentleman. She needed to speak to him for hours. Maybe hold his hand, rest her head on his shoulder. She didn't know why she felt those emotions. Sometimes there was no logic to feelings. There were just right or wrong ones.

'Can't we go somewhere where we can talk without getting interrupted every five minutes for what else we would like?' Ayesha asked, a little boldly, she realized.

'Sure.' He looked up and his bodyguard called his secretary and they mumbled something in his ear.

Then he turned to her. 'Would you like to go to a suite in this hotel and have a little more coffee? Or would you like to go for a drive somewhere and chat on the way?' And then with an afterthought and smile, 'I'll have people around if you like, if you feel unsafe with me.'

How could Ayesha tell him that she felt most safe with him? She felt that he was the only person who could keep her safe from her own life. 'Let's go to the suite. It's cold outside. And foggy.'

'Is the family going to be okay with you gone for so long?'

She nodded her head. 'I told them I would be out for the whole day running errands. No one is questioning me since we're leaving for Switzerland tomorrow afternoon.'

Harshavardhan nodded his head. 'You go first. The man from the lobby will escort you upstairs. I'll follow in ten minutes. Is that okay? For safety reasons. If you change your mind halfway, you can always leave and I won't question you about it. Okay?'

Ayesha thought that was very gracious of him. He was giving her the option to leave at any time if she felt uncomfortable.

A few minutes later they were sitting in a large Presidential Suite, enjoying the view of the fog that covered a large part of Lutyens Delhi. It looked beautiful in the early evening with a few twinkling lights coming on.

Harshvardhan admired her as she walked around in her black silk sari. She was one of the few women who could look elegant in trousers and a sari while being comfortable in both. She was petite and flower-like with eyes of fiery determination. Her long dark hair fell gracefully over her shoulders and her nose ring sparkled in the light. She was serene and mesmerizing. There was no way a man wouldn't be in love with her. He dared not make a move.

But as Ayesha turned back from the window to look at him she saw that his gaze was fixed on her. He sat there, devilishly handsome, his hands folded in front of him. He had a ruggedness that attracted her. In his plain white shirt and khaki trousers, he looked simple but rich. He smiled and inclined his head as he looked at her. His mouth curved into an unconscious smile.

Ayesha walked over to him and sat beside him on the bed, looking out the window. He shifted to see her better. She shifted as they faced each other. His burning eyes held her still. She leaned in, tilted her head and closed her eyes. She knew she was crossing the line.

Harshavardhan leaned in to kiss her gently on the mouth,

holding her by the waist and nudging her toward himself. She kissed him back. She moved her body towards him and held his hair, longing for him even more. He could feel her desire as he held her and stroked her hair.

When he let go, Ayesha pulled away. 'Is this right?'

'No. But we've done so many right things in our life that never felt good. Why not do a wrong one that makes us feel right?'

This time Ayesha held him and kissed him as if it was the only thing that mattered in the world. A sense of urgency drove her.

'Don't get your sari crushed,' he whispered to her, as he didn't want to let her go and hardly cared about the sari.

She pulled away to go into the bathroom to remove her sari and wear a robe. Her heart was pounding and logic had flown out of the window. But Ayesha knew that for the first time in her life, she was doing something entirely for herself. Not her father, her husband or her son. Just for herself.

As she walked back to fall into his open arms, the night sky lit up. The fog over Delhi lifted as it did in her heart. This one night would save her from her dreary life and then she would be able to go to Switzerland and then Lucknow in peace.

16

The very next day Ayesha received a present at her doorstep just as they were preparing to leave for the airport. She opened the box and was thrilled at seeing a DSLR camera, a Canon EOS 60 D.

She instantly knew it was from Harshvardhan. She sent him a text: *I don't think I can accept this…*

Harshvardhan texted back: *Please, do accept. Consider it your professional fee for the consultation about the Metro.*

Well, thank you then.

Take photos of yourself too.

Ayesha was sure she would have a far more wonderful vacation clicking photos that sitting in a hotel room ordering room service, something that Varun loved to do.

Just then Varun walked in, announcing to everyone that a blizzard had hit their destination and they were cancelling their trip.

'Whaaatt?!' Adi came out of his room screaming. 'We're not going? But Dad! You promised! What will all my friends say?'

Varun yelled back. 'There's nothing we can do. Beta it's not in our control!' He stormed off as he told Ayesha, 'Tumhara beta hai. Tum hi sambhalo.'

Ayesha quickly kept her new camera in her closet and began making calls. The travel agent assured her that they would get a full refund on their tickets and hotel bookings.

Adi sulked in his room. 'Adi,' Ayesha coaxed. 'It's so unfortunate that we couldn't go right now. But at another time, we still can, right?'

'When, Ma? We're leaving for Lucknow! And you said we'll be stuck there for some time before we can take vacations.'

Ayesha understood, of course…'How about instead of skiing, we go bungee jumping?'

Adi was suspicious, 'When?'

Ayesha was feeling lighter, happier, more generous. 'Why don't we do the Lord of the Rings trail in New Zealand in March? And we can go paragliding and bungee jumping there too!'

Adi sat up feeling more excited, 'Seriously?'

Ayesha nodded, 'Yes. I will make sure we book in advance. And I know you will have two weeks then. I think the weather will be much better. And this way you can spend New Year's Eve here with your friends like you mentioned last week, right?'

Adi nodded and smiled, 'Thanks Ma. You're the best.'

Ayesha left Adi's room and texted Harshvardhan: *Trip has been cancelled.*

My prayers came true!

She laughed at his reply. Clearly they were more than friends and she knew this relationship was about to complicate her life.

17

That first night with Harshvardhan had been wonderful. After they had made love, they lay entwined in each other's arms for a long time. They spoke only when they felt like it. They kissed passionately and made love again.

Long after that evening was over its imprint scalded Ayesha, as the minutiae of her daily domestic life took over and she began the hurtful process of trying to forget him. She figured the Switzerland trip with her husband and son would make that happen. She was all set to leave. She was ready to forget the most loving man she had ever met. She had to. For the sake of her marriage.

But it was not to be. And it was Harshvhadan whom she texted first the minute she found out they were not leaving for Switzerland. *I must be mad!*

'Madam?' Ayesha was sitting in her room alone with a cup of tea when Savitri quietly knocked and entered.

'What shall we make for dinner?' Savitri asked. 'It's already 7 p.m. Sahib will be home soon.'

Seven! Ayesha had completely lost track of time. Adi had gone to his friend's house after some classes and without his presence she hadn't done her chores.

'Yes. Just make whatever sabji there is and a dal and rotis. We'll finish all the things in the fridge for now.'

Savitri nodded. She walked to the door to leave and said,

'Madam, it will be okay. This time we'll settle things slowly in Lucknow. No calling anyone over till we're ready.' She thought her mistress was concerned about how much work was needed for the shift to Lucknow.

Ayesha didn't say anything until Savitri left the room. As soon as she was alone again she heard Varun's booming voice, 'Ayesha! Ayesha!'

Her heart stopped. Fear knotted her gut. Had he found out about Harshvardhan? She came out of her room in trepidation. Her composure was a fragile shell.

He ran to her and embraced her in a tight hug. 'Guess what!'

She was completely bewildered by his happiness and hugged him back.

'We don't have to leave! My minister gave me an extension.'

'What?'

'Yes! He said I have a one-year extension for now and then he'll see. Isn't that wonderful?'

Ayesha's head reeled. It was wonderful. She won't have to leave the city, she could see Harshvardhan again. She said the obvious, 'I guess we'll continue Adi's school. I'll need to tell them we're not going. Gosh. I hope they haven't made his seat vacant! And all this samaan. I'll need to unpack it also. Oh God, Varun. I wish I had known this earlier!'

Varun didn't care about the logistics. He was only thinking about himself, 'Oh I'm so happy. I'm going to tell Sanjay and Rohit and Rahul. Maybe we can have a celebratory drink tonight. All of us? With the wives.'

Ayesha nodded. 'Yes, yes but tell me how it happened.'

Varun was already dialing his friends on his mobile. 'The minister felt my service was needed for another year. Where is Adi? Let's tell him. Let's take him with us for dinner. Oh Rohit, hey, guess what man…'

Ayesha went into the kitchen to tell Savitri that she didn't need to make dinner as they were all going out. She headed back to her room and found her mobile blinking with a new message. Even before she read it she knew it was from Harshvardhan.

I can't let you go so soon. I have so many issues that I still need help with. Meet me tomorrow. Same place. Whatever time you say. Reading his SMS, Ayesha guessed he was behind Varun staying. He must have spoken to Varun's minister and asked for a continuance. She was sure he had paid a heavy price for it.

She texted back: *4 p.m. Is that okay*? She hungered from the memory of his mouth on hers.

Of course.

Ayesha felt an unfamiliar peace. A cry of relief broke from her lips. She had a year with the man she loved.

KAVITA

18

Kavita: 39. Tall, sleek, smart. Delicate fingers. Wavy brown hair. Twinkling eyes. Sharp nose. Wears pant suits. Gynaecologist. No hobbies. Holds a dark secret. Had a love marriage to Gaurav. Regrets it till date.

'Just sign here, and here,' the officer was instructing Kavita though she already knew given this was her husband's third time in the last two years to be arrested by the police. Kavita couldn't believe this was happening again.

'And ma'am, drunk driving is an offence,' the police officer sternly reminded. 'Delhi drivers think they can always get away with it but not with me.' Gaurav sat sullenly at a table behind them. She paid the bail money, signed the documents, and took a very morose-looking Gaurav back to her car.

'No one ever gets caught in Delhi and I've got caught thrice. *Meri kismet hi kharab hai,*' he grumbled.

'What the hell were you doing driving drunk again anyway? Who were you racing this time, Gaurav?'

'Watch your tone, Kavita. I'm allowed to have some fun. I work hard for a living. I can't afford a driver.'

'You can take a cab. You haven't learned your lesson from the last two times? You could have killed someone!' Kavita found it hard to concentrate on her own driving with all the anger boiling inside her.

'It's not my fault people just cross the street in the middle of the night thinking they own it. It's the bloody population of this country. They live everywhere. They feel they own the streets. No one looks left or right anymore.'

'So you think what you did was okay?'

'No I don't,' Gaurav sighed. 'But I'm stressed. I drank a little too much with the boys and was driving home. The streets were empty. It's Delhi for God's sake! Every street is empty at one in the morning. No cops are ever around.'

'Except Inspector Arvind, obviously and he is very vigilant. One wrong swerve and you could have been in a serious accident.'

Gaurav sulked all the way home and didn't say another word, not even to thank Kavita. He crashed into bed the minute they entered the house. Kavita changed and went to lie down with her back to him. He snored lightly as her eyes caught the clock: 3:00 a.m. She had to get up to get her son ready for school in four hours' time. And then head to work. It was going to be a long day. Now Kavita couldn't sleep. She wondered if things would have been different if she hadn't felt so lonely that day. *How did I end up being this lonely*?

It was nine years ago when they had first met. She was well into her medical residency by then and was working at AIIMS. She had studied all her life to be a doctor. She wanted to make her mother proud. She wanted to earn enough to look after her mother and younger sister. Her father had abandoned them when she and her sister were little.

One morning her mother said, 'Beta, you don't need to do so much. We're fine. I don't want you to wake up one day all alone. It's important to also have love in your life.'

She thought she had found that love in Gaurav. He had walked into her office, a Pharmaceutical Sales representative. Tall, broad shoulders, dark, wavy mop of hair. Like those men on the covers of a Mills & Boon. She was instantly attracted to him.

Though today when thought about it, she wondered if maybe it was only because of what her mother had said that morning, the idea of ending up alone.

'Excuse me, Madam,' Gaurav, the sales representative was saying. 'May I have a minute of your time?' He walked in and took a seat opposite her desk. It was just a coincidence that she was at her desk that morning doing paperwork. Otherwise she would have been on her feet visiting wards and performing operations. Kismet. *Is kismet another word for unhappy coincidences*?

She didn't even have time that morning but he was so good-looking that she had to give him at least two minutes. He was tall, had compelling dark, large eyes and his features were firm. His confident set of shoulders made him even more irresistible.

'I wanted to speak to you about a few drugs that we've just got FDA approval for. They're not out in the market and we wanted you to have them before the other hospitals.' His smooth olive skin stretched over his cheeks as he smiled. His voice resonated loud and clear but not overbearing.

This was not the first sales representative who had tried to sell his pharmaceutical products to doctors like Kavita, so she knew how they smooth-talked. And as much as she wanted to spend a little more time with him, Kavita knew it wasn't in her place to order drugs so she told Gaurav she was not interested.

'But this can relieve your patients from pain. Have you heard of an epidural?' He spoke almost immediately after she finished her sentence, not giving her a moment to get back to her work, but holding her attention for way longer than she had hoped. She liked how he challenged her.

'Every doctor has heard of it…,' she wanted to take his name.

'Gaurav. Gaurav Gupta.' His smile was as charming as his personality.

'Yes...Gaurav,' She remembered he had mentioned it earlier. 'I don't need an epidural.'

'What if I told you there was an alternative to the epidural that would not have such alarming after-effects? Would you still think about the drug?'

'Is it IV?'

Gaurav smiled. Now he had got her interested. That's exactly what he wanted. 'No. It's orally prescribed.'

'Does it have the same effect as an epidural? How? Isn't that unsafe?'

'I can leave some samples and written documents that we have on it. Here's my number,' he said as he took out the samples and his card from his bag. 'You'll have all the information on that. And I can tell you more about it over dinner, if you're free.'

She was offended by this man's gumption, asking her out for dinner!

Kavita shook her head. He may be gorgeous but he was a stranger. And love couldn't distract her now—not even the idea of it. Love took away from ambition. She would tell her mother that love would have to wait. She told Gaurav, 'You'll have to talk to the product manager. I'm not really in charge of this.'

But he was persistent, like any salesperson was. 'Once you approve, we'll head to the product manager and make a deal. Right now, I want you to see what this miracle drug can do and how you can ease the pain of your patient's lives! Wouldn't you like that?'

Kavita nodded and then shook her head. She was a renowned gynaecologist. She had delivered thousands of babies. She had performed hundreds of operations and her research was published in various medical journals. Why was she feeing like putty in this man's presence? 'Fine, Gaurav. I have rounds now. Thank you for your time.'

As they both stood up to shake hands, there was a strange electricity that passed between them. He smiled and left. Dinner would have to wait.

She sat looking at his card for a long time. This man had made her feel strange. She had been too busy all her life trying to study to be a doctor and then trying to prove she was a good one. Later she would tell her sister, Kaajal, 'I don't go for just good-looking men. I've seen enough of them. What was it about him?'

And Kaajal would reply, 'Sometimes, when you know, you know. There's no logic involved in knowing if he's the one. There's no logic for falling in love with a person. It just happens. And when you have love, you'll have it all.'

Now Kavita was in bed, trying to find sleep as Gaurav slept soundly next to her. She watched the digital clock turn to four. She stared into the dark, empty night. The house was completely quiet. Did she really have it all?

She was a successful gynaecologist in her mid-30s. She lived with her younger, unmarried sister, Kaajal, and their mother. Gaurav lived with them because her mother's was a large enough house for the entire family. Gaurav was staying in a rented place when they met. His parents lived in Jaipur along with Gaurav's two sisters who were also married.

He got by on charm. Kavita and he had had great sex in the beginning. And then work took over. Her time was spent in the hospital and that was when he lost his first job. Things went downhill from then. Two years into their marriage, Kavita knew it wasn't working. She wanted a divorce. She spoke to Kaajal about it. Kaajal was then finishing law school.

'It will devastate mom,' Kaajal had warned in reply. 'She's

too traditional, Kavi. Don't do this. Have a child. Maybe that'll save your marriage.'

Why is it that even when women know that it's the end of a relationship, they'll do whatever they can to save it for someone else? Gaurav was happy to have a baby. He was a pretty good father. He couldn't always change nappies but rocked Vansh to sleep every night. His career took a back seat. Not that it was going anywhere to begin with. He was fired from the pharmaceutical company when they had a class action suit against them. They thought it was his fault. He was unemployed for several months. That was the first time he got arrested for drinking and driving. Kavita and he went to marriage counseling and things were better for a while after that.

But Kavita now had to work hard to support Gaurav and the needs of a new baby. She hired a nanny to help. She worked extra hard. She didn't spend a single pie on herself. And yet Gaurav began to hate her more and more.

Gaurav eventually found another job as a sales executive in a TV channel. He enjoyed it for some time till he got fired again. His ego didn't allow him to take orders from a boss who was younger than him. Again he stayed at home with her mother and their son. Somehow through Kaajal's contacts, he got a job in an event management company and that's where he had been for the last two years.

Their son Vansh was now six and a half years old. He was quite independent, though he had the luxury of having enough family members and maids around to manage his life.

But Kavita felt she should have known better. If she hadn't called Gaurav about those samples, if they hadn't gone out for those few dates, if she hadn't so desperately wanted to be in love for the first time in her life, if her mother who had raised her and her sister single-handedly had not wanted her to get married so quickly, none of this mess would have happened. There were too many factors. A lifetime of reasoning and pondering.

Gaurav was so good with their son. He was brilliant as a son-in-law. He looked after her mother the way she herself never could. She was always at the hospital. He was the one who drove her everywhere, took her for anything she wanted, and spent hours listening to her. Even Kaajal, who was a lawyer and several years younger than Kavita, didn't have time to be with their mother as much as Gaurav did. How could she divorce such a man? On what grounds? Love is always the stupidest factor to get married. And falling out of it is the stupidest factor to get divorced. If only couples realized it before it was too late on either accounts.

And what would Vansh say? He would definitely choose to live with Gaurav. Kavita would die if that ever happened. Marriages weren't meant to be ideal, happy, romantic scenarios. They were a slice of life with two people compromising for a greater good.

So she let Gaurav be. She pretended it was a great marriage. She found common ground. She forced herself to have sex. She let some things go for the greater good.

The clock showed six o' clock. Kavita was already awake. She took her pink yoga mat and went to the balcony. She practiced yoga every morning before the house woke up. It was her time to exercise in peace and gather her thoughts. She did one hundred surya namaskars before she went to wake up her son.

'Mama, you're all sweaty,' he said as she snuggled next to him.

'Hmm. I love you, my pudding pie.'

'Mama. Please don't call me that now. I'm a big boy.'

'Okay okay, baba. I won't.'

'Mama, can I ask you a question?' Vansh said feeling shy and looking away from his mother who was lying next to him. She nodded her head. 'Can I have a sibling?'

Kavita sat up, 'What?'

Immediately Vansh changed the topic, 'No no. It was just that all my friends have brothers and sisters. So they can play with them. Otherwise you always have to fix play dates and tell Maasi or Papa to play with me…It would be easier if I had a sibling na?'

Kavita sighed. After last night, she never wanted to sleep with Gaurav again. Thinking about having another baby was far from her mind. 'We'll see. And everyone likes spending time with you and your play dates are for you to have fun. Now go get dressed please. Let's not be late for the school bus.'

Vansh jumped out of bed and gave his mother a hug. For him, she hadn't said no. He would work on her later. He would also talk to his father!

Kavita saw her son off to school and sat at the kitchen table with her cup of coffee. She couldn't have another child. She was just too tired. Even though she delivered babies for a living, she didn't plan on having another one herself. It would stunt her career and there was no love between her and Gaurav anyway. She decided to stay at home that day and clear her head.

19

It was a large house. Both Kaajal and Kavita had been born and brought up there. When their father left them for someone else, their mother got the house. She never chose to leave, believing with all her heart that he would come back one day. She worked really hard to make sure they went to medical and law school. She raised them well. When Kavita began to earn, she handed all her pay cheques to her mother. Since then they had managed to renovate their four-bedroom house and turned it into a modern abode. A large lawn was in the backyard. Vansh had good friends in the neighbourhood, not to mention so many people at home who made sure he felt loved and that all his needs were attended to.

Kavita's current worry was Gaurav: he had to put an end to all the risqué behaviour, engaging in shady deals and having near-misses that almost landed him in jail.

The morning after she bailed him out of the police station she decided to talk to him. She found him in the kitchen making himself coffee. 'Gaurav, what's going on?' He didn't answer. He continued making coffee, not looking at his wife, slowly put a teaspoon of sugar in his cup and then poured in some fresh milk. He tasted it and added a little more sugar.

'Is it something at work?' she pushed. 'You can't keep doing these things, Gaurav.' She stood at the corner of the kitchen, watching the hall for any sign of her mother emerging from her bath. 'It's not good for our name. If people find out about your brushes with the law, my career could be in jeopardy. Even Kaajal's.'

Kavita's was a commanding figure as she stood at the kitchen counter. She meant business and she would not have Gaurav ignore her. She had always been all about no fuss. Whether it was at home or the workplace, she got the job done efficiently and didn't bother about sentimentality where it wasn't needed. She was caring towards her family members but she was practical and pragmatic when it counted. She worked hard to spend quality time with her family. She took them on holidays and gave them attention. Last year she had taken them to Bali for a week; another week in Paris, too. Two long breaks when her son's school had vacations.

Right now she needed answers from Gaurav. She had tried everything, speaking to him, taking him to a counselor, giving him a roof over his head. She had even considered moving out at one point but figured it would be an added expenditure on her head as he just spent all his money on himself and his car. It was wiser they stayed here where Vansh had support instead of their only son coming home from school to an empty house and a nanny.

'Why don't you ever think of me?' were the first words that came out of Gaurav's mouth. 'It's always about your reputation, *your* career. *Your* family.' Gaurav sat with his cup of steaming hot coffee and did not give her a glance.

'That's not true. You chose to move in here. I had one condition when I got married and it was that I would not leave my mother or sister alone. And your parents live in Jaipur. My work was here. Or don't you remember that I was already working when you met me? We thought about moving out long ago. Is that it? Do you want to move out, the three of us? Will you pay for the house then? Because all my money goes into this house. I need to pay back the loans my mother has taken for Kaajal and me.'

'Yes yes, you're the big shot. You're the one who throws money at our faces.'

'I don't throw money. I use the money to make everyone happy. It's not easy for me either.'

'Yes, earning all that money isn't easy. Showing your family how successful you are isn't easy. Rubbing it in my face isn't easy.'

Kavita didn't say anything until he finished ranting. She just looked at him, wanting him to look at her as well. *How could this be the same man I fell in love with*? His face was still as handsome, sure. But the love had faded. Was this a natural progression of all relationships? Does romantic love always eventually fade to companionship, and companionship to resentment, which would then, inevitably, fade into apathy?

Why did I believe that Gaurav can change? Kavita scolded herself for being naïve, for thinking that their marriage would improve. For being in denial for so long that perhaps she had made the wrong choice. Whatever it was, she was determined to find a solution.

When Gaurav ended his rant she said, 'Why don't you tell me what you want me to do? I can't seem to get through to you anymore.'

'Maybe you should spend more time at home.' He looked straight in her eyes.

'I can't. Why can't you understand? I have my own ambitions, Gaurav. I want to make something of my life.'

He kept looking at her and said nothing.

'You have to accept that I am not only a wife and mother, or daughter and sister. I am a doctor. Doesn't that mean something to you?'

'First, you're a mother and a wife, Kavita.' He was just as sure about his position. 'You have responsibilities towards us.'

Kavita sighed, 'Okay, Gaurav. I will try. But then you will have to contribute to the house. You will need to give your salary to this house instead of spending it on your parents. I will come home early to be with you. I will make it work. But I need you to promise me you'll make it work too. You'll stop drinking and spend time with me too.'

'Let me think about it.'

His nonchalance peeved Kavita. 'What is really bothering you, Gaurav? Talk to me.' She wanted to save this marriage.

'It bothers me that you're financing us.' *There, he had said it.* 'It makes me feel small,' Gaurav continued. Kavita pulled up a chair and sat down. 'And you keep showing our son how great you are. How many lives you save. Things that you've bought for him. Mummy bought you a new toy, a new book. Hey look, Mummy bought us a new car!' His sarcasm was so thick you could cut through it with a knife.

'But your financial struggles are not my fault. They are all because of the choices you make. Don't blame me for your own failures. If I was an ordinary housewife sitting at home we would not know where to get our next meal from!'

'The recession hit so many people. Everyone suffered. Don't blame me.'

'I'm not. But my profession didn't suffer. And thank God I had a job that could pull us through.'

'Again you're pushing it!'

'I'm not.' Kavita sighed. This argument was going nowhere.

'Yeah, well that may be better as a wife than being so driven and manly.'

'Manly?' Kavita was aghast. *Was that even a word?*

'Yes, Kavita, I said stop being manly. It's the man of the house who buys the cars, provides food, looks after the family. Not the wife.'

Kavita felt even more furious. She felt Gaurav was being

extremely unreasonable. He couldn't get himself a decent, stable job, and because she was stepping up and providing for their family he resented her? She had felt this for a long time now but it was only today that Gaurav had finally let the words out: He wanted them to play the traditional roles of husband and wife.

No, she couldn't give that to him. She had never taken to domesticity and never would. It was just not her. That's why her mother was there. To be the backbone of her life while she went out to deliver babies.

She was angry at Gaurav but maintained her calm. 'How does it matter who provides for the family, Gaurav? I'm working to secure our future while doing something I love.'

'It matters, Kavita. Your mother won't always be around. When she's gone, what then? When Kaajal gets married and we're both working, who will look after Vansh and the house?' he thundered. 'It's time you take a step back from your career and look after your house and family. There's nothing wrong with being a housewife.'

Just then her mother emerged in the hall, making them stop their argument. He left the house without saying another word.

Can I really save this marriage? Kavita didn't know how. She was being punished for being true to herself. For knowing what she wanted, for being ambitious, for providing for her family! One thing he had said moved her to tears—If something did happen to her mother, she would then need to be that housewife.

He would never sit at home. And if she chose to divorce him and lead a single mother's life, who would look after the house? No one would really understand the hell she went through in her marriage. He was a complete Dr Jekyll and Mr Hyde. Everyone would be sympathetic towards him. It might even affect her career. A single mother as a doctor? Would patients be sympathetic towards her as a gynaecologist? Would families want to have her around? Wouldn't they fear that she would influence the expectant mother? Who knows how people thought. And she hated the thought of being on thin ice at her job if she was already having a shaky marriage. She hated the thought of divorce but she felt helpless. She didn't know what she could do.

What she now knew was that anyone who said they had balance in their life must be lying. Why was it expected more from a woman to have balance in her life? Why did she need to justify herself to society? When a man worked long hours, he was only doing what was natural. But when a woman did the same, she still needed to prove that she was a great mother and wife. Why did women have to open joint accounts with their husbands when they got married, putting whatever they earned or didn't in that account. Most housewives didn't even have a bank account of their own. Did they not want that independence, that freedom, that identity? Kavita had always known and earned independently. She had put every asset in her mother's and daughter's name. Gaurav had resented her for it. But she was the one who gave him money to spend as he wished. Shouldn't he have been grateful, appreciative, loving about it?

Was a man supposed to give money to his family? Was a woman supposed to give up her career if she got married or pregnant? Kavita hadn't been like that at all. Even though she had gotten pregnant, she had worked till the last day and had gone from her rounds straight to the maternity ward to give birth to Vansh. Three months later, she hired a full-time nurse to take care of the baby as she went back to work. She had cut down on her hours at the hospital to come back to her child early and then nursed him and slept with him through the night, only to go back to work the next morning. It was exhausting but she did it. She thought she had found her balance. She had killed herself for the first year. Why was she being punished?

Maybe a housewife's role is never simple. It's not about cooking, cleaning or looking after the family. It's not even about finding balance between keeping your boss happy and your husband, too. *Maybe what society expects of me is to keep my husband's ego inflated*?

But Kavita didn't know how to do that. She didn't know how to save Gaurav, or this marriage. She had a sinking feeling that something bad was about to happen.

20

'Bhaiya, naap liya theek se? Bust pe tight mat karna. Loose hi rakhna. Growing child,' a woman was telling the tailor as Kaajal and Kavita entered the shop, much to the embarrassment of the woman's teenage daughter.

Kaajal and Kavita were at South Ex market to shop and have lunch. They found the shop teeming with people taking advantage of a sale. Everything was at half price and the shoppers were ecstatic. It didn't matter that many of them had tons of money, evident in their Louis Vuitton bags and the diamonds on their fingers; a sale was a sale!

'Oh my God!' Kaajal shrieked as she twirled around in a red paisley skirt. 'Do you like this one?' Kavita thought it was lovely but she looked bored. 'Honestly I think you have too many of the same kind.'

Kaajal made a face. 'How many black pants do you have?' she teased as she went back inside the trial room.

'Well I need them for work.'

'All fifteen of them?'

'I don't have 15 pairs of black pants!' Kavita laughed. 'You're such a drama queen!'

Kaajal came out of the trial room with a pile of clothes in her arms. She put them on the counter. 'I'm taking these, please,' she said to the man behind the till. 'Cash. Thank you.'

She turned to Kavita. 'You wear only pants and jackets.

How boring are you? You have a million white shirts. Why don't you try something ethnic? Look, there are so many lovely options here!'

'I wear your clothes sometimes, don't I? But shirts and pants have always been more comfortable.'

They roamed some more and Kaajal happily shopped.

Kavita and Kaajal had always been completely different from each other. Kavita was more like their father and Kaajal got more of their mother's genes. Even physically you couldn't immediately tell they were sisters. Kaajal was far more curvaceous than Kavita. She was shorter, in a typical Indian kind of way but softer. Her nose was straight, short and charming unlike Kavita's that was sharp and long. Kaajal's hair was coarse, brown and curly, falling in ringlets around her face. Kavita's was silky, straight and black, falling over her shoulders when she left it open. Kaajal's beauty was exquisite, fragile, soft and warm. Kavita's beauty was like a wild flower, a powerful attractiveness that left you looking at her wondering what made her so compelling.

What they shared was ambition; they both were passionate about having something of their own. Kaajal studied law and worked with an international law firm in Delhi. She was slowly but surely moving up the ranks as she worked hard and remained focused. Kavita never allowed her to spend her money for the house even though Kaajal had demanded that she give her share. But Kavita had put her foot down. Kaajal's money was saved. She needed it for her marriage and her own financial security. Kaajal had been seeing a man for a year now and Kavita thought it was time to talk to her about marriage.

Kavita didn't waste any time and took advantage of their quiet time over lunch. 'Kaajal, what is going on with your love life?' She asked as soon as they had placed their orders. They were sitting at a corner table at their favourite Italian restaurant.

Oh, no, Didi is giving me 'The Talk'. 'How is he?' Kavita asked. 'At least tell us his name?' Kavita had always taken charge of the family. Ever since their father abandoned them, Kavita had felt like the head of the family. The sisters had become closer over the last few years since Kavita's marriage wasn't doing so well. They had held on to each other for years when they couldn't share their sorrow or disappointments with their mother, who was herself hurting from being abandoned. And for the past year Kaajal had confided only in her sister that she had someone special in her life. She never mentioned his name. Kavita never probed; she felt that her sister was genuinely happy with this one, unlike with the many flings before him. Before Kaajal could break it off with this man for some stupid reason, Kavita wanted to plan their wedding. Some excitement in the house would also give her happiness.

'My love life is fine. His name is Salman Khan. Now will you leave me alone?'

Kavita smiled. Such a drama queen Kaajal could be! She was sure this was because of her obsession with Bollywood movies and songs. Kavita, on the contrary, never understood the need for cinema.

Kaajal looked out of the window.

'Seriously, what name should we write on the wedding cards?'

'Wedding cards?!' Kavita shrieked, startling the woman sitting at the next table. 'Are you mad, Didi?' she lowered her voice but glared at her sister. 'Right now all you need to know is that he loves me and we're happy. There is no wedding for you to plan. Thank you very much.'

Their food came and as soon as the waiter left, Kavita spoke again; she was not one to give up easily. 'Okay,' she said carefully as she picked up a lettuce leaf from her salad, 'but have you two at least discussed your future?'

'You mean whether we're getting married or living together?' Kaajal said as she started on her own salad.

Her sister's bluntness didn't surprise Kavita. She had always spoken her mind without any regard for tact or diplomacy. That's what made her razor-sharp at work.

'Yeah,' Kavita replied. 'Don't you want to get married or are you afraid to leave us here?'

Kaajal flicked an imaginary speck of dirt from her yellow FabIndia kurta. She looked lovely in everything she wore. Her well-rounded breasts and her slender waist made men desire her wherever she went. 'I'm not afraid. It's just that marriage is complicated. I've seen what it's done to mom. And you. I don't want that. I'm having fun in life. Marriage kills it.'

'I know I sounding like mom but she's been talking to me about you. You're 30. It's time that you think about marriage. You'll want kids as well. If this is the guy you want to settle down with, let's meet him. Let's see what he has to say.'

Kaajal kept silent. She set her fork and knife down and leaned back in her chair, soaking in the sun that was falling from the window next to her. She did want more of a commitment from him but she didn't know if he was ready. She didn't want to lose him if she asked him and he got scared.

Kavita's voice was warm. 'Is there something you're not telling me?'

Kaajal pressed her lips together in deep thought. When she spoke her voice was deceptively calm. 'No. Not at all, Kavita.' She went back to eating her salad. 'See, I know what you're saying. But I don't think I'm the type to marry. I think marriage kills romance. And I don't want to be tied down by legality. If I love a person I will be committed to him. If tomorrow he cheats on me, I have the option of leaving him without getting families involved. Love and marriage are two different things. I can love someone forever. I don't need to devote my life to him. Besides, I want to be there for Mom and Vansh too.'

Kavita took her sister's hand. 'I understand what you're saying and I'm not taking that away from you. But we need to face facts. One day Mom will die. Vansh will grow up and want to travel the world and leave us behind. Where will you be then?'

'Where will you be, Kavi?' Kaajal asked, looking at her sister with piercing eyes. 'With a man you don't love?'

Kavita looked away. 'This isn't about me.'

'But I'm asking you anyway. What do you want to do with him? I know what you guys are going through. I'm not dumb and walls have ears. You guys are not even having sex anymore!'

Kavita kept quiet. 'I'm fine.'

'You stopped loving Gaurav long ago, Didi. And you never go out. You barely have any friends.'

'I have you.'

Kaajal got up from her seat and embraced her sister in a long, tight hug. 'You need to find someone who loves you as well. Divorce Gaurav. Start over. I'll look after Mom and Vansh.'

'No Kaajal. This is your time now. I want you to find someone who loves you, cherishes you, and wants to spend his life with you. It's time you got married and had kids.'

Kaajal started to interrupt, 'Kavi…'

'No, listen…if you've found this man who you love, talk to him. See where it's going. Everyone needs stability in their lives. And yes, my marriage isn't perfect, but it's not important right now. I love my job. I'm happy at work.'

'I love my job too.'

'I'm not talking about your job. I'm talking about being in

your mid-30s and realizing that you have everything in the world but love. And sometimes that love comes from a child. And you can't have one till you get married.'

'Well then you can help me find donor sperm and we'll have a baby outside wedlock, eh?' Kaajal grinned from ear to ear. 'You've helped thousands of couples conceive. Now help me!'

Kavita laughed with her sister. 'Yeah we could do that. And let our mother have a heart attack, hai na? Imagine that, a traditional woman does one hour of bhajans every morning in the mandir, and her younger daughter is conceiving without a husband? Oh, the shame!' Kavita smiled.

Then in a grave tone, 'But seriously, think about it. Think about what you want from life, who you want in it and then work towards it. Everyone needs companionship. Not just in their old age. Now. We need someone to talk to, spend time with, be comfortable with, share our silences with, our sorrows, our joys. And sometimes a marriage is the only way we can have that. So think about it, Kaajal. Not all marriages are bad. There are just phases when it's not good and they do go away. Living with or loving someone can never give you the kind of security and stability that marriage can.'

'What if it isn't a phase? What if the happiness never returns?'

'You don't give up when you're in love. You don't give up when you fight. You don't give up when you don't agree. You give up when even if he's doing something right, it has stopped making a difference to you.'

'Does it still make a difference to you?'

'Right now, it still does.'

'You won't divorce Gaurav then?'

'No.'

'Not even if he makes you so unhappy?'

Kavita pondered. 'Not unless I find a replacement. I don't want to be alone. I don't want to be a single mother. I need a partner. I need love. I need an entity around. Even if it means I need to compromise.'

Kaajal didn't push Kavita any more. Kavita also left it there. They both knew they had given each other enough to think about. And they would need each other again very soon.

21

Attending conferences was part of Kavita's work as a physician. She had tried avoiding as many conferences as she could so she would not have to leave her household too often but when she fancied the opportunity, she took it. She always came back . more knowledgeable.

This coming conference was to be held in Goa over four days. She sat at her desk reading the programme in her email. Her first thought was her son. She hoped he would be alright without his mother for so long. Her next thought was Gaurav. After the last few days of heated arguments, Kavita had promised to spend more time at home but when she was at home, he was out doing something. He didn't discuss work and she noticed that even though he was still drinking, he was getting dropped home. Things were very confusing at home. Kavita felt like she had the weight of the world on her shoulders. She needed some intellectual stimulation. She needed to get away from the burden of her family.

As soon as she landed in Goa, Kavita called home to check on Vansh. Without any consideration for the household Gaurav had scheduled his visit to his parents at the same time that she would be in Goa. Kavita worried about Vansh. Only the thought of her mother and Kaajal being there reassured her.

'Hello Mummy,' Vansh said from the other end. 'I'm fine.

I'm playing with my cars. I read in the morning and I've done some Maths as well. Can I please watch some TV now?'

'Sure, baby.'

'Hi Maasi,' Kavita heard Vansh say. 'Mama, Maasi has also just got home. Don't worry!'

Kavita smiled. She had raised a good child. 'I love you my Pooh Bear. You call me if you need anything. Mama's phone is on, okay?'

'Okay Mummy.'

'See you soon, okay, sweetheart? Now please put Nani on the line.'

Her mother told her not to worry. 'Have a good time at that conference,' her mother said.

'Thank you, Ma.'

They said goodbye and Kavita thought again of how fortunate she was for having her mother. It was through her mother's hard work that she had become a doctor. It would have been financially impossible to pursue the degrees she had completed without a working father in the house. But her mother had never allowed either her or Kaajal to feel they needed to step back from life just because their father had abandoned them.

Kavita was staying in a large business hotel with several conference rooms. The first two days comprised of a series of conferences from ten in the morning till five in the evening, with doctors from across the globe presenting their medical findings. Every evening cocktails were scheduled where the attendees could relax and mingle. The last two days were free for doctors to do some sightseeing before they headed back home. Kavita wondered if she should head back home immediately after the first two days.

She settled into her room and took a long, hot shower. The only thing scheduled for today was dinner, as the international participants were still arriving and would need to rest. After showering she unpacked, and then went for a massage. She headed back to the hotel and went straight to bed, skipping dinner altogether.

Kavita's presentation, on the need for surrogacy and the importance of adoption in India, was scheduled on the first day after lunch. She had researched this paper over a long period of time from when she was working on her PhD dissertation many years ago. She freshened it up and ended up giving a well-received presentation.

One doctor marveled at her more enthusiastically. He would later come up to her as she sat alone during dinner at the poolside.

'Hi, you're Kavita, right?' said the stranger.

Kavita looked up from her glass of white wine. 'Yes?'

'I'm Dr Imam. You may have seen me at the conference. May I take this chair?'

'Sure, Dr Imam.'

She asked as the stranger sat, 'Are you making a presentation too?'

'Yes, tomorrow afternoon. I'll be one of the last few. Everyone will be wanting to leave by then so I can say anything and get away with it.'

Kavita stifled a giggle.

'Though maybe I can speak in different accents. Then maybe you all will be enthralled.'

'You can speak in different accents?'

'Well not only have I not lived anywhere but Mumbai my entire life, I have not studied in any other country but India. So that makes me well-versed with accents from across the globe like this.' The absurdity of the statement wasn't lost on Kavita but the doctor changed from an American to a French and then a South Indian accent fluidly.

'And Punjabi?' Kavita asked as she rested her chin on her hand.

And Dr Imam did a Punjabi accent as well.

Kavita kept asking for more accents and Dr Imam spoke effortlessly.

'You're really good at this!' Kavita didn't hide her amazement.

'Yeah I should have been an actor. I do excellent impressions, too.'

'Why aren't you?'

'Oh I realized I liked dissecting things more than dancing.'

'You don't like dancing? I love dancing!' Kavita realized how uninhibited she was. Was it the wine? Was it the million stars lighting up the beautiful night sky? Was it that no one around here was about to pass judgement on her? Or had her ego received a great boost after the presentation? Whatever it was, she soon found herself on the dance floor with Dr Iman, showing her moves to the latest Rihaana track.

She felt light-headed after some time. 'I need to sit down,' she said to Dr Imam. She held the doctor's arms lightly and said, 'Let's sit there.' She noticed how attractive Dr Imam was. Dark hair. Light eyes. Fair skin. A fabulous body.

Another doctor came up to her as they walked. 'Dr Gupta, nice job today. I am most impressed with your work. It touched the heart.'

'Thank you so much,' Kavita said, breaking into an open, wide smile. She was a doctor because she believed she wanted to change the world, make couples happy and bring healthy children into the world.

'Don't you think our profession is defeating the purpose of population control?' Dr Imam asked.

Again Kavita laughed, with a depth to her smile that had been missing for too long, as the doctor continued resting a hand over hers, 'Maybe we should be tying more women's tubes than encouraging them to have a healthy pregnancy! See that would force me to go into acting. Poverty.' Kavita let the hand rest. A warm feeling tingled across her body.

Dr Imam had a wicked sense of self-deprecating humour. There was this inherent pleasing quality about the doctor. Kind eyes, a warm smile and gentle hands. It wasn't aggressive or ambitious or lazy and indolent. Kavita felt drawn to the doctor, in words she couldn't explain. There was something stirring deep inside her. Again. It had happened once in college and she had suppressed those urges. She was too scared to deal with those emotions. And when she got married, she had plunged herself so shard into loving Gaurav and working that she never let them surface again. Until now. Now it was as if her primal instincts were telling her that this is who she was. She needed to feel her emotions completely. She couldn't hide them any longer.

And so Kavita gave in to the night. She succumbed to the moment. She spent time with this handsome doctor; they spoke about their life, their work and their future plans. A drink became two and then a few more. They sat together for dinner and continued their chat. Dr Imam would lightly touch Kavita's arm, hands and hair and strangely, Kavita liked it. She didn't feel it was creepy and unwanted. When the party was winding down and most of the doctors had left, they were the only two people left by the poolside while waiters cleared up.

'Would you like anything else, Madam?' A waiter hinted that they needed to leave.

'No,' Kavita replied. 'We were just leaving.'

Dr Imam got up. 'Do you want to go for a walk on the beach?'

'Which beach?'

'The beach adjoining the hotel premises.'

'Oh I didn't know that.'

'Your room doesn't have a view of the beach?'

'No, I guess I never checked since I've been in the board room all day today and went to sleep yesterday.'

'Well would you like to see the beach, Dr Gupta?'

'Yes I would love that, Dr Imam.' Kavita said as she got up and the red dress she had worn slid slightly higher up her thigh, a movement that was not lost on Dr Imam.

Kavita took off her high heels as she walked on the beach, holding her shoes in one hand and holding on to Dr Imam's hand with the other. It was a gorgeous, clear night. Kavita had finished her presentation and she was finally enjoying herself in a land far away from her duties and routine existence. She was enjoying herself with a person who connected to her mind, who was clearly attracted to her and who enjoyed spending time with her.

For the first time in a long time, Kavita felt a kind of unfamiliar peace. And with a complete stranger! She was more herself than she had been with the people who had known her for years. She was enjoying every minute. She couldn't place her finger on why she was so attracted to him. Maybe it was because for the first time, no was expecting anything from her.

'You know, you're very beautiful, Kavita,' Dr Imam said softly.

'Thank you.' A tumble of confused thoughts and feelings assailed Kavita. Where was this going?

After a few steps of walking on the beach, with a deliberate, casual movement Dr Imam turned and faced Kavita. She looked to see that no one else was around. 'Kavita, would you mind awfully if I kissed you? I promise not to do so if you disagree and will never bother you again. We can remain friends.'

Mixed feelings surged through Kavita. This was the college experience she had never spoken to anyone about, all over again. She was cheating on her husband. And if she kissed Dr Imam back, would it mean she was a bad woman? She fought to control her swirling emotions.

Dr Imam saw her hesitating. 'I'm sorry, I shouldn't have done that. Please forget I asked. Can we still be friends?'

But Kavita wanted to take a chance. She had a feeling that it would be the best thing she ever did, even if it meant spiraling her world into the unknown. A sense of urgency drove her as Kavita leaned in and kissed Dr Imam with fervent ardour. Kavita's insides jangled with excitement. Dr Imam's mild flirtation through the evening, and now this straightforward proposal, was certainly a turn on but she didn't think she would have reacted so positively to it. She felt like a breathless girl of eighteen. As she pulled away, Kavita studied the lean, beautiful, fair-skinned face and piercing grey eyes in front of her. Kavita couldn't believe she was falling for someone at this time in her life. She was too old to be having a new, whirlwind romance.

She would have a few problems explaining this new romance to anyone. Dr Imam lived in Mumbai, to begin with, and long-distance relationships never work.

And two, Dr Imam was a woman.

22

Kavita was beginning to understand. She was attracted to women, too. *They have a word for it, what is it? Bisexual!* Yes, she was bisexual. Somewhere deep down, she had always known. But she had denied it to herself. How could a traditional woman be so different? Weren't 'good' housewives supposed to be heterosexual? Just loving their husband and attending to their children? How could she have desires that were not normal? How could a woman who was so focused on her career be so sexual? As if these things mattered anyway. None of them did. You are what you are.

And now Sara Imam had awakened her hidden self in a beautiful way.

She had loved it when a woman had made love to her in college. It was that night she knew she enjoyed being with women as well as men. The pleasure from a woman was so different. So unusual. A woman could touch her the way a man never did. And yet, she needed a man in her life too.

She had never spoken to anyone about it and buried it so it would never surface again to damage her career or her marriage. But Sara had evoked feelings in her that had made her realize her true self.

Instead of only staying for the two days that she had initially planned, Kavita stayed for the entire length of the trip and then took an extra day off the following Monday, citing networking reasons at home to stay back. This wasn't entirely untrue. She was trying to network, just not in the professional manner. She hadn't realized that things would move so fast with Sara.

Sara was a dynamic woman, supremely intelligent and excellent in what she did and yet creative in many other aspects. She made Kavita laugh and look at things like she'd never done before. She quoted poetry and music. Her jokes were witty. And her body, her body was simply smoking.

The first time Sara made love to Kavita, she was gentle and kind. It was in Sara's hotel room. A much bigger suite than Kavita's, with plush, soft couches and cushions. Lemongrass candles. Clean, crisp white sheets on an inviting bed. A large balcony that overlooked the expanse of the beach they were just on, where she had asked Kavita if she could kiss her.

'Drink?' Sara gave Kavita a glass of neat vodka without waiting for a reply. Kavita took it and swallowed it in one gulp. She needed it. The thick, musky liquid burned down her throat and gave her a warm, fuzzy feeling. They spoke for hours, stared into each other's eyes, rubbed their fingers on their palms.

Sara leaned forward, placing her lips gently on Kavita's. It was affectionate. Gentle. Intimate. It wasn't a kiss that was imposing, wanting, demanding. She pulled back to see her reaction. 'We don't need to do this.' Sara was giving Kavita a way out. She ran her finger across Kavita's lips, resting her fingers delicately around her ear.

Kavita shook her head. 'I want to.'

Kavita looked into Sara's eyes to tell her she was ready. Kavita took Sara's hands to admire them. She had perfect nails. Bright red nail polish. Unlike her hands—rough with chewed off nails. Why do we admire someone for the things we don't have? Kavita wondered. Random thoughts raced through her mind. But mostly how beautiful Sara was.

She ran her fingers through Sara's hair, admiring how well the woman looked after herself. Her hair, her smell, her beauty. Soaking it in, Kavita looked deeply into Sara's eyes. Sara ran her fingers down Kavita's face, across her cheek, down her throat and over her clothes. It sent shock waves through Kavita's body. The kissing must have lasted for two hours. Lovemaking with a woman was very different from that with a man. It was almost tantric. The slow movements, the gentle caressing, the languid pace of touching, fondling, licking, took hours and it was erotic, sensuous, and highly orgasmic.

'Have you done this before?' Sara asked after hours and hours of kissing. She slowly took off her shirt.

Kavita nodded. 'Once. Long back. It didn't mean anything then.'

'Do you want this to mean something?' Sara asked as the tight black shirt fell to the ground, exposing her bright red bra. She had large, full, voluptuous breasts. She held Kavita's hands and placed them on her breasts. Kavita was ready. Sara unclasped Kavita's bra and let her fingers move around her breasts under her dress, cupping them and taking them in her mouth. Sara swiveled her around slowly and pushed her against a wall. Kavita was hesitant.

Sara said, 'You want me to go slower? You okay?'

Kavita nodded.

Sara gently touched Kavita with the tips of her fingers from the nape of her neck, slowly moving down across her back and gently placing her thumbs right above the crack of her ass. As she moved back upwards lingering slowly on the side of her breasts, Kavita let out a long moan. Sara spent several minutes with her fingers and mouth over Kavita's back, arousing every sensuous nerve in her body.

'Oh you are so good with your fingers.' She deliberately

turned and pressed herself against Sara, kissing her as she moved her fingers through Sara's hair, feeling confident that she could do no wrong.

They went and lay down on the bed. Sara's hand slipped under Kavita's red dress. She held her breast and squeezed it. She moved slowly, taking her time. She spread her legs as she began rubbing her hand over Kavita's thighs, making small concentric circles with the tips of her fingers, slowly moving towards her panty. Slow, web-like motions.

Kavita knew this should be the moment to pull away if she didn't want her life to change. But the feel of a woman kissing her was so overpowering that she lay back and enjoyed the moment. Sara's fingers moved slowly inside Kavita, exploring her dark side, rubbing her thumb in the sweet spot. Kavita let out a soft moan. Her body tingled. Her resistance weakened. Sara pulled Kavita's dress over her head, leaving her breasts exposed to the cool air around them.

'God Kavita, you are so beautiful.' Sara sucked on Kavita's breasts slowly, gently tugging at her nipples as she licked them. Kavita moaned softly as she moved her hands over Sara's back. Sara slowly moved on top. She started kissing her breasts, gently kneading them as her lips moved downwards blowing soft kisses on her stomach with her lips barely touching Kavita's skin. Kavita's body was on fire.

Sara spread Kavita's legs with her one hand as she continued rubbing her breasts. Kavita fell back on the pillows with her hands behind her head. Sara's mouth slowly moved down Kavita's thighs as she parted her legs. She slipped two fingers inside, slowly moving them. Then went faster, harder. She found Kavita's clitoris and rubbed her thumb against it. She removed her fingers and used her tongue. Slowly licking her, probing deep inside. Kavita's body was on fire. She held on to the sofa as one leg fell casually on the floor. She could feel

waves of passion soar through her body. Sara continued to
stroke Kavita, kiss her gently and talk to her while she made
love. Kavita had never felt this way with a man. She reached
her climax and was in heaven.

Kavita looked up, caught her breath. 'That was so good
that I think the neighbours need a cigarette!'

They both laughed. They knew they had something special,
more than sex.

'I want to clean you up now,' Kavita said as she held Sara's
hand and led her to the bathtub. 'With lots of hot soapy
bubbles. Get in. Let me run the water.'

Sara smiled. Kavita felt complete right then. This would be
a night they would never forget.

23

Sara was everything Kavita wasn't but wanted to be. And yet there was this nagging feeling in the pit of Kavita's stomach that she would suppress this part of her again when she went back home and her daily chores took over, no matter how much she loved being with Sara. There were certain things one didn't do. One was to declare you were bisexual! Not when you were married or had a child. No matter how much happiness it gave you.

Sara understood that aspect of Kavita. How she wished Kavita would realize that the longer you live for someone else, the more you kill your own soul. If you didn't stand up for who you were, you would regret it all your life. So when Sara parted ways with Kavita at the airport all Sara could say was, 'Don't let your head rule over your heart. You'll regret the decisions you make if you make them for someone else.'

But when Kavita got on the airplane, she had mixed feelings. Was this her escape from the drudgery of her life with Gaurav? Wouldn't it be easier if she sorted out what she needed from Gaurav rather than escape into a world that was taboo? The conference had opened up her mind to such new possibilities that her head felt like it was going to explode. She took a pill and went to sleep for the rest of the journey.

When Kavita got back home she plunged herself into work and family duties. She took Vansh for soccer practice and even passed on her procedures to other surgeons so she could spend more time at home with Gaurav and her family. She cooked and hosted a party for their friends. She became the 'perfect housewife' as Gaurav wanted. It lasted a whole month. Until the depression set in.

Somehow she needed more. More than just the job or her family. She needed Sara. And the more she tried to push it out of her mind, the more Sara's face kept taunting her. Kavita wanted out of her confusion. She rediscovered her yoga mat and began going again to her favourite garden.

She went to Nehru Park or Lodhi Gardens early in the morning to do her surya namaskars and watch the sun rise long after her pranayama was done. She found solace amongst the trees. She loved Delhi for this—the winter season. The beautiful gardens that allowed anyone to enter and find themselves. The wide roads that accommodated every vehicle from a bullock cart to a BMW. Delhi was truly the melting pot of India.

One day after her yoga at Lodhi Gardens she decided to roam the shops of Khan Market to spend more time with herself and clear her head.

'One black coffee please and a slice of pound cake,' Kavita said to the waiter. She was sitting at Café Turtle, her favourite haunt for coffee and pastries.

As she waited for her coffee she got an SMS from Sara. 'She was visiting Delhi the coming weekend, could they catch up?' Kavita didn't know how to reply so she didn't. She finished her coffee and roamed the bookstores. She also popped by the Good Earth shop for some more items on the Buddha. Somewhere she felt that it was because of this that she had gotten so far. Learnings from Buddhism made her more calm and focused. She always picked up a painting or a statue of Buddha in many forms to decorate her house. No one in her family understood why she did so. While they would all sit and pray to idols during festivals, Kavita would read more about Buddhism and find solace in meditation.

After hours of sitting and reading at a bookstore and roaming the streets of Khan Market, Kavita sat down for a hearty lunch of pasta at Big Chill. As she ate, she pondered. Why was she scared of meeting Sara again? Did she think she would fall in love with Sara? Would it affect her relationship with Gaurav? But which relationship? Wasn't their marriage a sham anyway? Even when they slept together, Kavita didn't like it anymore. Didn't her teachings tell her that there was no wrong or right in life. There was no good or bad. And when you started seeing yourself through other's eyes, you would fall instantly. If you could remove judgement from life and stop becoming judgemental about the self, wouldn't that be the greatest liberation of the soul?

Kavita thought there was a reason why she was different from her family, from her friends. While everyone believed in one way, she always sought out something more. She had tried to conform for so long. With marriage, with motherhood, her beliefs, her sexuality. But she wasn't like them. For so long she had suppressed it. It was time she embraced it.

Kavita picked up her phone and replied to Sara. 'I'm looking forward to meeting you.'

And suddenly she was sure. This was the only way she could live. By being truthful to herself. By cherishing a feeling that was within her instead of admonishing it. She felt a heavy weight lift from her shoulders. The dawn of a new day.

KAAJAL

24

Kaajal: 30. Lawyer. Short. Slim. Beautiful. Curly brown hair. Smiling eyes. In a complicated relationship. Loves to shop.

'Are you on Tinder?' Kaajal asked her friend, Tarini, while they were eating momos at Chanakya Yashwant Place.

'Tinder?' Tarini asked as she took a bit of spicy chutney onto her plate.

'Tinder. It's an app for meeting random people.'

'For random sex?'

'Yes.' Kaajal took a sip of her Thums Up. How she loved these momos, the spicy chutney, and then washing it down with a Thums Up. Her sister thought it was vile and she never understood the delight in sitting in a restaurants while food was served on plastic plates by young waiters.

'Why would I be on Tinder? I'm married.'

Kaajal smiled. 'Many married men are on Tinder. Why can't married women be on it too?'

'Because that's cheating.'

Kaajal stuck her tongue out at her friend. 'As if married people don't cheat. They're the ones who are most bored and want random sex. Single people still want to get married.'

'Where is this conversation going?' Tarini asked as she polished off the last piece on her plate.

Kaajal shrugged her shoulders. 'I'm just saying. I saw a profile of your husband on Tinder and was wondering if you knew he was on it.'

'What did you just say? You must be mistaken.' Tarini shuffled in her purse for some money to pay for their momos.

'No, no I'm paying,' Kaajal said. 'And don't stress, babe. The best way to get over a man cheating on you is to cheat right back!'

Tarini didn't say anything.

'So what do you want to do about that?'

'So what happens then? Does he meet you?'

'Are you mad? I ain't doing your husband. I'm doing someone else's!' Kaajal said as she burst into giggles. She had confessed to Tarini about her relationship long back. Kaajal and Tarini had met at a play at Kamani auditorium. They had been so ravenously hungry by the interval that even after the play started they were the only two people eating the greasy samosas outside. Then they decided to watch the rest of the play sitting in the aisle since their front row seats were taken. Since then they became friends who often went for performances at the Kamani auditorium to get their culture fix and to eat greasy food in different places across Delhi to fill their street food craving.

When Kaajal started sleeping with a married man, it wasn't Kavita whom she confessed to. It was Tarini. Initially it was an emotional upheaval but soon things settled down to a comfortable level.

'Actually,' Tarini said, 'I don't need to be on Tinder to find a man. I already have one!'

Now Kaajal was interested. 'So I don't really care what Sanjay is up to. He can sleep with whomever he wants!'

'So,' Kaajal said as she took a bit of saunf from the bowl that came with her change. 'Who is it? Tell! Tell!'

'Varun.'

'Who's Varun?'

'A friend of mine.' Tarini was nonchalant.

Kaajal was a little more sceptical. 'Where have I heard this name before?'

Tarini looked a bit sheepish as she said, 'All I'm saying is that if Sanjay wants to go out and screw people, well screw him because I am getting as much as he can! Now do you want to go to Sarojini or not?'

Kaajal stood up to go. 'Yes let's do that. I want some new scarves for work.'

As they walked to the auto stand Kaajal shrieked. 'Oh my God! I just realized where I've heard that name before. Isn't that Ayesha's husband? Varun?'

Tarini smiled coyly. Kaajal shoved her. 'Good for you. Sleeping with your best friend's hubby!'

'Ex-best friend!' Tarini said quickly. 'We haven't spoken for so long. We barely meet except for her Diwali parties, you know? Those lavish parties she throws so everyone sees how powerful she is. And besides, I think she's having an affair too. I haven't told Varun, obviously. But I think everyone in this world is entitled to have some fun.'

'So you are going to have an open marriage?' Kaajal asked.

'No, an open marriage is when both parties know that the other is sleeping around. This is just a happy marriage!'

Kaajal and Tarini both laughed as they got off the auto at Sarojini Nagar. Like most of Delhi's middle class, the two of them loved Sarojini Nagar for its great bargains. And it was never just about the clothes, when one went to Sarojini Nagar; it was about the experience of hunting around for great quality and low prices. It was a time that would be remembered later when women bought things from Jimmy Choo and Louis Vuitton at DLF Emporio. If a woman didn't have the shakarkandi at Sarojini Nagar with extra masala and nimbu, the delicate waffles at Emporio would never taste as sweet.

Kaajal said, 'I agree that marriages get boring. People should just live together. Then at least you can walk out whenever you want to. And then the reason to stay is because you believe in the love. Not the paper that binds you.'

'Look, sometimes paper binds you and sometimes sex does. The fact is that you choose what life path you need. I love Sanjay. He's a great guy. An amazing father. He's loving and caring. He gives me the freedom to be what I want. He gives me money to spend as I like. Why should I leave him? Just because we've lost interest in sex with each other? Well that's a stupid reason.'

Kaajal thought about it. 'But don't you want your person to be faithful and loyal?'

Tarini shook her head. 'In bed? Why? What is faithful? The Shiv lingam is worshipped by millions of women. Why should one woman hold on to one man then?'

Kaajal shook her head. 'I don't know. You know I am in a relationship with a married man but I would still want him to be faithful to me. I know he's not sleeping with his wife. And he's planning to leave her. You can say that's my warped notion of fidelity.'

Tarini picked out a bag from a stall as she said to Kaajal, 'Marriage is more than sex. You know sooner or later, people get tired of the same type of sex. They know each other's moves. Even if you've experimented with stuff, your bodies get tired. Sex is more mental then. I now need to psych myself into having sex with Sanjay. Only then can I be wet and ready. No matter what he does, if in my head I don't want to, I can never have sex. And after some time in a marriage, one just doesn't want to psych themselves up anymore. That doesn't mean he's a bad guy. I mean he's wonderful with my parents and family. Why should we separate or divorce for such a silly reason as sex?'

'Hmmm,' Kaajal pondered aloud. 'I hate to admit it but are you making sense there?'

'The only problem will be when Varun is transferred back to Lucknow. Then I'll just have to get on Tinder, right?' Tarini said with a laugh.

Kaajal wondered if she should speak to her married man about this. If he never planned to leave his wife, then what would she tell her family? Ultimately she wanted a companion in her life. It need not be a marriage certificate, but just someone to depend on. She had hoped her love, her passion and her dedication would have proved how much she needed him in her life and vice versa. She didn't know whether it was the spicy momos or the conversation she just had, but Kaajal was feeling like she was going to throw up!

25

It had been a long day at work before Kaajal could speak to her boss. She had kept a vrat for him and she needed to tell him that.

'Sir, may I come in?' Kaajal said as she entered his cabin. They had been extremely professional about their relationship in the workplace. She called him Sir and he treated her as a junior as all bosses did. Otherwise the firm would kick both of them out.

'Yes, Kaajal,' The boss looked up from his desk and smiled at her. 'Shut the door behind you.'

He thought she looked amazing. He had never seen her like this. Decked up in a salwar kameez with mehndi on her hands. 'What the…' He fumbled for the appropriate words.

'It's Karwa Chauth.'

'Oh Dear God! Not you as well!'

'I thought you would like a bit of devotion from me. You rarely get it,' Kaajal said as she put her hands on her hips and raised one eyebrow.

The boss came around to her and put his arms around her before she moved away, looking towards the door which was unlocked. She locked it. Checked it again to make sure.

'The only devotion I want from you is what you know best.'

Kaajal smiled. 'So you want me to break my fast?'

The boss pulled her towards the bathroom. 'Isn't Karwa Chauth about making the man happy? How about I tell you ways in which you can do that without starving yourself?'

Kaajal protested a little while he dragged her towards the adjoining loo, 'But this is for your long life.'

'Well, let's see what other long things can come out of this fast.'

He pulled her to the bathroom and Kaajal knew she could take control then. He started kissing her. Then, she just slapped him. Kaushik stared back defiantly. She unleashed a volley of abuses, including one for his mother. Kaushik smiled. 'Now you're asking for it.' Kaajal slapped him again. This time, he slapped her back. Hard.

Kaajal cried out in pain. She dared him to do it again. He slapped her across her face. She wanted more. Harder slaps. The tension built. He pulled her hair and slapped her again. She pulled him and kissed his mouth. Bit his lips. Pulled his hair. She dragged him outside to his sofa.

She leaned close over his face, her tongue in his mouth...she kissed him...she moved her hands up, pinned against a wall, face-first, he held both of her arms above her head and dug his nails into her back, ripping her dress and leaving marks.

He took his belt off. She bent along the top of the sofa. Her hands were tied together with a leather belt and she watched herself in the mirror on the opposite wall as Kaushik moved behind her, spanked her hard, causing her to cry out again. She begged for more. She begged for Kaushik to call her his whore. She bent over some more. Tears started to roll down her cheeks. He hit her harder, called her a filthy slut. She is stretched, spread-eagled and face down on the sofa, her heart hammering inside her chest. Her back arches back...back...her head tilts back...she extends her arms...he enters her. Sweet taste of blood in her mouth. He pushes and rams himself inside her hard. She reaches a climax. She's never felt so complete in her life.

He gave her some water as he pulled his trousers up and put on his belt. 'Thank you. This was the best Karwa Chauth I've ever had.'

Kaajal smiled. No wife could do that for him.

26

Kaajal heard the phone ring while she was playing Connect Four with Vansh. She put a red coin in the slot and said, 'There, connect four! I beat you!'

Vansh threw a fit. 'No fair, Maasi. You cheated!'

Kaajal smiled and ruffled his head before picking up the phone. It was Tarini.

'What are you doing? Want to go for drinks later?' Tarini rattled off without waiting for a reply. 'Let's go to that Gurgaon place. Raasta na? We liked it last time. Shall we go there again or try something new?'

Kaajal rolled her eyes as she got up from the kitchen chair to make herself a cup of tea. 'We just met yesterday, Tarini. Don't you have any work? Such a housewife you are!'

Tarini felt offended. 'Fine if you don't want to go then it's okay yaar. And what's wrong with being a housewife? You know how much work we do?'

'No! No. I'm kidding. I'm sure you have lots of work!'

'Stop being sarcastic yaar. Not all of us want to work hard for the rest of our lives. Working at home and managing children is also a big task.'

'How you people have no ambition is beyond me. But whatever floats your boat, honey. Of course I will go.' Kaajal wondered if Tarini seriously had nothing better to do than spend all her husband's money. Was this her life's purpose?

Kaajal had seen her mother suffer from being just a housewife. Their father had abandoned them when they were younger. It had left an indelible scar on her. She had promised herself two things. One, she would never succumb to marriage. And two, she would always be financially independent.

Tarini defended herself. 'Not everyone is as ambitious as you are, Kaajal. Some of us enjoy looking after our families. That's what gives us purpose.'

Kaajal didn't interrupt Tarini. She loved her friend but honestly never understood her. She often asked Tarini probing questions like, 'what would happen if your husband died and you had to look after yourself?' Tarini would only laugh and say that wouldn't happen. Kaajal would ask Tarini what she would do when her two children grew up and stopped needing her? Tarini would answer, 'Find more friends to party with!' Kaajal felt it was a waste of a life. Such an intelligent, talented person like Tarini could do so much with her life but was wasting it.

Tarini, meanwhile, often wondered why Kaajal was so judgemental and couldn't bring herself to accept her for her choices and be happy for her. Maybe Kaajal needed some security in her life, like a good man and a happy marriage!

Kaajal didn't want to argue. 'Should we call a few people we haven't met in some time?'

'Like who?'

'Varun and Kaushik?' Kaajal laughed at her own joke. Wouldn't it be absolutely delicious to go out with married men in a public place!

'Yeah right. As if they'll come.'

'These bloody affairs I tell you. There's never any dignity in them at all. Anyway, see you at Geoffrey's at eight?'

'Okay.'

Kaajal put the phone down and thought about it. Even

though she loved Tarini, sometimes she felt their conversations were stilted. Tarini spoke about food, her husband, her affair, clothes, movies and the plays they watched together. She went on vacations with her husband and used his money to buy herself things. All the while she was having an affair behind his back. Somewhere Kaajal felt that was morally wrong. And yet society would always see her as the 'other woman' who 'stole' the man who had stood rightfully behind his wife. How strange society was.

Society applauded women who chose to get married, stay at home, raise children and live off their husbands. And yet it looked down upon women who chose to work to fund their own expenses, be suspicious about women who dated to find happiness and ridiculed women who chose to live alone and not be a burden on anyone. Housewives were applauded and single women were creatures the society didn't know how to handle.

'Strange.' The only words that escaped Kaajal's lips.

'Maasi, can I go to Ameya's house for a play date?' Vansh suddenly asked, startling her a bit.

Kaajal asked, 'Has his mother given you permission?'

'Yes you can speak to her now.'

Kaajal took the mobile that was given to Vansh to talk to Ameya's mother. It was stranger that Kavita and Gaurav had given their only child a mobile phone at the age of six. But since she wasn't a parent, she hadn't raised the issue. She thought it was too young an age for a child to get a phone. But Kavita felt that it was a small device that allowed him to call five numbers that were most important at any time and if he was in danger he could just press any number for an emergency. Kaajal thought this was exactly why she didn't want to get married and have kids. It was a dangerous world to bring your child into. And you would never be able to do anything if all your thoughts and actions were on how to keep your child safe.

She hung up the phone and told Vansh to put his shoes on. She walked down the road to drop Vansh for his play date and was assured by the mother that she would drop him home by seven thirty. By that time Kavita would be back and she would be able to leave for her drinks date with Tarini.

As Kaajal walked back home, she felt acutely aware that she was being followed. She looked down at her Anokhi skirt and her full sleeve shirt. There was not a single inch of skin showing. Oh how she hated Delhi for this reason. Boys on bikes.

They passed by her and whistled.

She ignored them. She kept walking, her head held high.

Then she saw them take a U-turn and head back.

Her heart started pounding. She hadn't carried her purse. She didn't have a mobile either. She had simply walked out of the door with Vansh and a set of house keys.

The boys were coming back towards her.

Blood throbbed in her veins. Her head felt light. The sun was still out. They wouldn't do anything. Would they?

She looked around. There was no one else around on this street.

The bike got closer. The boys were laughing. They had a plan.

Kaajal was scared. She knew she was defenceless. She had no pepper spray. She didn't have a weapon. And there were two of them. Generally in such situations one goads the other. It was always about power with boys. They didn't think about anything else at that time.

She didn't know whether to scare them, as she had read once. Or should she just surrender so they would let her go? What did that article say? Why couldn't you think of the correct thing when the time came. *I had a lot of information but I was stupid enough not to protect myself before coming out of the house!*

The boys came close and slowed down. Kaajal did what came naturally.

'Kya hai?! Kya chahiye?' Suddenly she found confidence. She was carrying a set of keys. She knew she could at least use that to gouge out their eyes if she got the chance. Boys always thought women would be weak. Women Intersection would never harm a man if it came down to it. Yes, they were taught to ram their knee into the penis or poke their fingers into the boy's eyes for self-defence but they were taught to be 'good girls'. And that moment of split-second doubt was what allowed men to overpower women.

She ground her teeth and made her face red with anger. She showed them she was ready. And boys don't generally like a fight. If they know a woman is strong and they'll have to put up a fight, most often they'll let the woman go.

The boys drove off, laughing and talking about her.

Well, bitching about me is better than anything else, Kaajal thought as she ran back home and locked the door behind her. She had seen the faces of the boys. She would report them to the police so they wouldn't harass anyone else.

She first called Tarini, 'Hey. Let's chuck the evening plans. What are you doing now? I need you to come with me to the police station. We need to put some goons away.'

INTERSECTION

27

'Bhaiyaji! Bhaiyaji! Yeh kya hai?'

'Madam, this is an enchilada.'

'Inch ki ma ki?' Simran asked as she looked at the dish in front of her.

Naina turned to her and said, 'Simi, we've come to a Spanish restaurant. This is Spanish food.'

'Rabba! Tum log bhi na. Kahan kahan se jagah dhoondh lete ho. Simple butter chicken nahin kha sakte kahin pe bhi? Bhaiyaji please take this back. What is this green thing? Yeh toh bilkul disgusting lag rahi hai mujhe.'

The waiter stood with his hands folded. 'Sorry Ma'am, we can't take it back unless you tell us what the problem is.'

'The problem is ki mujhe nahin khana yeh vahyaat cheez!' Simran's voice became louder while Naina tried to solve the situation. 'How about you try my paella?'

Simran and Naina exchanged dishes as usual and Simran still didn't like it. 'Yeh bohat bland hai.'

Naina told the waiter, 'Can I have a dish of this chicken? Yes, please can you get that fast? This will go well with the paella. And please can I have two long island ice teas? Simran and I need them!'

Simran smiled at her friend, 'Tu kitni badmaash hai. Drinking in the middle of the afternoon!'

'I can't believe she is having an affair!' another friend piped in louder making Naina's head turn towards the other end of the table.

Naina was at her monthly kitty party. It was a social group she had made when she put Shonali in school. Shonali, her firstborn, was just two years old then. She left her in play school the first day and stood outside the school the entire time. She howled as Shonali went into class. And soon enough she saw many mothers through the course of the week who howled alongside her. They became friends and started meeting once a week for a cup of coffee after dropping the kids. It eased their pain. They would discuss children and husbands and recipes. None of them were working then.

Soon they started having lunches, scouting new places to eat every Monday afternoon. From Hauz Khas restaurants to the latest theme cuisine at Khan market, Naina loved roaming with them. After she won Masterchef, she invited her group of eight girls home and cooked a lavish meal for them. But after that she got so busy that she had to stop going for weekly luncheon encounters and stick to meeting them once a month. You could either be social or be sensational. You couldn't achieve success with both! So she decided to give it up. She took the occasional cooking class but the rest of the time she wanted to be a housewife. And she loved it.

Naina was meeting her gang after a long time. They had stuck together for eight long years. From raising children, to criticizing husbands, diets to disorders, miscarriages to mother-in-laws, renovating houses to plastic surgery, they did everything together and talked about everything. Everything except how bad their marriages actually were. Or how lonely they were, if at all. Those were things you didn't discuss at happy lunches.

Once one of them had confided that her husband was having an affair and Naina had counseled her to go to a marriage therapist. There was no further conversation after that. That woman stopped coming to the group and shifted to a house far away. Naina wondered why women needed to be tough all the time. Why they needed to show this great pretence to each other that they were super women. Would vulnerability be such a bad thing? Would it come back to bite them?

'Anjali, is that a new Louis Vuitton bag?' one woman asked.

Anjali nodded. 'I was getting tired of the old one. It was too big. I wanted something for just a few things, you know. I got it this time when we took our annual vacation to New York.'

They were all sitting in a new place started by Ritu Dalmia, Cordon Bleu Chef. It had lovely décor and the food was exceptional. Except for Simran, who didn't like anything to eat anywhere, all the girls were enjoying themselves.

'I'm watching my weight. I'll have the grilled chicken please. No wine,' Anjali told the waiter. But all the girls protested, 'Oh please yaar. One glass of red wine is good for the heart. It has less calories than your bread in the morning.'

'Yes but I need my bread. I don't need wine,' Anjali spat back.

'Actually you don't need any grains,' Nandita remarked. 'Our bodies are meant to eat everything raw.' Nandita was a staunch believer in wholesome food. 'I ferment everything. Vegetables, bread. It's so healthy.'

'I love fermented grapes!' Naina said as she sipped on her wine, inciting giggles all around. 'I'm not eating. At all. I'm on a diet. Only salads and soups!'

'Grilled chicken is healthy yaar! Come on. It's not as if you're going to be an actress and all,' Anjali chided Naina.

'Arrey but she was on TV no?'

'She looked lovely the way she was. Our own Indian Nigella Lawson,' Anjali said as she winked at Naina.

'Well she's not on TV now. She can easily eat. As it is she doesn't meet us no? So when she does, she should just enjoy herself.'

Naina smiled as she looked at all of them. This was her own group. Chatting and making sure the other person ate as much as the next woman so the guilt wouldn't come down heavily at night. 'You all have such bad relationships with food. We must treat it with respect.'

'You want me to pray to it now? Is that also going in your new book?' Anisha piped in as they all laughed.

'No it's just that when we know we'll have enough tomorrow, we will stop overeating today.'

'Arrey bhaiya kya bol rahi hai!' Simran remarked with a wave of her hand and a slight nasal twang. 'If I die tomorrow I shouldn't feel I didn't eat what I wanted. I want to be happy today. Not starving!'

'If you die tomorrow, how will you know if you didn't eat something? You'll be dead na?' Naina asked with a smile as wide as a Cheshire cat's.

'Hai Rabba! What you talk! Such nonsense, Naina. Like you want me to die. Chal katti,' Simran said and didn't mean a single word as a platter of deep-fried mozzarella sticks was passed around and they all took a helping, ignoring their diet and conversation completely.

Naina came back to the gossip, 'So who was having an affair?'

Anjali said, 'Apparently there is a girl called Kaajal, Kara, Karia, something like that. She works at this law firm. I don't remember the name. She was caught sleeping with her boss and the partners have threatened to fire her. How come all women are blamed for such things? Wasn't it the man's fault as well? Why aren't the men getting fired?'

'So true. So unfair no?' Naina said, shocked at such behaviour. In London there would be one policy and it would apply to both genders. Her mind raced back to when she was working as a chef and a manager had hit on her. She had immediately threatened to go to HR or sue the hotel. She was loyal to Kaushik. The manager had backed off and had been made to quit by the hotel. Even though she was much lower in the ranks, the organization had taken her word against his.

'Hey Naina, tera pati bhi wahin pe kaam karta hain na?' Simran asked and made her return from her reverie.

Anisha laughed at Simran. 'There are so many law firms in this world, Simran! As if her husband will be in the same one.'

Simran instantly corrected herself. 'Yes. But wouldn't it be better if we got more gossip? Naina, ask your husband if this K woman is in his law firm. Give us some gossip on her.'

'Arrey but who is she? Why are we so concerned about her?' Naina asked, getting slightly perturbed that Kaushik could be working in a firm where such immoral activities were taking place.

'She's my sister-in-law,' said Ishita suddenly. She called the waiter for another glass of water. 'My brother is married to Kaajal's sister.'

Naina was befuddled at the venom. 'But why are you gossiping about your sister-in-law?!'

'Because I just don't like her. She has never gotten along with me. She makes fun of my accent and is jealous of everything I have. The new Michael course bag I got?'

'Kors, yes,' Anjali corrected her and asked her to continue. They always looked out for each other and a little correction about pronunciation never mattered. If it was coming from Kaajal it would be an insult; Kaajal looked down at her and laughed at her whenever she made a mistake.

'Well, she said mine was a fake. From Bangkok! The little bitch. I can afford to buy original stuff.'

'But I thought you liked your sister-in-law?' Naina asked as she cleaned her hands in her finger bowl. They were all done with their meal.

'I like my other sister-in-law. My brother's wife, Kavita. She is so sweet to me. She gives me a free checkup anytime I want and she gives me important information, like which pill to take to delay my period if I'm going on a vacation to Monte Carlo. Kaajal is her sister. She is good for nothing. So old and still living with all of them.'

'Girls, chalein? The kids will be waiting for us,' Simran said as she looked at her watch.

'Oh is that a new Dior watch?' Anjali noticed.

'No. No. Very old. You've not seen it? I only wear this.'

'No you were wearing your Omega the last time we met?' Anjali asked.

The chatter continued as they all dispersed from the restaurant and got into different cars.

'Chal,' Naina said as she air kissed all the girls on both cheeks, never touching her lips to their faces, 'I'm headed home. I'll catch you guys soon. My kids come home in a bus.'

'Bye Naina. Now don't be a stranger huh? Next Monday we're going to Shamrock. It's a new Irish pub. Maybe we'll see some Irish men!' Simran giggled.

'Ab tum Irish khana khaogi?' Naina was surprised.

'Oh ho. Next time you only order for me. We'll have fun. Come, come.'

Ishita said, 'I'll be back in Jaipur but I'll see you next month, Naina. You know I can come only month mein ek baar. Because I do all my legal work here with my lawyer.'

Naina suddenly put two and two together, 'Which law firm is it?'

'Mukherjee,' Ishita said. 'That's how I know Kaajal got thrown out. Her boss is in trouble now. Okay bye. Love you.'

As Naina got into her car, she dialed Kaushik's number and he disconnected. She was dying to know who Kaajal worked for. Kaushik would tell her all the details in the evening. She couldn't wait to find out all the gossip. And then tell her friends next Monday. Maybe meeting her friends was a good idea after all; it had kept her mood light and engaged her time. Friends really made her world go round.

28

Kavita was finally in a wholesome relationship. She met Sara at her hotel and spent two days with her. Now she knew what true love was. It was a feeling of being complete, of wanting to spend time with someone, of knowing and respecting each other's silences, of having the same hopes and dreams, of sharing ideas and encouraging each other. And it had nothing to do with age, or gender. The thought blew her mind.

'So where do you want to take me?' Sara asked as Kavita got into her car.

'I'll take you to a place that means a lot to me,' Kavita said as she started driving. She had decided to take Sara to a lovely place she would ordinarily not visit. She figured if Sara understood this part of her life, maybe she could start believing in the possibility of being with this woman.

Kavita drove Sara to the Lotus Temple in Delhi. It was a beautiful place that was peaceful and sacred for those who believed in it.

'This is beautiful,' Sara said as they walked up the lawns. Kavita was glad.

As they sat inside in silence, with their eyes closed, Kavita felt a deep sense of peace. The fact that she could share the one thing that was closest to her with another person for the first time in her life meant that she was connected to that person in many different ways. The universe was trying to tell her that she needed to believe in herself. But she felt she still needed to let Sara know a few more things.

In bed that night, Sara asked, 'Are you committed to me, Kavi?'

Kavita brushed a stray hair from Sara's face. 'Yes. I don't want anything more with anyone else. But I need to go back to my marriage. I'm a mother and a wife. I move in an elite, traditional society. My reputation can get ruined if this comes out.'

Sara let out a sigh. 'Where do I stand then? Am I just a fling? I need you to be honest with me.' She paused. 'I need you to tell me because I've fallen for you. I want you in my life, Kavita. To me you are not a fling.'

Kavita understood but right now she couldn't give more. Her world was tumbling around her. She needed to find a strong footing again. She was questioning her identity.

Sara asked gently, 'Will you ever leave your husband, Kavita?'

Kavita replied in a grave tone, 'I cannot leave my husband or child, Sara. My life is in Delhi with them. I'm saying this again, I am reputed in my field and my society knows us too well. My mother would be horrified if I was to tell her I'm leaving with a woman. She's very traditional in her ways. She supported me with all my decisions and I can't go against her. She raised me by working two jobs. Knowing her daughter is a bisexual would kill her. So please don't expect more than what we have right now.'

Sara was crestfallen. How could she tell Kavita that she wanted to spend the rest of her life with her? It had only been a few days and Kavita was just beginning to understand this. For Sara there was nothing more to understand. She had already experienced love with a woman. She was sure of herself. She knew what she wanted. How could she tell her that she knew love? She knew what it did to you. How it could change you and mislead you. How could she tell her that she had never felt this way about anyone and could see them together for a long time? Kavita herself refused to accept the thoughts about the future. They had only had three days together but they had had the most wonderful time.

Who wouldn't fall for Sara? She was beautiful beyond words, had a charming smile and lovely eyes that drew you in. She was intelligent, warm and funny. Any man would fall for her. Kavita asked, 'Have you ever slept with a man?'

'Yes. I've had two men in my life. A very close school friend who I've lost touch with now and who asked me to marry him. And one more. A random one night stand just to make sure that I wasn't heterosexual.'

Kavita almost choked on her juice. 'You almost got married? You slept with men? But aren't you a lesbian? How do you not know?'

'Well my parents didn't accept that I was a lesbian so I desperately tried to please them. I ended up dating a man for some time. I slept with him but hated it and felt really violated, you know. And I broke up. I didn't want to do it anymore. Then a whole bunch of girls went on a Bangkok trip and it became awkward. They didn't know how to be around a lesbian when I told them I was one. So just to make things better, I went and slept with a guy after a really drunken night to show that I was joking. Two times in my life I've lied to someone, Kavita. My parents and my friends. To make them happy. It left me bruised and shaken because I couldn't stand up to who I was. I vowed never to do it again. I don't want to live like that. I want to be true to myself. Maybe society will judge me and hate me. But at least I won't hate myself.'

Kavita thought about it. That same society would never

accept the fact that she was bisexual. No one even understood it correctly. It wasn't as if she would be with both men and women at the same time. It simply meant that when she was with one person, male or female, she would be loyal to that person. It was like any other relationship. Except that she was attracted to both genders. So when she was with Gaurav, she enjoyed sex with him. And when she was with Sara, the lovemaking was pleasurable too. Both were different and unique. And she didn't want the term 'bisexual' attached to her identity. In this conservative society she would lose everything. She'd rather say that she was 'flexible.'

God forbid her secret came out! What would she tell Vansh? Her mother? That she was leaving Gaurav for another woman? What would they all say? What would her mother or her child do? The thought sent shivers down her spine.

She didn't need to tell. The truth was to come out soon enough.

29

Kavita took the file the nurse gave her and started reading the medical history before the patient walked in.

The patient was slim, petite. She wore a cotton kantha sari with a red blouse. She had two large diamonds in her ears and nothing around her neck or hands. She came alone. She was covering her face with the pallu, as if to wipe off sweat but Kavita knew she was hiding something.

'Hello Ayesha, I'm Kavita,' Kavita said, as shook her new patient's hand. 'I see your pregnancy result has come back positive?'

Ayesha nodded her head. How could she have let this happen? She thought her tubes must have dried up by now. She couldn't have another child. Not if that child was Harshvardhan's, a bachelor politician. And she herself married with a ten-year-old son. It was the most disgraceful thing to have happened!

'So should we do a sonogram, right back there? We can see the results.'

'I need to get rid of it,' Ayesha spoke quickly, cutting Kavita's speech. 'I don't want to keep it.'

Kavita had heard the argument before. She hated performing any abortions that were not necessary. Here was a respectable-looking woman who could clearly look after the child financially and physically. She needed to convince her to hold on to the baby. She knew she was contributing to the population of the country but abortion wasn't the answer to the problem.

'Ayesha,' Kavita spoke softly. 'Would you like some tea?'

Ayesha shook her head. The home pregnancy test result had come back positive and she had panicked. It had been Friday. Then she had to spend an entire weekend attending some farmhouse party with Varun and Adi. Many couples socialized and Ayesha played the 'happy marriage' farce with Varun, a show of how they were the perfect couple, to other couples. And all the while Ayesha was dying inside. Dying to call Harsh and tell him. The harder she tried to ignore the truth, the more it persisted. The wheels of her brain churned to find an answer. How would she explain this at home?

Then on Monday she had taken a blood test to confirm the pregnancy. Her last hope was that the home pregnancy test might've been wrong. But it wasn't. So she booked an appointment to meet Kavita, who came with high recommendations.

'Ayesha?' Kavita asked her again as she had wandered off into a daydream. 'Tea? Coffee?'

'Don't you have other patients?'

Kavita shook her head. 'It's a quiet day for a change. Sometimes I feel this is like a metro station. So many people. Buzzing around. It's quite maddening. Tiring. So much energy expended. So I welcome days like this, when I can have a cup of tea with a patient and talk about them rather than just their case.'

She had buzzed the nurse to come in and Kavita asked her, 'Please can you ask ward boy to get me a cup of tea and for Ayesha…'

'A tea please.'

'Two teas,' Kavita said as she smiled, knowing that by the

time the boy came she would have had enough time to convince this patient to keep the child. 'Where's your husband?'

And that's when Ayesha broke down and wept. Kavita came around her table and put an arm around Ayesha's shoulders. Maybe that was the reason she didn't want to keep the child? Her husband wasn't supportive. Or she was divorced. But Ayesha gave another answer.

'It's not my husband's.' Ayesha said between sobs, her hands hidden from sight, twisted in her lap.

Kavita then understood the reason. 'It doesn't matter. Should we try to find a solution to this together? You know men can always be tricked. If you have sex with him within a week, I can give you a due date and then later push it up. Due dates change all the time. Men don't know all that.'

Ayesha shook her head. 'No. No. I can't have this child.'

'Why Ayesha? Don't worry about the pregnancy. I'll help you through it. Children are a gift. So many women in the world want children and can't have them. They spend lakhs on having a child. There are other options.'

For the first time since Friday, Ayesha felt like she could talk to someone. 'I love children, Doctor.'

'Kavita. Just call me Kavita.'

'Kavita, I love children. I have a son. He's ten years old. He's turning eleven at the end of this year. I tried to have another child a long time ago but I couldn't. I had complications and then I gave up. My husband is not a very responsive man. He's happy with his one son.'

'Maybe if you bring him here we could speak to him about how it would be lovely to have another child.'

Ayesha thought about it and shook her head. The tea arrived. She took a sip and almost scalded her tongue. She hadn't been thinking correctly. These last few months with Harsh had been blissful. They had met often in hotel rooms during the day and she had even spent a few nights out, leaving Adi at a friend's house or telling Varun she was out with Pinky. No one had bothered.

Then there were some vacations and Adi had gone on a field trip with his school, leaving an entire weekend free for Ayesha. So Harshvardhan had taken her to Kerala. They had gone on a houseboat; made love on the deck where no one was looking. She recalled the smouldering passion that thrilled her. Three days in a marvelous five-star resort where no one knew the politician. That was when she had gotten pregnant. It had been exactly four weeks since then. She hadn't told him about the pregnancy, avoiding his calls for the last few days since she was unable to make small conversation and she didn't want him to know. He would ask her to run away with him. Marry him. She knew him. He was madly in love with her. He needed her with a ferocity that she hadn't seen in Varun. He held her face and would say, 'I love you, Ayesha. I love you with all my heart.' And she knew he meant it. He was saying it from deep within his soul. Nothing could mitigate that. And this child, this love child, was a validation of that. So if she told him, he would want her to have it. And she would be conflicted. She was a married woman. She was a simple housewife. What would her industrialist parents and her reputed in-laws say? This would bring shame to the family!

Kavita completed the sonography and spoke to Ayesha. 'In any case an abortion can only be done when the foetus is a little more developed so we can extract the whole thing. You'll need to wait another two to three weeks before we perform surgery. Here's my number. Call me if you feel like talking. I'll give you an appointment for April 16. Alright?'

Ayesha nodded and left. That would give her enough time to figure out her life. She didn't know how she had gotten into this mess. But she knew she needed to end it soon.

30

It's funny when you look back on life and wonder where the time went. Life decisions are made so quickly because we go by instinct most of the time. We trust our gut. And that's where we go horribly wrong. Sometimes we need to back our instinct with logic before we make our life-altering decisions.

Finding a life partner was one of those decisions. Kaajal had been dating a man for over a year now. She was ready to settle down. Yes, she had told her family that marriage was for losers but honestly she felt she needed more companionship. She still didn't believe in marriage but she wanted some permanency. She knew she needed to confront the man in her life now. What were his plans exactly?

They were lying in bed in a hotel room one night after making love when Kaajal broached the topic.

'We met over a year and a half ago. Things have changed so much since then. Don't you think so?'

He knew exactly where the conversation was going but didn't say anything. Kaajal continued, 'Do you love me, Kaushik?'

'Yes I do, Kaajal. I love you tremendously.'

Kaushik first met Kaajal in his office at Mukherjee & Associates some two years ago. She had just joined them. He was immediately attracted to her but he was her boss. He couldn't make any moves. But she was bright, talented, young, and very sexy. She was motivated and driven. Like Naina had been. Why was he attracted to women who wanted to do something with their lives?

They had started their affair when he took her for a legal conference out of town. She had come on to him. He had walked into her room to discuss their arguments with the client the next morning when he saw her in a satin robe and nothing underneath. She had listened to him intently, giving him a glass of scotch while taking notes. He had been very distracted then.

'What people don't know won't hurt them right?' she had said as the robe fell off her shoulders and she slipped under the covers of the big, bouncy bed.

It had been so long since Naina and he had made love. Or had any passion. She was such a mother now. Her body had changed. Her mind had altered into that of a 'behenji.' And she was always tired. Morning, noon or night. At one point he had given up on Naina. She lay there now when they made love, squeezing her eyes shut as if she wanted him to get it over and done with. They hadn't been like that. Now he could barely stand her. Marriage changed everything. But Kaajal wasn't asking for marriage. Till now.

He asked her, 'Do you want us to get married or something?'

Kaajal shook her head. 'Not at all, Kaushik. I want to have the option of walking out on you. But this kaleechadi can't be the only ring I wear. I want a ring from you.'

'I'll buy you a ring. What is that anyway?'

'It's a ring the sister's husband gives when they get married. It's called a kaleechadi. And Gaurav was sweet enough to give me an emerald ring. I want a diamond one. And I want it to mean something. I need to know if you're committed to me. All I've been hearing for the last two years is now bad your marriage is. If it's so bad, then why don't you get a divorce?

Kaushik remembered when things were easier. When these conversations didn't happen.

It was the first time they had slept together he knew he was in love with Kaajal. Kaushik had stood there, running his hands through his dark, wavy hair, 'You're not going to sue me for sexual harassment or anything, are you?'

Kaajal laughed, a tinkle in her voice, 'Only if you promise not to get me fired.'

Their lovemaking had been wild and passionate. They had sex in the shower in the morning before they went to meet the client, a raw energy that gave them razor sharp confidence and acumen. Since then Kaushik realized that being with Kaajal pushed him to be a better lawyer. He thought better, he argued better, he was more suave and confident and was rising in the ranks at his company when he slept with Kaajal.

Kaajal became a part of his daily life. But he didn't know how to tell Naina. What would happen? She would leave him? What about the kids? He couldn't be away from them. But Kaajal had never brought it up.

At the office, she was diligent and thorough. And in bed later in the night, she was still diligent and thorough! That's what he liked about her. Her raw primal instinct at her job was equivalent to her need with him in bed. Kaajal had never wanted anything else. He had given her a 100 per cent bonus and a 50 per cent raise within two years of her working at the firm. He had told her that he was married. He had confessed but he had also said there were severe problems in his marriage. She had hoped that one day those severe problems would become 'irreconcilable differences' on paper in a court of law.

Kaajal was in love with Kaushik. She loved him for his ambition and drive. She had daydreams of when they would be together; she would still work and make partner in the firm. She knew he was married. He hadn't hidden that from her. She had seen his wife in the office one day during lunch. He had seemed flustered. Stupid man. They never knew when to play it cool. The wife had gone home. He had spent extra on that night with her. A lovely dinner and a better hotel. He had pampered her till she allowed him to go home. What she didn't tell him was that she wasn't jealous. She knew in her heart that he would come to her. Sooner or later. Bad marriages never recover. They only get worse. And that's why she needed to finally bring up the topic. So he understood her intentions. Until now.

'Kaushik, you and I are good together. I need to know where we're going. I want to have a deeper commitment with you.' Kaajal didn't want to use the word 'marriage.' She wasn't stupid enough to scare Kaushik away until she knew he was ready for the deepest commitment. *I will lead him into it, eventually*.

Kaushik sighed deeply, unable to figure out his life. Kaajal was right. They were good together. Better than he was with Naina. But he loved Naina too. He had some great memories with her. And they had two beautiful daughters who would be devastated by a divorce.

'If you're not going to take legal action, let me know. I want to be on Tinder, this new app that makes me hook up with a man every night. I'm sure I can find someone who will fuck me and then obey me! I just thought I should give you the first right of refusal,' Kaajal said with a flash of humour crossing her face. A seduction done right is so subtle that the seduced thinks they are the seducer! Women had power over men but only some knew how to use it correctly. Kaajal was one of those women.

Kaushik dragged Kaajal into bed. 'How can you do another man? You belong to me.'

Kaajal looked him straight in the eyes and whispered just inches away from his face, 'Then prove it.'

'Kaajal.'

Kaajal took out her belt and stood on top of him on the bed. 'Mistress.'

He swallowed hard. 'Yes, Mistress.' She smiled. Were good girls into BDSM? Maybe women who understood their sexuality and wanted to explore the highest level of what an orgasm could do to them would try it. The rest? The rest were housewives who were happy with missionary sex. No wonder so many married men strayed!

Later, Kaajal went for a shower and emerged to remind him. 'This is the last time we can meet, Kaushik.'

Kaushik looked up from his phone. 'What? Why?'

'Because I need to move on. I can't be in a meaningless relationship. And with a job that's shaky right now because someone has spread rumours about us...'

'I told you I'll handle it,' Kaushik said, knowing that the rumours would subside if he just got in one more client. He would declare he needed Kaajal around and things would settle down. He thought he had it all figured out.

Kaajal came and sat on Kaushik's lap, straddling her legs around his waist, letting the towel that was wrapped around her fall open as her breasts and perfectly shaped body was left half visible to the man she loved. 'I want you to safeguard my job, Kaushik. But I also need to know what your future plans are. Are you going to be with me? Or am I always going to remain a mistress?'

Kaushik moved her aside before he got up and paced the room, 'I don't know how to leave Naina.'

'Do you want to?' Kaajal asked, wrapping the towel around her again.

'I don't know.' Kaushik said honestly, his expression a mask of stone. 'She means a lot to me. I can't just give up a marriage like that.'

'You gave it up when you decided to sleep with me. You've been unhappy for so long. A marriage is a never-ending commitment to a person. You want to make it work even if it gets boring or dull. You've not wanted to make it work with Naina for over two years.'

'I have two children with her.'

'Come on, Kaushik. You told me that you stopped loving her even before the second kid came along. You just wanted your first one to have a sibling. Was that a lie?' Kaajal wanted a confrontation.

'No it wasn't a lie. But now that I have two kids what am I supposed to do?'

'There is such a thing as child support. I'm not asking you not to give her what she wants. I'm just asking you not to give her yourself to her. Give yourself to me. Choose me. Because I drive you. I motivate you. I make you a better lawyer and a better man. You're happier with me. And isn't your happiness what will make your children happy and healthy too? Do you want them to see two people who don't get along?'

'No.'

Kaajal was indeed an excellent lawyer. 'Are you going to spend your entire life trying to bring back a romance? Just because you have memories with a person? Because you have children?'

'Children get affected by divorces.'

'Yes. And murders. And bullies. And the news. But eventually they are okay. And they see it all around them and get immunized to it. This world has changed. Children are used to their parents being divorced. And who knows, Naina might be having an affair too. I'm sure you don't think she's being faithful do you?'

Kaushik remembered the conversation he had had with her a few days earlier. How she had said she wanted to have an affair. Maybe she was already having one. Maybe his wife was making a fool of him.

'How long are you going to live in a dead-end marriage, Kaushik? I love you. I can make you happy. I do make you happy. Why can't you see that?' Kaajal played her broken damsel in distress game, and instantly Kaushik felt bad for her.

She had stuck by him for so long. Kaushik knew he needed to confront Naina. He was madly in love with Kaajal. He knew that he would lose her if he didn't take steps for them to be together. He would have to speak to Naina about a trial separation. He needed to get out of this boring marriage. But he didn't know how to tell his parents or hers. Because underneath the killer lawyer he was, he was mighty afraid of his parents and the consequences of separating from his wife.

31

The most significant day of your life doesn't have to be an entire day. It might be a single conversation, one that changes your perspective towards everything you know. Or perhaps the thoughts and feelings you've had till that moment when they finally come together like the pieces of a jigsaw puzzle that you can now see clearly to understand what your choices are.

Naina rushed back home to find out more gossip about her husband's firm. She knew it would connect Kaushik and her. Maybe he would think she was interested in his work. She rarely understood anything about law. All she knew was cooking and he was not interested in that anymore. He loved to eat her food. Not talk about how she made it. Or what her plans were. Maybe some office gossip would get them talking again.

But by the time she could speak to Kaushik, it was eight thirty in the evening. The girls had gone to sleep and as usual Kaushik was sitting and watching TV in his room. Naina and Kaushik hadn't eaten their supper yet. She asked him, 'Do you want to have dinner now or later?'

'Later. I'll have a drink first.'

Naina went to the bar and got him a scotch on the rocks. While she was giving it to him she said, 'Hey, you know I met the girls today. And one of them told me that there is this girl Kaajal, in your office. She's having an affair.'

Kaushik's hand froze. The glass dropped from his hand and the contents splashed on the floor as the shards of glass cracked on the cool floor of Naina's bedroom. Naina noticed it, of course, the shocked reaction, and that was her clue that there was no coincidence. She needed to be sure.

Kaushik looked at her and tried to cover up his mistake. 'Oh shit!' he exclaimed over-dramatically. 'The glass is all over. Naina! Why couldn't you give me the glass properly?'

Naina didn't know whether it was the shards of glass that had cut into her skin or his reaction that had cut into her heart.

'Who is she having an affair with, Kaushik?' she asked. She didn't care about the mess for the first time in her life.

'I don't know, Naina. These are just rumours. How many employees does our firm have? How am I supposed to keep track of all these rumours?'

Naina didn't buy it. 'Who is her boss?'

'Look, let me clean this. I know you're tired. And this so-called affair that you're upsetting yourself with—this is just stupid gossip!'

She stood still and didn't say anything.

'You sit here. I'll get this cleaned.'

'I SAID, WHO IS HER BOSS, KAUSHIK?'

Kaushik who had almost got up from the bed to clean up the glass that was lying between them sat back down and replied in a low voice, 'I am. But…'

'Oh my God!' Naina shrieked. 'Are you having an affair with her, Kaushik?'

'Naina, I think we should not get hurt because of this glass. Let's get Pushpa to clean this, please.'

'You haven't answered my question. Are you having an affair with her?'

Kaushik sighed. 'I'm sorry. I fucked up.'

Kaushik got off from the other side of the bed and moved her away from the glass pieces. She felt as if she had been struck by lightning.

'Don't touch me,' she hissed. 'How could you?'

'Naina, I…'

'Shut up. I want to know how long you've been having this affair.'

'What difference does that make?'

'I WANT TO KNOW!'

'Naina, please. You'll wake up the kids.'

'I'll wake them up anyway. I want to know, Kaushik. How long has this been going on?'

'Naina, please.'

'Did you do it here?'

Kaushik was stunned. He had never seen Naina so angry and venomous. 'Did you do it in my room? In my house? On my bed?'

Kaushik nodded. Naina held her head in disbelief and shock. 'Oh my God, Kaushik. All these years. All these years I've given you and you…how could you? Why the fuck did you do this?'

Kaushik had never heard Naina swear. Sweet pretty beautiful mother Naina. He had only seen her as gentle, calm, and caring. Naina was filled with rage. She began to hit Kaushik with all her strength and wept with tears streaming down her eyes.

'You've changed, Naina,' Kaushik said.

Naina shrieked, 'I've changed? Now you want to blame me for your infidelity?'

Kaushik looked up at her. 'Tum badal gayi ho.'

Naina wiped away her tears. 'Main badal gayi hoon? Tum bhi badal gaye ho. Rishtey badalte hain. That's called a marriage. People need to change to become better. We move from a place of something that was…to something that we can be together. Zindagi mein log ek jaise nahin rehte hain, Kaushik.'

Kaushik wanted to hold her but she was too quick for him. She moved away. She wiped her tears. 'I don't know what to do anymore.'

Kaushik wanted to hold her. 'Naina.'

Naina stood there feeling helpless and burned. But she needed to know one last answer before she decided what to do. 'Do you love her?'

Kaushik shook his head, afraid of even his voice. He said softly, 'No. Please forgive me.'

She looked at him suddenly not believing what she heard. Not trusting the man she had spent ten years with. Not knowing what choices lay ahead.

What does a woman do when she finds out her husband is having an affair? Does she choose to give him up and start over again? Does she forgive him because that's all the life she knows anyway? Does she take him back for the sake of their children who need a father?

She would be all alone all over again. She would have two girls to look after. She would need to get back to full-time work. What would she say to her children? If he was asking for forgiveness shouldn't she give him another chance?

'I can't think right now.' It was all Naina could say. 'I can't sleep on my bed either. I'm going to my mother's place. You manage the kids tomorrow.'

'Naina, let's talk about this,' Kaushik pleaded as Naina went to the bathroom, changed her clothes in a matter of seconds and grabbed her bag to leave.

'No, I can't talk right now. Please leave me alone. Manage the kids, Kaushik, till I come back. Just do that for me.'

'Of course I will. They're my kids too.'

'Well you haven't made them feel that for a long time. You've been too busy with your mistress.' Naina banged the door shut behind her.

Naina knew she needed to get away from there. From her own home! She didn't think she would ever have to leave Kaushik like this. From the moment she had met him she was loyal and attached to him. She had never done anything wrong. And he had betrayed her. He had had an affair with his subordinate, fucking her on their marital bed. He had desecrated her home, the place which she had made for them. She didn't know what to do. She didn't know if she should call her mother.

Sometimes parents get so involved with their children's lives that they will never forgive the son-in-law even if you yourself do, eventually. There was no point in talking to the family. She knew she couldn't go to her friends. No matter how lovely they all were they would tell her to just grin and bear it. She didn't feel like having a conversation. She needed to get even. She needed revenge. She wanted to show Kaushik that he wasn't the only one who could have an affair. She was just as desirable and just as wanted. She needed to be appreciated. She desperately wanted a man.

She knew exactly where to go.

32

Gaurav had come back from his parents' house and decided to start a business with his father's money. He went to work one morning and quit his job that very day. Even before consulting Kavita. It was on that day that Kavita felt completely fed up with Gaurav and his decisions. They were sitting in the large lawn of their house, having a drink and talking.

Gaurav was explaining his motive to Kavita while she listened quietly, slowly getting more drunk and angry. He spoke with great pride, 'I think it's a great business plan. It was something I needed to do.'

'You should have taken my opinion before you quit your job.'

'But I don't need your opinion. I'm sure about this. This is what is going to make me happy.'

'It's not that. Couples need to consult each other before they take drastic steps like start a business, quit a job, have a baby, move residences. It's what couples do. It's called mutual respect.'

Gaurav was quiet. He took a large gulp of his drink. 'Why must everything be your way, Kavita? Why can't things be for my happiness too?'

'I'm not asking you not to be happy. I'm just asking for a little respect.'

'And so am I. I see how our son looks at you and how he looks at me. I want to win his respect too.'

'He does respect you.'

'Not as much as he respects you.'

'Why are we even talking about this? I was talking about your job.'

Gaurav raised his voice. 'Yes. MY job. I'm starting a business with my money. I didn't ask you for money. All I asked you was for support. And you can't give me even that?'

'I do support you, Gaurav.' Kavita could feel the beginning of a migraine attack.

'Then let me do this and just be happy.' Gaurav took his empty glass and stormed inside the house, leaving Kavita alone again to finish her drink and ponder their relationship.

She stared at the stars and remembered how wonderful it had been with Sara on the beach. She took her mobile out of her pocket and dialed her number. 'Hey.' She whispered into it even though there was no one around. 'Did I wake you up?'

'No,' Sara said. 'I was up. Just reading.'

'What were you reading?' Kavita made light conversation, not wanting to talk about the fight with Gaurav or the fact that she was missing Sara so much.

'Murakami.'

'Murakami?'

'Baby, Haruki Murakami is a Japanese writer who writes very esoterically. I'll lend you some books when you come. Have you booked your ticket yet?'

'Yes. It's still a week away. Like I told you on the mail.' Kavita's sentences were short and brief. How could she tell Sara that she couldn't wait that long anymore? She felt angry at herself. She felt frustrated with life. Why was God punishing her for her dead marriage? Why was the burden of this pretence so hard?

'Listen, baby.' Sara's voice was gentle and calm. 'I know it's difficult for you to live in this world where you need to prove you have the perfect marriage. I know how difficult it is to sustain long-distance relationships when everyone knows about the relationship and supports you. It's even more difficult when no one knows and it's still a long distance.'

'So what am I supposed to do, Sara? That's no explanation!'

Sara could hear Kavita's voice choking. 'It's a week, Kavita. How about we focus on the good things. What's upsetting you?'

Kavita spoke about how Gaurav had quit his job, his new absurd business plan, her responsibilities as a mother, how she knew her sister wanted to get married but hadn't told anyone, how she needed a change in her job.

Sara listened patiently. 'Why don't you leave him, Kavita? Come to Bombay. Stay with me. I will look after Vansh.'

'You've never met Vansh.'

'If you love him, why wouldn't I love him?'

'And my mom?'

'She can come too.'

Kavita laughed. 'How many people will you look after?'

'As many as will make you happy.'

Kavita realized that Sara's love for her was unconditional. Unlike Gaurav's. Her husband had put conditions since the day they had met. She spoke so that Kavita would come to the conclusions about her life herself. She allowed Kavita to speak about what she needed. When Kavita put the phone down, she felt light-hearted, liberated even. Sara was indeed a good positive light in her life. She wondered how she would keep it a secret from everyone in her life.

Kavita didn't know that someone was eavesdropping on their conversation.

33

'Oh I love G. K. Market!' Kaajal swooned as she strolled into Goldy's to look at some bangles and kitschy clothes.

'I've grown out of it,' Tarini said as she fingered the bright, zardozi work on a long fuschia skirt.

'What?!' Kaajal took out a halter neck and put it on herself. 'No one can ever grow out of this.'

Tarini rolled her eyes. 'Jab We Met days are over, Kay. Seriously, you need to move to the other block. N block has far better stuff than this market. M block is for teenagers. Filled with silver jewellery, bright, garish clothes sold on the pavement, nighties and stuff in shops. Puhleez.'

'Oh dear Madam hoity toity prefers the Indian weaving of FabIndia and the upper class tea at the cafes of N block now, is it?' Kaajal said in a fake British accent.

'Well look at the fast food places in this market. It's for fast food teenagers, babe. At least N block has the best restaurants.'

Kaajal smiled as she put the choli down and paid for it. She knew she could wear it to bed when she met Kaushik later that evening. He would flip when he saw her wear that and a matching thong. She would be a dominatrix made in India. She giggled to herself as Tarini got on the phone and went outside.

Kaajal loved coming to G. K. M block market. She knew how much Tarini hated it but she dragged here there to have the gol gappas and Prince paan every now and then. She also shopped for clothes she could wear at home. Somewhere she felt it was important to save her money on useful things later than waste it on materialistic things right now. Kaajal was practical and meticulous. While her sister had a Louis Vuitton bag and had bought herself a new SUV, Kaajal still travelled in autos and used a jhola she got from FabIndia.

'Who was that?' Kaajal asked.

'Varun.'

'Oohh lover boy,' Kaajal teased.

Tarini smiled. 'Look, I'm really sorry but he wants to meet. You know married men and their timings yaar. And I'm really horny. Can we catch up for dinner later? Hauz Khas maybe? Somewhere decent where there is no fast food and wine is served in correct glasses?'

Kaajal smiled and hugged her. 'Go, Miss Hoity Toity Horny. WhatsApp me later. Tell me all the gory details.'

Tarini left while Kaajal got into an auto to get to the metro station. She loved the Delhi Metro. And now that there were special trains running for women, she felt she could easily get a seat and get more done in a metro than when she was stuck in traffic in an auto or cab. She hailed Harshvardhan as a new-age leader, telling herself that she would vote for him if he ran for Prime Minister.

As soon as Kaajal got home she called out to her mother, 'Ma, are you home?' But her mother was apparently out. Kaajal and Kavita had given their mother her own car, driver and mobile phone. That way she could be independent without the girls worrying about her. The driver was like a caretaker for their mother, and helped her whenever she needed it and ran errands for her as well. Kaajal presumed her mother had gone out for work.

She went into her room and dumped her bags. It was so

nice to have the house to herself. There were so many people around most of the time that she could never enjoy the place where she was born and grew up. While many houses around had been developed and made into high-rise buildings, her mother had held on to this house from several builders. There was no other place that could boast of a garden. Theirs had a vast green garden that was filled with trees and plants that Kavita and she had planted when they were children. Their mother loved her garden and spent many hours planting new things, taking out weeds and pruning shrubs. It was what kept her young. Kaajal smiled and said a prayer of thanks to God that her mother was still alive even after the devastating loss of their father from their lives. She changed into her shorts and a ganji. Delhi was too hot in the summer. She put on the air conditioner in her room.

She heard someone rumbling in the kitchen. She walked out and saw Gaurav hunched over the fridge looking for food.

'Need something?' she asked.

He got startled. 'Oh, you scared me.'

Kaajal smiled. 'I think there's some chola in the fridge. I'm making some tea. Want some?'

'No. Thanks.'

Kaajal made tea while he sat and ate some chola with toast. He grumbled to himself, 'Why can't Kavita cook sometimes. This maid knows nothing. I hate this chola.'

Kaajal ignored him. He picked up his plate of food and dumped it in the sink while Kaajal took her cup of tea silently towards her room.

'What's your hurry? Don't want to sit and chat?' Gaurav asked, smiling at her as he grabbed a glass of water.

Kaajal shrugged her shoulders and sat at the kitchen table.

Gaurav sat too. 'So um…how's work.'

While they made polite conversation, Kaajal saw that he

had begun to open up to her. He started speaking about his new venture. He was excited. She felt she needed to encourage him a little. It wasn't easy living with such strong women. She smiled and asked him more questions. He felt happy that there was someone who was not chiding him for his decision.

'So you think it was okay to quit my job?'

'Absolutely, Gaurav. If this is what makes you happy and motivated then go for it. You won't know what you're capable of doing if you don't try, right?'

'That's exactly what I told Kavita but she refuses to listen.'

'Oh, don't get me in the middle of your spousal problems. I don't want to know!' Kaajal said as she finished her tea and kept her cup in the sink. They had people who lived in the servant quarters in Delhi. Harish, the cook, came in the morning and evening. His wife cleaned in the morning and washed dishes in the evening. And during the afternoons they rested in their own small rooms slightly away from the main house, where they could be reached by a simple bell that was in the main house near the kitchen and in Kaajal's mother's room.

Suddenly Kaajal could feel Gaurav close to her. A little too close. She turned around. He was standing right behind her, smiling.

'You know, Kaajal, I've always thought you were far prettier than your sister.'

Kaajal rolled her eyes and pushed past him, 'Yeah right.'

He held her hand and she swiveled around, shocked. 'Listen.' He let go of her hand. 'I just wanted to tell you this. I've not been able to before. Please can you just wait a minute to listen to me. I mean, no one in this house has time or patience to hear my point of view anymore. I feel so suppressed. It's like I don't exist for anyone.'

Kaajal stopped and crossed her hands.

He continued, 'You know I'm the one who moved in here. I didn't want to. I wanted to stay separately with your sister. But she couldn't leave you or your mother. And then I made all the adjustments.'

'No one stopped you from leaving later, Gaurav,' Kaajal said sarcastically.

'Now don't get angry. I'm just saying it was a good decision. I got you as a friend, didn't I?' Gaurav said with a big smile. Kaajal nodded.

'I'm just paying you a compliment. I think you're wonderful. Thank you for listening to me. I need a friend sometimes,' Gaurav said and then asked, 'Can I get a hug? Please?'

For a split second Kaajal was reluctant but she had known Gaurav for so long that she shrugged her shoulders and went to give him a hug. But instead of letting her go, Gaurav held her face and kissed her on the lips passionately. 'You're so beautiful, Kaajal.'

Kaajal pushed him back but Gaurav held her tight. 'Let me go, Gaurav.'

Gaurav pinned her to the counter and kissed her neck. 'You smell so delicious,' he murmured into her hair.

Kaajal fought him but he had strength that she could not match. 'I've always found you so attractive, Kaajal. Like a flower. I know you like me too.'

Kaajal fought him off, tears rolling down her cheeks. Her phone was far away. There was no one to help her.

'For so many years I've wanted to do this. You know no one has to know. I'm not sleeping with Kavita. I can be all yours, baby,' Gaurav said as he thrust his pelvis into her shorts, unzipping her slowly with one hand while pinning her to the counter.

His mouth moved slowly down her neck and between her

breasts. Kaajal wondered for a second if she should just give in rather than fighting. Just when you had to fend off people on the streets, the home became a danger zone as well. Just then she heard a car in the driveway. She shouted, 'Mama's home.'

Gaurav stopped for a brief second and let her go. In that split second, Kaajal ran to her room and locked it. She sat on the floor next to her door as she heard her mother enter the house and greet Gaurav. Tears streamed down Kaajal's face. How could she live here anymore? She didn't feel safe. How could she tell Kavita about this incident? Kavita would divorce Gaurav. Or she wouldn't. She would have to choose. And what if she chose to stay in the marriage because of Vansh? Where would Kaajal go? She didn't have a husband. She didn't have enough money to live alone. She needed to stay in this house. But she couldn't. Kaajal didn't know what to do. She couldn't call anyone. For the first time in her life she felt angry and betrayed.

34

'Tum jaante nahin ho mera baap kaun hai?'

'Sir, please calm down. This is a hotel.'

'I can own this hotel. My father is a politician. He will shut you down if I tell him how your waiters behave with me! Do you know that? Now get me another drink.'

'Yes alright, Sir. Sorry for the confusion.'

Ayesha looked at the conversation that the manager and a customer were having. She wondered if the child she was carrying would become like that. After all, his father was a politician too! Ayesha shook her head. She couldn't think about all this. She had decided that she would not keep the child. But she needed to tell Harshvardhan. If he ever got to know from somewhere else, then their relationship would be in jeopardy.

She was waiting for Harshvardhan in a hotel coffee shop. Delhi had so many hotels that she felt she had seen most of them in these last few months. All Delhi hotels had beautiful, lavish decors with specific cuisine restaurants that catered to a variety of Delhi palates. She had loved eating in different restaurants and going to different hotels. It was so different from the Habitat Centre or IIC that she and Varun frequented for drinks or lunch. How societies changed in Delhi. From business-class people who lived in certain colonies and enjoyed visiting new restaurants in the elite places of Delhi, to bureaucrats and their families who loved Lodhi Gardens, Habitat and IIC and enjoyed visiting each others' houses that were beautiful, large and artistically decorated. And then there were politicians who loved going to five-star hotels and had parties at farmhouses where the press weren't allowed and businessmen were invited. Each society kept to itself, never truly opening up to another. And here she was, mixing different worlds until her own world collided.

Ayesha needed to tell him that this child would jeopardize her marriage. And that she could continue the affair anymore. It was getting too complicated and she didn't want another accident. She would not know what to tell her parents and her in-laws. It would be embarrassing. Not to mention that she really didn't want to get up in the middle of the night for potty changes. She was done with that. Her child was a pre-teen. She was happy that Adi was independent. She had spent her entire life raising one child and giving him proper values. Now she wanted to spend the rest of her life doing things for herself.

And after watching the conversation with this brash young man, she was sure she didn't want to raise any more children in today's world. Why were they all so rude when they were drunk? Why did they have this attitude that things could go their way just because their fathers were in power? Maybe she should talk to Harsh about that.

Harsh walked in to the hotel discreetly with a bodyguard and joined Ayesha at the table to have a pleasant dinner.

'You look lovely, Ayesha. How have you been?' he asked as a waiter came around to serve him water.

Ayesha smiled. 'I'm fine. Thank you.'

'What is this? This is not whiskey!' the brash young man a few tables down spoke again in a loud voice as Harshvardhan and Ayesha looked at him, as did the entire restaurant. Then the brash man threw the whiskey on the waiter and the manager came by again.

'Sorry Sir, I have to ask you to leave.'

'Leave? I'll tell my father, Jaisingh Waadria, and he'll come down and buy this place out.'

'I'll call the cops, Sir.'

'Oh call them, bloody asshole. They won't do a thing to me! Call! Call!'

At seeing the manager getting perplexed, Harshvardhan thought he should be gallant and step in to help. He told Ayesha, 'Excuse me. I can't just sit here and watch this naatak.'

He got up and went to the table. 'Hi. Young man, I think there are plenty of places you can go to and there are only old people here. Their whiskey is also not good. I suggest you leave.'

The man with his group of friends got up and looked Harshavardhan staright in the eye. Ayesha's heart was in her mouth. She didn't want them to fight. Oh God. She thought she would throw up.

'You know my father?' the young man spoke.

To which Harshvardhan replied, 'Yes I do, son. He's in the cabinet with me. My name is Harshvardhan. You can tell your father I said hi.'

Then the young man paled and spoke loudly to his friends, 'Let's go. This place is a dump.'

They left without paying the bill. The manager ran after them begging them to pay the bill but the young man just slapped him across his face. Harshvardhan watched all this and told the young man, 'You will pay for this. Sooner or later.'

The young man turned to him and spoke in a threating tone, 'No, old man. You'll pay for this sooner than you think.'

Harshvardhan came back to the table. Ayesha's face now had gone ashen white. Her breathing was heavy and she was feeling sick. Maybe it was the nausea of pregnancy or it was the entire affair of Harshvardhan that made her get up and run to the bathroom to vomit.

When she came back, Harshvardhan was paying the bill for the man who had just left. Ayesha saw it was fifty grand.

'What! Why are you paying his bill?' Ayesha asked.

'Because it will go out of the poor manager's salary who probably only earns that much every month anyway. These Delhi boys can be a pain. Their ego is so high that they feel they can get away with anything. Anyway, how are you feeling? What happened?' he signaled for the waiter to get them some more water and all the waiters and the manager were at his attention.

'Can you afford to spend so much, Harsh?' Ayesha asked knowing that ministers didn't make as much money as the private sector.

'I can't. But I can't see grave injustice happening either. It's alright, love,' he said as he finished paying the bill and looked up. 'Money can't buy happiness. Karma comes back to you in many ways. It's important to do good karma. God always recognizes it.'

The head chef brought out a few starters and a cocktail for them.

Ayesha turned to them to say, 'Oh, we haven't ordered these.'

'It's complimentary from us, Sir. Please enjoy your meal.'

So Harshavardhan laughed and dug into his food as Ayesha picked at it. 'Tell me. What's been going on? Why aren't you eating? You're behaving very strangely Ayesha. Is everything okay? Do you want to go someplace else?'

Ayesha shook her head as the whole situation made her

feel like weeping. Here was a man who was so generous, so loving and so understanding. A man who would make a great father. A man who was a great protector, nurturer, caregiver, lover, friend and strength for Ayesha. And he would never be a father. He had never found anyone. He had told Ayesha he had never loved anyone the way he loved her. And even if she chose to remain married for the rest of her life, he would take care of her as she wanted. He needed nothing from her. He was a man who only gave. And here was an opportunity for her to give him something in return and she couldn't.

The dam burst as hot tears rolled down Ayesha's cheeks. Harshavardhan immediately took her hand in his and passed her his handkerchief. 'Ayesha, whatever it is, I'll solve it, baby. Tell me. What's wrong? What's wrong, jaan? I can't see you like this.'

Between sobs Ayesha confessed, 'I'm...I'm pregnant.'

Harshvardhan's hand did not move from hers. He looked into her eyes as she saw a flicker of joy pass through them. He gulped hard. 'Oh Ayesha...that's won...well what are you going to do? You know I'll support you with whatever decision you make.'

Ayesha moved her hand away and leaned back in the chair as the waiter brought their pasta. Harshvardhan said to the waiter, 'Can we please have a minute? We can eat it in a while.'

Ayesha looked at all the food that was going to waste. Maybe she should eat, if only for her child. What was she thinking? She wasn't going to have this child! Why were these thoughts entering her head? What did she really want to do?

As if he read her thoughts, 'What do you want to do?'

'What are my options?' Ayesha's mind blurred.

Harshvardhan took a sip of water. 'It's not what I want, Ayesha. It's what you want. Your happiness is important to me.'

Ayesha paused. 'I can't keep it. I'm married. What will I say?'

Harshvardhan nodded his head. 'I understand.'

Ayesha took his hand. 'Should we stop seeing each other?'

Harshvardhan replied, 'Not at all! Please never leave me. How about I tell you I love you, Ayesha? Will that change your decision? What if I told you I would marry you. I want to marry you. No that's not a good proposal. Let me try again. Will you marry me, Ayesha?'

Ayesha felt the corners of her mouth turn. That was such a sweet thing to say. 'I don't want to trap you, Harsh. I'm not asking you to marry me.'

'I know. But I want to. I want us to be together. I'll look after Aditya. So many people get divorced. You can too. I'll wait for you.'

Ayesha looked at him as if he had gone mad. 'And what happens to your political career? Won't the press have a field day when they know you had an affair and got a married woman pregnant?'

Harshvardhan was quiet while Ayesha continued, 'You've worked too hard to let this go. You'll become the prime minister one day. I know it. And I and this baby will only stop you from doing that. So let me be. We can meet when it's convenient. And let this incident just pass.'

Harshavardhan had tears in his eyes. 'I have always wanted to be a father. I never found the right woman because I was so interested in becoming a leader rather than a husband. And now that I've found the woman and I can be a father, I need to choose if I still want to be a leader? Why is this so cruel?'

Ayesha wanted to pacify him. Reach out to him. But she couldn't. She couldn't give him words of encouragement. She wanted him to succeed. It was her fault she was pregnant. She couldn't ruin his dreams. And even though he was sad and upset right now, he would get over it. His campaign would suck him in. His ideals needed to go higher. He wouldn't succeed with his ideas if he was stuck at home with a child. His destiny was to become a great leader. He was trained for that. All his life he had worked for it. She couldn't have him sit at home with her. She knew he would and she would be his downfall.

Ayesha had made a decision. She would go back to Dr Kavita next week and remove this burden from their lives.

Harshvardhan called for the cheque and said, 'Let's go somewhere else to discuss this.'

Ayesha desperately wanted to get out of the hotel. She needed fresh air. As soon as they both stepped out of the hotel, there was a flash from the paparazzi who had followed Harshvardhan there. A reporter was there to ask questions. Ayesha had worn a sari that day and she covered her face with a pallu and sunglasses so no one would recognize her. Harshvardhan reacted on his feet as he whispered for her to go back inside and hide in the women's loo. She immediately turned back to go into the hotel while Harshvardhan was bombarded by the news channels.

'Sir, are you having an affair?'

'Sir, will you be getting married soon?'

'Do you think your personal life will affect your public ideas now?'

'Sir, is she married? We got news from an unknown source who just left the premises that she was a bureaucrat's wife. Is she?'

Harshvardhan replied, 'No comment.' He got into his car and immediately called Ayesha who had gone back inside the hotel to hide. He called her from his car and told her to stay in the hotel bathroom. 'I'm sending someone in an ordinary car to take you from the ladies room on the banquet floor to the

exit outside. He'll make sure you reach home safely. I'm so
sorry about all this. That stupid Waardia's son must have
leaked it to the reporters. I'll call you soon, love. Are you
okay?'

Ayesha could only nod as he put the phone down. What
she was most worried about was the fact that someone had
taken her photograph. If it appeared on the news, her marriage
would be over. She would be a disgrace. She would lose her
son!

And that's when she felt a sticky substance between her
thighs. She knew something was wrong. And she was afraid
for her life, in more ways than one. She dug into her purse
and found her phone. She dialed a number.

'Dr Kavita. This is Ayesha. I'm bleeding. What do I do?'

35

The origin of an affair is loneliness.

It's lack of attention from the person who you want attention from.

An affair starts when you're so unhappy in your relationship that you feel you deserve something more.

An affair could also start from revenge. An act to prove that you're still desirable in the eyes of another man when your partner can't see it. An act to get even and feel better.

Naina had been giving Arjun cooking lessons for over three weeks now and they had become quite close in an extremely platonic way. He was a perfect gentleman, never overstepping a line, always being polite, patient and eager to learn. He treated her like a teacher during the class and as a friend when they sat down for lunch every day. But he never treated her like a lover or behaved lecherously with her. She was comfortable around him. There was a general camaraderie and respect in their relationship, something that had been missing from her life for some time.

Naina couldn't bring herself to go to Arjun's house in the middle of the night. She needed to sort out her head. So she called Pinky, told her the entire story about Kaushik's affair and crashed at Pinky's house that night. Pinky gave her breakfast and a hot cup of coffee before she gave advice. 'Dekh, all this love shove and all na fades away. You must decide what is important to you. What are your dreams and goals? What do you want from life? Aur agar woh tumhare pati ke saath nahin hai, toh usko chod de. You know why in the entire mammal kingdom God gave human beings the sharpest brains? For us to use them, Ma Ki Aankh. Aur hum, we give that up for love. Go do your work. And be open to new people in your life, Naina. Poori zindagi pachtayegi.'

So Naina went back to work the next afternoon and gave Arjun a cooking class. Her mind was a million miles away with her home, children and her life and somehow Arjun just made her feel lighter and happier by his clumsiness in the kitchen and by admiring her beauty from far.

'How do you maintain yourself so well? I mean you love eating all this stuff and yet, look at you, you're so fit!' Naina asked as she dug into the Thai curry rice they had made together.

Arjun ate well. He wasn't one for nibbling at his food. 'I work out. I go for a run every morning. It burns everything off. I can't diet. I love to eat. And now I'm loving how to cook.'

Naina smiled, extremely conscious of his virile appeal. 'I'm so glad. You've become pretty good at it. But you still have four more weeks to go.' He noticed her hair tumble carelessly around her back, her perfect oval face and cocoa eyes.

'By then I can be a trained chef. I'll run and cook in my own restaurant.' As Arjun smiled, light wrinkles formed around the corners of his eyes. He was charming, elegant, athletic. She felt an immediate and total attraction towards him.

'Why would you want to do so many things? Software, art, events and now a restaurant?' Naina asked, wondering how their dreams could coincide like this. 'Don't you ever want to settle down and just have children or relax with a family?'

'Of course,' Arjun said. 'I have a daughter. From my first marriage. She's ten now. She lives with her mom in Mumbai. I moved from there because there was a bigger opportunity for me to do events here. I get her to fly in whenever she has holidays to spend time with me. I don't do enough for her. I wish I could. I miss her tremendously but then divorce isn't just tough on children, it's tough on the fathers too.'

Naina looked at him, surprised. 'Isn't it supposed to be tough on single mothers?'

'The mother takes Rs two lakhs a month as alimony. I pay for my child's schooling and any extra expenses. I think the single motherhood thing is a bit overrated. If she was working and earning on her own and managing a child then it would be tough. But my ex-wife doesn't do anything. She is a...what do you call it...socialite. With my money.'

Naina was shocked. 'Two lakhs a month? But why?'

'Guilt,' Arjun said, as he took another bite of his food. 'I cheated on her when we were married.' He reached out for the salt shaker that was in front of them,

Naina stayed quiet. Kaushik was cheating on her too. She was sure she wouldn't get two lakhs as alimony from him. His lawyer instincts would be in full gear and he would do everything to put all the blame for the demise of their marriage on her.

'Do you have enough to manage after giving all that?' Naina asked, wondering if this man was truly benevolent or simply rich.

Arjun nodded. 'I do alright. I want my daughter to be happy. And she's a well-settled individual. She sees how much I do for her mother and never begrudges me.' Every time his gaze rested on her, her heart skipped a beat.

Naina thought it was incredibly noble of him. She was enamoured by this mild-mannered, good-natured man. He was incredibly handsome, fit for his age and kind-hearted. Her face felt flushed with the anticipation of something new.

Naina helped clear the dishes once they had finished lunch. Arjun observed her closely. Her silky hair tumbling around her shoulders. Her dark, intent eyes, warm and loving, keeping things away.

'You don't need to do all this,' Arjun pleaded as he helped her clean up, his eyes riveted to this woman who was an ethereal, natural beauty.

'I want to.'

Arjun looked at her as if he was photographing her with his eyes. Suddenly she looked up and their eyes were held in a locked gaze. She didn't miss his obvious examination and approval. She let out a soft breath. His arresting good looks totally captured her attention. Her body ached for his touch. Several moments passed without a word, a sound, a movement.

People say an affair doesn't begin with much thought, rather on impulse. It's the heart leaping forward when it gets an opportunity. The head has nothing to do then. As for Naina, well Naina had always been the wild child of London. The smut queen. The smart mouth who could make everyone laugh with her lewd jokes and loud remarks.

And here she was, quiet, bashful, uncertain. There was a tingling in the pit of her stomach. Her heart jolted and her head pounded. He radiated a vitality that drew her like a magnet. She longed for him to say something. Because she wouldn't. She would wait. She had changed.

Why is love so clichéd? Why does it always start the same way? It's an instant attraction between two people who play a game to see who will make the first move. All along, Naina had made moves on men. Now she wanted to wait and see what this man would do. Arjun saw the hesitation in her eyes. He had wanted her from the moment she had first entered his house, the beautiful, bright, delicate creature who had captured his heart with a swish of her hair and the magic of her fingers. He had been trying to impress her ever since. She was warm, funny, loving and, it seemed to him, very unappreciated.

Suddenly, he leaned in gently and brushed a gentle kiss across her lips. The slow movement sent shivers down Naina's spine. He stepped back. The house was silent. A vast space all around but just inches between them. His extraordinary eyes blazed. Her body felt like it was being pushed by a force alien to her. She took a step forward, giving him silent permission to continue. His nearness was overwheleming. His cologne hung in the air.

They locked their eyes as Arjun gathered Naina in his arms, as his mouth swooped down to capture hers in a passionate embrace. Her heart hammered in her ribs as he lay soft kisses around her face, the corners of her mouth, her eyes. Her eyelashes fluttered against his cheek as her hands wrapped around his head, holding his thick hair in her long, delicate fingers.

'Oh, Arjun,' she moaned as he ran his fingers down her back. 'I need to go.'

'Don't go,' he said, his breath soft against her ears. 'Stay. Please.'

She felt her blood course through her veins like a raging river. She knew this was wrong. She was married. She had taken an oath. Made a commitment. Followed her husband around a fire seven times. So why did this feel right?

Naina buried her face against his throat, giving in to her most primal instinct. His kiss was slow, thoughtful, tracing the contours of her mouth. 'Whatever. You. Want.' Between each word, he planted kisses on her mouth, her neck and her ears. He was running his thumb deliciously up and down her thigh. She closed her eyes and threw her head back, surrendering to the moment. Aroused now, she drew herself closer to him, matching his intensity with her own. He slowly unbuttoned her crisp black shirt, planting kisses along the length of her neck, her cleavage, her breasts, across her silken belly. She felt conscious of her weight. The added kilos over the years. The ones Kaushik didn't want to see. But Arjun held her body as if he needed to possess it, own every part of it, desired it as if he would burn if he didn't get it. Her nipples hardened instantly under his touch.

She unbuttoned his shirt and slowly let it fall to the ground. For a moment, she wondered if she should pick it up, the hundred dollar designer shirt that was lying on the kitchen floor.

Arjun slipped her bra off and explored the rosy peaks of her breasts. She let out a soft moan. He picked her up in one swoop in his immense, strong arms and placed her gently on the sofa in the living room. Arjun slowly removed the rest of her clothes. His tongue began a lust-arousing exploration of her soft flesh. His one hand traced concentric circles around her thigh. He used his thumb and tongue alternatively to probe into the deep, dark crevices of her soul. Slowly. Tantalising. Teasing. Moving faster. Sucking. Deeper. Harder. She threw her head back and begged him to stop. He rubbed harder. Held her breast. Squeezing. Rubbing. Licking. Probing. Until she exploded into a downpour of hot, fiery sensations that came in a wave as darkness and light embraced her. Over and over again.

The light rippled from outside. The scent of sandalwood floated in. The tinkling sound of wind chimes from far away. Laughter. A dog barking. Naina had never felt so complete. Not after her children were born. Not with a man who so selflessly gave to her over and over again on his sofa, in the middle of the afternoon, without a care in the world. But he never entered her. She begged him but he was happy to just give her wave after wave of rapturous pleasure.

Naina didn't go home or to Pinky's that afternoon or that night. She spent several more hours with him, getting pampered. She didn't know revenge sex felt this good.

36

Kavita's mother was an extremely traditional woman. She was raised in Amritsar with eleven siblings. Her father was a truck driver and her mother was a housewife. After having Kavita she had two children who died at birth. Then Kaajal was born. She loved being a housewife and just wanted to bring up her children well. But when her husband left her for another woman when Kaajal was just two years old, Kulwinder Kaur decided that she would not only go back to work but she would make sure that her two daughters never suffered the same treatment from a man.

Kulwinder stayed in the same house that her husband had brought her to. It was a beautiful house with many memories. She had chosen to stay in the same house, in the same colony in case he ever chose to come back to them. But in time she had realized that he didn't care and when he came back that fateful night to ask for forgiveness and for her to take him back it was her daughters who had said no. Then it was only memories of him that were in the house. It was in this house that she had her children, this house that saw her older child get married. It was to this house that she brought her grandson from the hospital. And she knew it would be this house from where her younger daughter would get married and settle down happily.

She wasn't particularly happy with Kavita's decision to

marry Gaurav and she knew all the times that she had bailed him out. She wasn't stupid. But she refused to interfere in her daughters' lives anymore. They were grown up enough to make their own decisions and understand the consequences. She often wished they wouldn't be so protective about her. She was only sixty years old and quite healthy for her age. But they all treated her with great care and tremendous respect.

It was one of the mornings when Vansh had left for school and Kavita and Gaurav were sitting at the dining table, that she made a decision. A decision that would change all their lives. It was because of the conversation that she had overheard.

'Kavita,' Gaurav said as he sat down with some toast and coffee. 'I want to talk to you about something.'

That night when Kavita had spoken to Sara, Gaurav had heard everything. He had come looking for her. And he had heard her speak to Sara about how much she loved her. Gaurav hadn't thought much about it. It could just be a friend. All these girls said the same thing. It was different for men. But soon he discovered that she was acting strange. Kavita didn't want to sleep with Gaurav anymore. She would make some excuse. He was getting frustrated. And then the email landed in his inbox. With her travel plans and their loving exchanges of messages. He was horrified. He didn't know how to react. He would never have assumed his wife was a lesbian. So he decided to confront her.

With her cup of coffee in hand, Kavita sat next to him.

Gaurav bit into his toast and said calmly, 'Are you a lesbian?'

Kavita was shocked. She had never imagined he would ask her such a question. How had he guessed? 'Why do you ask that?'

Gaurav was cold. 'Because I heard you speaking to your lover the other evening.'

Kavita scoffed. 'What are you talking about?'

Gaurav finished his toast and took a sip of coffee. His voice was laced with sarcasm. 'I also got an email about your travel plans to visit Sara. Do you want to keep on denying it or do you want to tell me the truth?'

Kavita felt trapped. She didn't know what to do. She had visualized this situation several times in her head. She had never had an answer.

'Gaurav...,' she started and stopped.

Gaurav was enjoying this. He knew he had her in a place of weakness. Finally. Finally he could dominate her.

His dark eyes darkened as he held her gaze. 'What would your mother say?'

'Gaurav, please don't. Please don't tell anyone. I'll do anything. Promise.'

'Will you have a threesome?' Gaurav asked, with a wicked look in his eye.

Kavita was shocked. He was vile. How could he even ask such a thing?

He continued to taunt her. 'I'll forgive you if you have a threesome.'

'Gaurav,' Kavita fought with the nightmares of this cobweb conversation and tried to make sense of what was happening. 'That's not possible. That's not who I am. Who she is. Stop being vile and disgusting.' A permanent sorrow seemed to be weighing her down.

'I'm disgusting? You're the one who's sleeping with a woman. How do you even do that? What do you use? How can she be better than a man?'

'Gaurav, you won't understand. So let it go. Now what do you want?' Kavita asked him firmly, trying to solve the situation before her mother emerged from her room. Thankfully Vansh was not around and Kaajal had already left for work.

'What do I want? What do I want? I want you to be sorry. I want you to realize that you were the imperfect one here. I want you to finally admit that you are weak.'

Kavita bit back her tears. 'I am weak. I'm sorry. Please don't take away my child.' A new anguish seared at her heart.

Gaurav looked at her with contempt. 'No court will give you your child, Kavita. We live in an archaic society where sons aren't given to mothers who are lesbians. The father becomes the primary caretaker.'

Kavita pleaded with him as tears stung her eyes and rolled down her cheeks. 'I can't live without Vansh. He's everything to me.'

Then Kulwinder Kaur emerged from her room. She had heard enough. She needed to finally interfere in her daughter's life and take responsibility for her as her mother.

'GAURAV,' she thundered loudly as Gaurav and Kavita looked at her. Kavita froze. What had her mother heard? Swallowing the sob that rose in her throat, she looked up at her mother.

She imposed an iron control on herself. 'Kavita, kya hua?'

Kavita faltered. 'Ma, please. Leave it.' Her head was bowed, her body slumped in despair. How could she explain this to her mother? This deep dark secret that she felt was shameful.

But Kulwinder Kaur had seen enough in her life to not let her children suffer the way she had. 'Kavita. Daro mat. Don't be afraid. Tell me everything.'

Kavita dropped her lashes quickly to hide her shame. She spoke in a soft voice, 'I'm bisexual, Ma. It means…'

'It means she loves men and women,' Gaurav spoke with an amused look. 'And she's having an affair with a woman.'

Kulwinder Kaur had never heard of these things. It was all strange to her. This new-fangled world where people loved anything or anyone was very alien to her. But she loved her daughter and she would support her. 'No issues. If she loves a woman, she can love a man back na?'

Kavita said, 'Yes Ma. But…It's complicated.' A blush like a shadow ran over her cheeks.

Gaurav was determined to create havoc in the family. 'What will happen when all our friends find out, Kavi?'

Grief and despair tore at her heart. 'Gaurav, please. You wouldn't…'

'Oh but I would. Because you have had an affair. I haven't.'

'You've not been the perfect husband, Gaurav,' Kavita said, steeling herself against this barrage of accusations. The embarrassment quickly turned to annoyance.

'And you've never been the perfect wife, Kavita. But that doesn't mean you go and have an affair.'

'I stopped loving you, Gaurav. And you stopped loving me. People deserve love. They deserve happiness. Just because we're married doesn't mean we stop living and wanting and feeling. I'm sorry, Gaurav. Let it go. Don't let it affect our relationship. Let us remain married. For the sake of our son. We'll go to a counsellor and sort it out.' She shriveled a little at his expression.

'Why, Kavita?' Kulwinder asked. 'Why do you want to remain married?'

Kavita looked at her mother and replied in a state of shock, 'Because what will happen to Vansh?' A sense of intense sickness and desolation swept over her.

'Haven't you always looked after Vansh? Won't you look after him even if you're not married?'

Kavita nodded as a raw and primitive grief overwhelemed her. Her mother continued, 'Then?'

Gaurav wanted to break this little camaraderie between mother and daughter and asked, 'Well I won't let Vansh go. I need him too. But I'm willing to give you a divorce, Kavita.'

Kavita started crying. She wrapped herself in a cocoon of anguish. Her mother put an arm around her and said, 'Kavi, mujhe yeh bisexual cheez samajh mein nahin aati hain. But all I know is that I will support you. Pyar ek aisi cheez hai jo kabhi bhi zindagi mein aa sakti hai. Aur agar tum keh rahi ho ki it's with a woman, mujhe kuch farak nahin padta hai.'

Kavita looked at her mother in amazement. This simple woman could be so progressive and so strong. Kavita had seen so many women who had been afraid of the consequences of not having a man in their life and her mother had shown her how it was to manage without one. Why was she feeling as if she needed to tie herself to Gaurav when her own mother was a great example of how to live well without a man?

Her mother asked Gaurav, 'What if I gave you enough money to start your new business, Gaurav?' Gaurav looked at her sceptically as she continued, 'You needed money. You didn't want to ask your father. What if you had enough money to start any business you wanted? On one condition. Kavita gets sole custody of Vansh.'

Kavita wiped away her tears, crimson with humiliation and resentment. 'Ma, what are you talking about?'

Kulwinder ignored her daughter and looked directly at her son-in-law. 'Don't ever tell Vansh about his mother. Let Kavita do so in time. And take the money and start a new life. Kya yeh tum kar sakte ho?

'Ma, what are you saying? From where are we going to get this money?' Kavita felt a wretchedness of mind that she had never felt before.

'Kavita—you don't love this man. Remember what you told me when your father came back? You told me that I've done so much on my own that I don't need a man to validate me. So now believe in it yourself, beti. You've done so much with your life.'

Gaurav sniggered. 'But in this society she still needs a man. This is Delhi. And she is already well known. All our friends are group friends. They are all couples. Even if I don't tell them they will get to know. Everyone gets to know when a couple gets divorced and they all ask why.'

'Let people talk, Gaurav,' Kavita's mother quickly said. 'You will not. You will not say why. Can you agree to that?'

'What do I gain from this?' Gaurav folded his hands at his chest and smirked at the two women.

'How about this, Gaurav. How about you take this house. It's worth at least ten, fifteen crores.'

Kavita shouted out in astonishment, 'Ma, no! You can't leave this house. This means everything to you.'

Kulwinder looked at her. 'No. You mean everything to me. This house means nothing if you're not happy. So what do you say, Gaurav? It will solve all your problems. You will be free again. As long as you leave Vansh and not talk about Kavita to anyone. Okay?'

Gaurav pondered and nodded his head. 'But I want to visit my child whenever I like.'

Kavit felt relieved and in pain at the same time. She couldn't believe her mother had just given up her house. What would Kaajal say? Should she have been here to argue the finer details? Maybe they could have saved some money.

Kavita whispered to her mother, 'What about Kaajal's wedding?'

Kulwinder whispered back, 'I have enough for that. You don't worry.'

And Kavita knew that she had enough saved as well if her sister ever wanted to get married. But for now she felt relieved that she was free of Gaurav and that she could keep Vansh.

She knew she had to make a call. To the person who had changed her life. And she had to ask if she would welcome her mother as well. Kavita knew her life was going to change over the next few months and she was anxious, nervous, excited and looking forward to the new change. It was as if a huge burden had been lifted from her shoulders. Nothing felt as good as finally being free of this secret, this marriage and this old life.

37

Ayesha didn't realize how drastically her life would change. Her photo was splashed in the newspaper with Harshvardhan and the headlines screamed: 'Potential Prime Minister having affair with married woman!'

Thankfully her face was partially covered with her pallu. She was so thankful that she always wore saris and had by chance been wiping her face when the flash went off. Within a split second she had turned and exited. Fear, stark and vivid, glittered in her eyes. Harshvardhan had always warned her that the media might follow him and to be careful.

When she came back from the hospital, she had taken the sari she had worn that day and given it away to a bai. She didn't want any evidence in her house. She had rushed to the hospital that same evening and gone to meet Kavita, who had fixed everything for her. Her stomach had been clenched tight and the sudden fear coupled with her age had made her body go into shock. Ayesha had realized then how precious life was and how important family was to her.

She had called Pinky to help her back home and it was Pinky who had stayed the next day and managed the house as well. Varun was surprised but Ayesha told him that the papers were about Pinky and she was just hiding away from the paparazzi for a while. Varun had bought her story. After all, Pinky was also married and the face in the paper couldn't clearly be seen, though Pinky was a larger woman than the one in the photo. But Varun didn't pay much attention to it. He indulged in the office gossip about the politician and soon forgot about it.

It was Ayesha who was dying inside. She couldn't message or call Harshvardhan, feeling afraid that his phone might be tapped and people would find out her real number and follow her to her house. It was impossible to steady her erratic pulse. She just lay low for a few days, refusing to go out of the house and feigning illness. It was in the middle of this that Varun asked her, 'Have you had yourself checked? You know I didn't use a condom. It's just…'

Panic like she'd never known before welled in her throat. Ayesha had her heart in her mouth as she nodded and said, 'I'll do that.'

She kept the news hidden from Varun. She needed to heal before she could say anything.

Finally, after a week of not hearing from Harshvardhan and the news reports had died down, he called her from an unknown number. She finally heard his voice on the other line. Immediately her eyes welled up with tears. It was so good to hear his voice.

'I'm so sorry, Ayesha, for putting you through all this.'

'What are you talking about? It was my fault. I'm so sorry you had to go through all this mess because of me.' Her heart churned with anxiety and frustration.

Harsh was quiet for some time before he answered, 'I've taken this extra number in case you ever want to get in touch with me.'

'What do you mean?' Ayesha was apprehensive and her heart was in her mouth.

'I will need to break some ties for some time. The media is following me, my love. I don't want you to get involved. I don't know what else to do.'

'Of course,' Ayesha said, trying to find logic and reason. The tight knot within her begged for release.

His voice broke as he asked her, 'Have you decided about the child? My proposal?' He spoke with a slight hesitance in his voice.

She stammered, bewildered. She didn't want him to think she didn't love him. 'I'm staying with my husband, Harsh. I am a housewife. I can't do this. I'm sorry. I'm too old to start again.'

Harshvardhan's voice choked. 'I love you.'

Ayesha sobbed into the phone. 'I love you too, Harsh. I'll always love you.'

'Will you meet me one last time?'

When she tried to speak her voice wavered, 'Where?'

'Today. Ten p.m. Metro. Same place as last time. For the last time.'

Ayesha wasn't sure if she could get away. 'I'll try. But how will you manage to escape all the photographers again?'

'I'll manage that,' Harsh said. 'Please come. I'll stand where you found me that time.'

She swallowed hard and managed a feeble answer. 'Okay.'

Ayesha hung up and sobbed her heart out. She couldn't get in the way of his career. The scandals would rock him and eventually he would be bitter and angry with her. She wanted him to remember their relationship for what it was, a beautiful time when two souls connected and meant something to each other. She hoped that he would remember her for giving him wings, for pushing him towards the right things, for making him a better man, and forgive her for the choices she made.

That evening her composure was a fragile shell around her. She broached the topic hesitantly with her husband. 'I want to step out for a bit. Is that alright? I've been cooped up in the house for so long. Tarini was planning a girl's night at home.

I will probably just go there and chill. Adi has finished his dinner and is playing in his room. Savitri is around if you need her.'

Varun was still watching TV as he said, 'Yes go. Have fun. You've been stressed out a lot. Meeting some girls will do you some good.'

Ayesha wanted to confide in someone. What if something went wrong? She dressed very carefully that evening, a simple salwar kameez, solitaires in her ears, a little kaajal and lip gloss. For her petitie build she could pass off as a college student. She took a dupatta and carried her sunglasses. She found a cab and went to the metro station where she had met Harshvardhan.

His black car was parked in the parking lot but he wasn't there. She climbed the steps alone and walked on to the platform from where they had taken the ride. She noticed him standing next to a pillar in disguise. He was wearing crumpled office clothes and a moustache and geeky thick black glasses. She smiled. If they had been alone she would have laughed out loud. Then he would have taken her in his arms and kissed her passionately, rubbing the fake moustache all over her face till she squealed and ripped it off his upper lip.

But Ayesha didn't say anything as the train arrived just then. It was nearly empty. A few passengers boarded it and Harshvardhan was one of them. Ayesha quickly raced down the steps and caught it in time. Harshvardhan sat in a corner and Ayesha went to sit next to him. He looked the other way as their bodies touched. She looked around the compartment. There were no plainclothes security guards around. This was dangerous. Anything could happen to him. She wanted to speak but he didn't seem as if he wanted to. She leaned in closer to him, her back touching his shoulder. They rode the entire route of the metro till the end of the line without exchanging a single word.

With each stop Ayesha's heart sank further and further. She knew this was the last time they would be together. How desperately she needed him. She knew he couldn't get out of his office to meet her. The reason why he had not told anyone that he was there with her today was because he didn't trust his security to not leak it to the press. He would always be in danger if he indulged in clandestine affairs. If she couldn't be with him with all her heart and soul then he couldn't continue to live half a life. It would ruin his career. And she knew he understood how important that was. But here he was. Making this one last effort so he could hold her hand in a compartment of strangers. Wanting to prove he was there for her even when she had not chosen him.

A raw and primitive grief overwhelmed her. Her throat ached with defeat. Ayesha wanted to laugh her pain out. Wasn't it funny. The people whom we consider family sometimes remain strangers in our lives. And the people who walk in and stroll out hold such a significant place that we can never forget them. Harshvardhan had changed her life. She knew he would be a part of her forever. She knew she would love him till the day she died. And yet she needed to fulfill her duties to the world. To her society…to her huband…to her parents. She was a dutiful housewife. There was no alternative.

As the last stop arrived, he turned and kissed her on her lips, a kiss that lingered for a few seconds and felt like tiny drops of heaven on her mouth. She opened her eyes as he got up and left the compartment, not looking back at her as she sat alone in the train for several minutes. She sat crying her heart out, not caring what any passenger thought of her. She felt alone and desolate. She knew this was the end of a great romance. And she needed to head back to the grim reality of her life.

The train started again to go back to where it had started.

But Ayesha knew she could never go back to where it all began. She would always remember the last train ride she took with Harshvardhan. It would be seared into her memory forever. It would be the last metro ride she took for a long time.

38

'You can't leave me!' Kaajal screamed at Kaushik. 'You can't!'

Kaushik hung his head. He didn't know what to say. He had booked a hotel room one last time to be with Kaajal and to tell her that he couldn't continue seeing her and that he was staying with his wife.

'Kaajal…,' Kaushik started but had no words. He was stuck between two women. He honestly had no idea what to do. On the one hand he wanted to stand by his wife, who he had loved dearly and who had given him two children. Yet he also wanted to be with the woman he loved now. The confusion was gnawing at his insides. He had spent two days with his children and not questioned Naina about where she had gone. She couldn't be having an affair. That was not like her. She had been wild in her time but she had always been loyal. He had betrayed her and now he didn't want to see her hurt. Oh, his head was spinning from all this. Why did relationships have to be so confusing?

Kaajal had tears rolling down her cheeks. She had presumed he would tell his wife he was leaving her and that he'd be with her. She hadn't told him about the incident with Gaurav. But after that she knew she didn't want to be alone. Not for now. Maybe later, when she was stronger.

'Do you love me, Kaushik?' Kaajal asked to which Kaushik took her hand, made her sit in the chair that was adjoining the bed and kneeled in front of her.

'I love you with all my heart, Kaajal. I'm just fucked up.'

Kaajal slapped him hard across the face. Kaushik was stunned. He sat back on his haunches as he held his face with his hand. He was getting the wrath of two women. He supposed he deserved it. But what Kaajal said next truly shocked him.

'Then why can't you stand up to your wife and be with me?' she asked with defiance, her tears drying up as thoughts formed hard and fast in her head. 'Tell her that you need a divorce. Tell her you love me.'

'I can't, Kaajal. Why can't you understand? She'll take the children away from me.' Kaushik was wondering if they would ever use the hotel bed that lay pristine clean. He was paying seven thousand rupees a night for this hotel room and if Kaajal didn't want to say a final goodbye to him then that money would go to waste.

'Do you want a life with me, Kaushik?'

Kaushik got up and sat on the bed, the red mark from her slap burning into his cheek. 'Yes I do. But…'

'There is no but!' she interrupted him. 'I will handle this then.' She got up and grabbed her purse.

'Where are you going, Kaajal?' Kaushik asked, hoping she would just come and have sex with him so he could feel happy with life.

'I'll be back. Wait here.' She stormed off. Kaajal was determined to see this relationship through. She couldn't give up on it. She had spent two years with this man. Just because he was scared to confront his wife didn't mean she couldn't. She needed to cancel out all possibilities. She wasn't a woman who had any regrets. It was because she took all steps possible to make her dreams happen. She had fought hard right from birth to not be a burden on her family. She had fought hard to get this job, and to find the man of her dreams. She had to fight one last battle to know if all of this was going to collapse or if it was meant to be.

Kaajal flagged down an auto outside the hotel and gave the driver the address to Kaushik's house. She wanted to see Naina. She had to know if Naina still loved Kaushik or not. And she needed to fight for her man.

39

As the auto took Kaajal to Kaushik's house, she pondered why Indian society remained highly judgemental against women. If a woman desired sex she was a wanton tramp. If she had an affair with a married man, society would blame only her, not the man. If she was sexual, aggressive, spoke her mind, wore short skirts, showed her cleavage or argued with men, she was called 'loose'. And if she ever went to ask for her man's love instead of the other way around, she would be slapped in the face. Unfair!

But Kaajal was prepared for the worst. She knew where Kaushik lived. She had gone to his place when Naina wasn't there. She didn't want to but Kaushik had insisted, saying that staying in hotels was becoming too expensive and the lust between them had only increased with the years. He had said there would never be a problem. The maids all went to sleep in the servant quarters and Naina was out for the entire night with the kids at her mother's place. It was the perfect time for them to relax at home. Kaajal remembered marveling at Naina's sense of keeping house.

The large drawing room with big colourful sofas and oil paintings on the wall. The cozy bedrooms for the children and the elegant master bedroom for her and Kaushik. Kaajal never wanted to make love in Kaushik's marital bed. So she stayed out of the bedroom. Instead they used the guest bedroom and the living room. She was playful. Kaushik loved that about her. She often wondered if he would be happy just staying with her, a woman who couldn't decorate, cook, or become a housewife.

Kaajal shook her head and gathered her courage as she rang Naina's doorbell. A maid came to the door and showed Kaajal inside the house, presuming that she was Memsahib's friend.

Naina came into the drawing room and froze. She had been playing with her children in their room when the maid had called her, 'Keera memsahib aayi hain.'

Naina knew exactly who she was. How dare she enter this house! She needed to confront her nemesis and give her a piece of her mind. She walked out, ready to scream at Kaajal. She found Kaajal standing in front of a painting instead of sitting down and waiting for her. Naina felt emboldened. She should be sorry for what she did. Stealing her husband. The cheek of the woman.

As soon as Kaajal heard Naina enter, she turned. The speech she had prepared disappeared. Her confidence dissipated. And she felt as if she should not have come. What a stupid act, Kaajal thought. Who ever did such a stupid thing? She had known Kaushik was married. Why did she think he would leave his wife for her? No one ever did. That was an urban myth. So why was she here?

'That's a beautiful painting,' Kaajal heard herself saying.

Naina nodded, forgetting her plan to trash her husband's mistress. 'It was the first thing I bought in India when we returned. We lived in a much smaller house. We only had a gadda and that painting.'

Kaajal sat down on the sofa and felt even more miserable. Kaushik and Naina had shared so many memories together. She only had memories of lust with Kaushik. She looked up at Naina and said what she felt from the heart, 'I'm sorry.'

Naina sighed. 'You know, I've always heard of stories of men straying. I never thought it would happen to me. I always thought that it would be the man's fault when an affair happened. Women and us housewives always blame the men. But it's not true. The man is a stupid creature. It is always the woman who seduces a man. A man looks at every pretty thing that passes by. It is only the woman who responds to any of a man's gestures and then the affair begins. Wouldn't you say so?'

Kaajal looked at Naina. 'In those moments it's only lust that happens. Sparks of lust can initate an affair and when the sparks die the lust dies as well. That's why you need to know if there is any love involved.'

Naina sat opposite Kaajal. 'Would you like some tea or coffee?'

Kaajal shook her head. 'Just water, please.'

Naina went to get her a glass of water. Kaajal almost had a feeling that she would pour it over her head but instead Naina graciously served it to her and sat back down on the sofa.

'Kaushik and I love each other,' Naina told Kaajal in a cold voice, even though a part of her had doubts. 'We are husband and wife. We've taken vows and made a commitment to our families as well. You will just be a blip on the scene. I suggest you apologize to me and leave. And never come back or try to bed my husband again.'

Kaajal hung her head. She would have done exactly what Naina asked except an inner voice told her that she was a fighter. She needed to speak her heart before she left. 'I'll do that, Naina. But I want to say something. May I?'

Naina nodded. She was willing to hear her out. Maybe she could use it later against Kaushik. Maybe it would make her affair with Arjun palpable to her mind.

'The thing is, Kaushik did love you. You were everything

to him. And he does love the girls.' Kaajal swallowed a deep sob before continuing, 'But he loves me now. You can ask him. He truly wants to be with me. He doesn't want to be married. He is unhappy, Naina. And staying married to you is making him unhappy.'

'How dare you,' Naina hissed, trying to keep her voice low. She was getting uncomfortable with the cold truth that Kaajal was speaking.

'Please let me finish. And then you can kick me out and I'll never bother the two of you again. Kaushik is motivated and driven when I'm with him. He's a great lawyer. He's meant to do great things and we help each other in our career. We're good for each other. But...because he is married to you he will stay with you. He will stay with you forever because he's committed to you. He's told me he can't be with me, Naina. Because he can't leave you. Even though he loves me.'

Naina was shocked. She hoped her two children wouldn't come out of the room to see this woman. Never in her wildest dreams did she think she would be consoling her husband's lover. She gave her another glass of water and Kaajal dried her tears as she spoke further.

'Sometimes we fall out of love with people. Does it mean we must stick to them forever?'

'That's what marriage is!'

'Is it only about being committed and unhappy?'

'No, it's about working through the unhappiness and letting time solve the problems.'

'What if you can't wait for time to solve the problems and you want to take destiny into your own hands?'

'Then you need to find an alternative.'

Kaajal summoned up all her courage for her next few words. 'Here's the alternative, Naina. Let Kaushik go. Let him come to me. Let him be free. Let him meet his children whenever he wants. You can take as much money as you want from him. Just don't bind him to yourself, this house and this marriage because you fear society.'

Naina felt sad and angry at the same time. 'I do not fear society.'

Kaajal asked Naina the same question she had asked Kaushik, 'Do you love him? Like really madly, passionately, can't live without him, love?'

Naina thought about it for a moment while Kaajal continued. 'If you don't, why do you want him to be unhappy in a place that he's not getting that. Why do you not want his happiness? He will love and respect you more if you let him follow his path than make him follow a choice he took so many years ago. People change. Destinies change. We have more choices. Aren't we allowed to seize them? Aren't we as human beings allowed to feel happy and complete at any age?'

Naina had always loved Kaushik. She had never envisioned a life without him. She had two beautiful daughters who looked like their father. What would she tell her parents, her friends, the help, even? She couldn't let Kaushik go so easily from her heart. She needed time to think. She needed to figure out what to do.

Naina said one thing to Kaajal, 'If you've finished what you needed to say, you can leave.'

Kaajal picked up her bag and got up. She looked at the painting again and said, 'I can never take away the memories you have with Kaushik. You'll always be the most important person in his life. You're the mother of his children. All I can be is a source of happiness for him. It truly is a lovely painting.'

Kaajal walked out of the main door as Naina watched her go. She knew Kaajal was right. But her heart was breaking into a million pieces. She took a pillow and cried into it, her

stomach in knots from the conversation she had just had. She
felt anger and sadness all at once. Naina got up from the sofa
and walked towards the painting. She removed it from the
hooks behind it. And with a fanatical, intense strength she
threw it on the ground and smashed it beyond recognition.

3 YEARS LATER

40

'Yeh kya hai?' Simran asked, as she looked around the table. The group was sitting at a new place in Hauz Khas Village.

Naina brought over a plate of naan before she sat next to her friend, 'Yeh butter chicken hai, Simran. Specially tere liye banaya hai chef ne.'

Simran held Naina's cheek and squeezed it. 'Now I will only come to your restaurant. There's no need to go anywhere else any Monday!' She took a piece of naan, dug into the butter chicken, closed her eyes and said, 'Oh my God. Meri toh death hi ho gayi. Yeh iti achchi bani hai. Tu toh sachi main Masterchef hai.'

Naina laughed as the other girls dug into their plates. Naina asked them, 'Ishita, is your pasta okay? Gauri, is your grilled chicken nice?'

They couldn't speak as they had already stuffed their faces with food. Naina looked around and smiled. It had taken some time but she had pulled it off. Her very own restaurant. Heaven in a Bowl, a new concept of getting a bowl of your own favourite dish. An upper class Haldirams and an Olive combined. And she couldn't have done it without the help of the man in her life.

She looked around to see where he was. He was donning a chef's hat and bringing out her dish. Her favourite, a mushroom risotto.

'Here you go, Madam.'

Naina tested him, 'Without cream?'

'Yes, Madam.'

'With basil, thyme and a hint of rosemary?'

'Yes, Madam.'

'With wild mushrooms, not packaged ones?'

'Yes, Madam.' She took a bite out of it and it simply melted in her mouth. The risotto was divine. She looked up and said, 'I've trained you well, Chef Arjun.'

Arjun smiled and leaned down to kiss her on her lips, 'Always at your service, my lady.'

She giggled as the other girls looked at the couple and said in unison, 'Ooooooohhh.'

She was so thankful to have Arjun in her life. It had happened suddenly. Things had changed the very night Kaajal had come to see her all those years ago.

She had tested Kaushik at night when he had come home from the office tired but on time. She had asked him, 'Do you love me?'

He had replied, 'Sure.'

And then she knew. He didn't really love her. She had been forcing him to stay with her for so long. He had already moved on from this marriage but felt stuck.

'If I had an affair would that be alright? I mean, I guess we could call it even then and go on with life,' Naina said with her hands on her hips.

Kaushik looked at her and said in a resigned tone, 'I have no authority to speak. It's really your life.'

'A marriage is one life of two souls. It's giving each other space enough to come back to each other, not breaking away forever. But you've already made up your mind. Your answer should have been no because you would be horrified and if I did, you would never touch me again.'

'You know monogamy is really overrated,' Kaushik said.

Naina had laughed, 'Why is that?'

'Mammals weren't meant to be monogamous. They were meant to be free. It's humans who have created this idea of commitment and marriage and being faithful to one person. It's ridiculous.'

Naina had decided what to do then. She knew her marriage was over. She felt relieved. She smiled and told him, 'You know why two people choose to get into a marriage or make a commitment? It's because they know that they have two choices in the world. One, that they can sleep with as many people as they like all their life and never find happiness. Or that they have found someone that they love and they don't need to find another partner to sleep with. Because honestly, Kaushik, sex is sex. But love varies. If you don't have love, you won't have anything. But you can always buy sex.'

Naina had taken her children and walked out of the house the next day. She had explained to them that their parents were getting a divorce. She had met a lawyer and got child support and alimony from Kaushik. She could prove he was having an affair and that meant she had a pretty comfortable life. She put away all the money for her children and decided to start cooking classes and doing ads again. She plunged herself into work and her parents supported her. Kaushik's parents pleaded with her to stay with their son but she had only one thing to say to them, 'He has found someone else to make him happy. And I want to give him the freedom to be happy.' They stopped pleading after that.

She also started meeting Arjun often. They had a wonderful time together. She didn't ever mix up the families. She didn't meet his ex-wife or his daughter and she didn't let him meet her family. She didn't want to make it messy. Not until he proposed the idea to start a restaurant together. And so they did.

Heaven in a Bowl was a quaint place in Hauz Khas that catered individual dishes to customers. It served both Indian and Italian food in small individual bowls. So a Simran could have her butter chicken while someone else could have a pasta. There were a variety of dishes on the menu. Portions were for one person. It was an amazing idea that Naina had thought of and Arjun agreed to finance it immediately. She was now booked out for an entire month. Most women loved to come to her restaurant since it had lovely outdoor seating with plants and lanterns around and an indoor air-conditioned area with soft black and white decor. On one wall she had her children paint, colour and draw what they felt like. After all, this was as much their place as it was hers and Arjun's.

That's when her parents and children met him and his daughter. The girls got along so well that Naina felt it was ridiculous for her to have been apprehensive. Arjun asked her father for her hand in marriage. It had been an emotional moment. All the girls had been present, waiting with bated breath as he had slipped a three carat diamond ring on her finger. She had gasped and cried. Was love possible twice in one's life?

Arjun sat her children down and said, 'I never want to take your Dad's place. I just want to be your friend.' He had given both of them a tiny diamond ring as well. 'This is your kaleechadi. It means I promise to love you and be there for you always.'

They were just happy with their rings. Shonali, who was the elder child, had given him a hug and replied, 'I'm glad you will be my friend. As long as you make Mama happy, we're happy too.' But even though Naina had said yes to him, she had fended off the date of the marriage for some time. She liked the idea of being in a relationship without rushing off to legalize it. She had no time anyway, with the restaurant in full swing and managing her children's lives, which she was now able to do perfectly since Arjun had quit his job and was helping her manage the restaurant full-time.

'Dessert mein kya hai?' Simran asked, as she polished off the last bite of her butter chicken with naan.

Naina smiled as she got up to bring out an entire dessert cart. 'Yeh sab hai! Maine sirf tumhare liye banaya hai!'

The girls squealed, 'We love you, Naina.'

Naina was happy that Arjun and her new venture had taken off so well. He had supported her through her tough days when Kaushik had moved out and they had filed for divorce. He had encouraged her to get back to work. She was also thankful that she could tell her friends about her divorce and the new man in her life. Surprisingly, they did not judge her or speak ill of her decision. They simply supported her and when the restaurant opened, they were the first customers who came regularly and always paid, no matter how often Naina told them it was on the house. And they told all their other friends and every mom in their school now had kitty parties in Heaven in a Bowl.

Arjun had not only been great at managing the entire restaurant, but he had learned how to cook as well. So when they were short of waiters, chefs or a host, Arjun managed it all.

He told Naina, 'Remember I told you I wanted to just do one thing with my life? Well, I finally found what that was. I'm home.'

He spread his arms as Naina hugged him close. 'Do you want a quickie in the store room?' he whispered in her ear.

She looked around and saw her friends were busy chatting amongst themselves and wouldn't miss her. 'Yes, let's,' she said as she started unbuttoning his shirt.

She pulled him towards the store room, letting her hands slip to his ass, giving it a small squeeze. 'Move it already!'

Naina smiled. She knew how she could be wild again. All she needed was someone who would let her be everything she wanted to be, without judgement, without expectation, with tremendous love.

41

'Can you please fix this?' Kaajal stood in her shorts and shirt as she balanced a shower rod in the bathroom.

Kaushik entered and helped her. 'Why do you always leave these things for the weekend? The weekend is a time when we can just relax with each other.'

Kaajal slapped him across his face. 'Relaxing is for the weak. Now do as I say.'

Kaushik smiled. 'Yes, baby.'

Kaajal slapped him again, 'Yes, Mistress.' She enticed him with her eyes. She dragged him to the bed and pushed him on it.

'Handcuffs or tie?'

'Tie.'

Kaushik smiled as she tied him up. Their sex was still explosive and violent. Just the way he liked it.

When they were finally done and had taken a shower, they both got dressed in their business suits. Kaajal said, 'I'll have to apply make up to hide these bruises.'

'You bruise easily.'

'You play rough!'

'Let's stay at home and play another game then. Weekends are also meant to avoid clients,' Kaushik said drawing her close to him. 'You're the only woman I know who has guts, Kaajal. What did you do to have me in your life? I must be really special!'

Kaajal shoved him away playfully before responding, 'Thank

God I'm not married to you. You know I can find anyone else if you're mean to me right?'

Kaushik laughed, 'Thank God. I think marriage is for losers.' He took her in her arms as she protested, 'My suit will get crushed.'

He held her tightly and said, 'You're sure about this living together thing?'

Kaajal nodded, 'I've always been sure. Why do you keep asking me?'

'Because all women at some point want to get married and have children. They want security. Commitment. Monogamy.' Kaushik remembered his last conversation with Naina and how she had walked out on him. He had been so relieved.

Later, he had told his lawyer that he wanted access to the kids as often as possible and he would pay Naina a monthly sum till she got married and child support even after that. Naina had agreed and for most weekends he took his children to the park or to the movies but never brought them home to Kaajal as Naina had forbidden that. Kaushik knew about her restaurant and Arjun. They had had a massive fight about that and for a very long time couldn't see eye to eye. Then she just came around and one fine day they met for drinks and just forgave each other. Communication is always the easiest way out of misunderstandings and it takes time and space to make that communication possible.

Some days he wondered if life was meant to be different. What if they had never come back to India, would they have survived their marriage in the UK? Maybe not. People change the way they're meant to with time. It's who they are. It doesn't matter where they are. If he had never met Kaajal, he would probably have met someone else. He was never meant to be tied down. And yet here he was tied down to Kaajal in every sense of the word except with a license.

Kaajal looked at Kaushik as he got ready. She had never

imagined she would have the guts to do what she had done. When she left Naina's home she came back to Kaushik in the hotel room and told him that he needed to go home. They said their final goodbyes with tears in their eyes. He left knowing she had tried and she knew he was too good a man to ask for a divorce.

She spent the night in the hotel by herself, not knowing the calamity that was occurring at her own home. The next morning when she had gone back her mother told her what she had done. Kaajal was shocked at Gaurav's behaviour. But Gaurav had already left for Jaipur. Kavita had spoken to Vansh about moving to Mumbai. And that's when Kaajal told Kavita and her mother about how Gaurav had assaulted her. Kavita had been furious. She called Gaurav up and told him that his things would be shipped to Jaipur and the deal was off. Her mother would keep the house. And if he ever tried to tell anyone about her, she would tell Vansh what he had done to Kaajal.

Gaurav kept quiet and all he asked was that he could spend summer holidays with Vansh. Kavita agreed. She was ready to move to a new city and start her life over. And she was glad that Vansh would spend time with his father as well. Kaajal had said she would move with them. There was nothing left for her in Delhi. Until Kaushik had called.

'She's left me. I'm free,' Kaushik said and lit up Kaajal's world. 'Will you be my permanent girlfriend?'

Kaajal had tears in her eyes when she said, 'That's all I ever wanted.'

She told her mother and sister that she would stay in Delhi. She told them she had been dating a colleague and she needed to be in Delhi. She didn't tell them he was married and would soon be separated and divorced. One explanation at a time, she thought.

Kavita had pulled Vansh out of school after the year ended and packed up her things and left. Their mother had stayed in the big house with Kaajal until Kulwinder herself told her to go stay with the man she truly loved.

So Kaajal and Kaushik had been living together for almost three years. Several times Kaajal had been asked by her mother, Kavita and Kaushik, 'Don't you want to get married?'

And Kaajal had thought about it and replied, 'Not at all. I'm happy where I am. And with who I am. I don't need marriage to validate my happiness or my stature.'

'But won't you face legal issues with money and rent, in case you want to buy a house, etc?' Kavita had asked.

Kaajal had responded, 'I'm a lawyer. And a damn good one. I'll work it out!'

Kaajal felt liberated. She had never wanted to be like her sister. She had never felt pressured to get married or have children. She was focused on her career and she liked spending her money on herself. She saved for her future and she spent on things that were important to her. She was driven at work and ambitious with her life. She enjoyed Kaushik egging her on to do better and her ideas were what made Kaushik senior partner at their firm.

It was only recently that they had decided they would start their own firm. She suddenly had an idea. She gave him a tie and asked, 'This client is based in London, isn't he?'

Kaushik nodded.

'Then why isn't he getting a London firm?'

'They're dealing with Indians. They need an Indian partner. Why are you asking stupid questions? You know this. We've been meeting them for a month now.'

'What if we set up an office in London. Get more clients like them. Run an Indian office with Indian lawyers. Have a broader vision.' Kaajal was coming up with a very ambitious plan for both of them.

This was what Kaushik loved about her. She pushed him to do better and think harder. She was smarter than him and far more ambitious. He loved that about her. He had initially thought that their romance wouldn't last more than a few months. But it had now been four years.

How many times had she told her friends, 'I prefer living with someone to getting married. I love him. I understand him. And if we ever break up, there will be no legal mess. Marriage means that families get involved. And divorces means courts do. It's never about the two people involved. Commitment comes by choosing the person every day. Not by a legal contract. Love binds us. Lust binds us. And the fact that we make each other better means we're together today. Kal kya hoga, kisne dekha hai?'

Her mother had agreed in the beginning because she wanted her daughter to test the waters before getting married but even when she eventually asked Kaajal again about a wedding she stood her ground. 'Pyaar shaadi se pakki nahin hoti hai, Ma,' Kaajal had said. 'Pyaar dar se pakki hoti hai. If he's scared I'll leave him, he will not do anything to make me go. If I tie him to me, he will definitely run away.'

Kulwinder had ultimately given in. She had seen how well her children were doing with their own choices.

Kaajal loved the fact that Kaushik still lusted after her. What Naina had not been able to achieve, Kaajal had. When people say 'men don't change'? They're wrong. Men did change for the correct woman. They were more attentive, caring and understanding if you knew how to play the game right. And Kaajal was a master at the game. She hadn't been with anyone since she met Kaushik. But she didn't rule out the possibility of anything in her life.

The world was her oyster. She was ready to rule it.

'Are you coming, Kaushik? I'm driving!' She grabbed the car keys from the corner-table in their lovely apartment and raced ahead of him.

Kaajal had found bliss.

42

Kavita was in her scrubs while Sara was lying in the operation theatre with beads of perspiration encircling her face.

'Come on Sara, push!' Kavita said, as the baby's head crowned.

'I can't,' Sara groaned. She was tired. It had been eighteen hours and she was about to murder someone. Kavita coaxed, 'I promise, one more push and I'll do night duty for the entire month.'

Sara almost laughed but nodded. Kavita looked at her partner and marveled at how far they had come. Life had completely changed in the last three years.

Kavita had resigned from AIIMS and settled in Mumbai with Vansh. They had taken a lovely two-bedroom place in Khar West somewhere close to Sara's clinic. Kavita had joined Sara at work and the clinic had just taken off. With two world-class gynaecologists at the helm of great new beginnings, Kavita and Sara became popular in no time. Soon they had clients from all over the world and eventually started another branch in Andheri West.

Kavita rarely missed her life in Delhi. She adapted to Mumbai like a fish to water. Vansh found it difficult at first, as he missed his old friends, naturally. But he soon found his ground and spread his wings, soon excelling in cricket and finding friends and peers who respected and liked him. He would later tell his Mom that he was happy in Mumbai. He still missed his maasi and grandmother but they visited often and Kavita made sure that they went back to Delhi every opportunity they got until she started sending him alone as well. Vansh also visited his father during his holidays.

When Kavita first introduced Sara to Vansh and her mother, she had used the word 'friend'. And soon, Sara became a fixture in their lives. Soon enough Sara expressed her desire to have a child. And Kavita agreed Vansh should have a sibling, finally. But Kavita refused to go through labour again and so Sara said she would get IVF treatment done. Vansh was ecstatic with the news that he would be a big brother. Kavita hadn't figured out how she would manage two clinics at the same time. Sara had insisted that she would take the baby to the clinic and manage. She would not give up on her dream and work as a doctor. Kavita had simply told her to take it easy for a few months while she did all the heavy lifting.

'Okay, here comes the baby,' Kavita said as Sara gave one last push. Kavita took their baby in her arms and both mothers burst into tears. 'She's beautiful!' Sara exclaimed.

Kavita cleaned up the baby and brought her to Sara's breast so she could feed on her mother's colostrum. She then took the baby away again to show Vansh and her mother, as well as Sara's parents, who were all eagerly waiting outside the labour room.

'Mama, is that Laila?' Vansh asked excitedly as he saw the baby.

'Yes, baby. Laila Imam Kaur. Your baby sister.'

Kulwinder gave Kavita a tight hug. 'I'm so proud of you. I've always wanted a granddaughter. I will be eternally thankful to Sara.'

As Sara recuperated, in the evening Kulwinder gave her, as per custom, a gold set of earrings and a necklace. 'For you,

beti. For the immense gift you've given all of us.' Sara was
touched. Maybe Kavita and she would never get married but
to be accepted by Kavita's mother was a blessing. She knew
relationships weren't defined by society. They're defined by
how you feel for a person. Whether she was married or not,
Sara knew she had a wonderful mother-in-law.

'Hi, Sara Aunty,' Vansh asked quietly as he came into the
room to see her.

'Come, baby,' Sara said. 'Did you see your sister?'

Vansh nodded as Kavita followed him with Laila close to
Sara.

'She's the most beautiful girl in the world,' Vansh said.

Sara smiled. She had never thought she would have a
family. She felt fortunate that Kavita and her family had
accepted her. She could finally claim to be a 'housewife'.

Kavita smiled, looking around the room. Maybe this was
the way it was supposed to be. Maybe some relationships
aren't meant to be conventional. A mother, a father, and two
children don't always make up the 'perfect family'. Maybe
relationships needed to redefine themselves and society needed
to be more accepting of the new definitions of the old
concept of a family.

Maybe housewives weren't always women who did nothing
with their lives. They were the ones who could accept any
role given to them. And they needed to be proud of that.

43

'Humara neta kaisa ho? Harshvardhan jaisa ho!'

The crowd went crazy as Harshvardhan came on the podium to make his inaugural speech. He was at Rashtrapati Bhavan where millions had gathered to hear their Prime Minister speak.

After a tumultuous three years, Harshvardhan had risen to the top to rightfully claim his place as India's 15th Prime Minister. It had taken some time and he had had to fight a grueling election but he had always been focused and driven to succeed. He took a deep breath before he climbed the stage. For a moment the woman he loved flashed in his mind as she had always done before any important event. Even though they had not stayed in touch, she had been his guiding light, always in his thoughts, goading him, chiding him, comforting him when he needed her. She was and would always be his love. How he missed her today.

Harshvardhan smiled and began, 'I am a firm believer in God. I am a firm believer in this nation. I am a firm believer in empowering women and that will be my first order as Prime Minister. I will make sure that each and every woman in this country will have freedom, independence and financial security. That each housewife will have power and that there will be safety and security for every woman. So help me, God.'

The crowd erupted with delight and clapped as chants started. He paused before continuing his speech.

'Can you make it louder?' Ayesha asked Varun as they sat at home in Lucknow watching the speech.

Varun turned up the volume. 'Where are the children?'

Ayesha turned to take her daughter in her arms. 'Mia was right behind me, holding on to my sari. You naughty little girl.' There was a huge age difference between her two children but when she had told Adi that she was having a child, he had been ecstatic. It was Adi and not Varun who had helped Ayesha in the early days of Mia's birth. He had helped with the nappies and put her to sleep while Varun had gone to play golf and supposedly 'network' to get better promotions. But he never had. Now their tenure in Lucknow was ending and it was almost time to head back to Delhi. The packing would start again. But this time Ayesha was looking forward to it. She had a reason to go back.

Adi came into the room and asked his mother, 'Mama, can I go to play at Dhruv's house?' He picked up his baby sister in his arms and said, 'Cutie. I love you.'

Mia laughed and pulled her elder brother's hair. Ayesha scolded her children, 'Mia, don't pull Bhaiya's hair! Adi, no you cannot go. It's time for lunch. And everyone keep quiet. I'm watching this.'

Harshvardhan continued, 'In keeping every woman safe, we build a safe nation. In keeping every woman secure, we keep families secure. In strengthening every woman's financial security, we build India as a financially secure country.'

'I can't believe we had gone to his house so many years ago,' Varun said as he looked at the TV. Then he got up and said, 'Chalo anyway, this is too boring. I'm off for golf. I'll see you in the night.' He called out to the kids, 'Bye kids!' He left without a hug, a kiss or even asking for approval from his wife, who was left watching the television alone and managing a house by herself, as she had been doing for so many years.

Ayesha hardly cared. She was now beyond concern for her husband. After Mia was born her whole world had been to look after this child. She saw Adi take Mia to play in her room. Thankfully, her daughter looked like her. Otherwise she would have quite some explaining to do. It was after she had started bleeding that she had decided to keep the baby. Kavita had sent an ambulance that took Ayesha away from the paparazzi and securely in a stretcher to the hospital.

She had asked Ayesha, 'Now is the time to decide, Ayesha. Either I can remove it, or you can keep it.'

Ayesha had closed her eyes and prayed. The only face she had seen was Harshvardhan's and his words had rung in her ears. *I'm with you, for you, always.*

Harshvardhan continued his speech as Ayesha stared into the TV screen scrutinizing him closely. He had greyed a little more and got a bit of a paunch. She wondered if he was eating correctly with the campaign stress taking over his health. He was smiling, but she knew there was something missing. How she had missed him every single day of her life.

It was as if he had never left her. She had remembered him when she had Mia. She had named her baby after Mother Mary and Mia meant 'my own'. She knew that was something he would have appreciated. She poured over the newspapers as she saw him grow from strength to strength in his party. She watched every news channel at night to hear him speak. She prayed for his success as she watched his daughter grow up. And she prayed to Mother Mary to forgive her for keeping this secret from her family and from the man she loved.

Ayesha knew that some loves weren't meant to happen in this lifetime. They were meant to show you who you could be. And Ayesha had only become stronger as a person with Harshvardhan in her life. Besides being a great mother, she had also started a safety and security group for women in Lucknow that personally went to look after women. They would meet government leaders and make sure that streets were well lit, that eve-teasers were punished, that women had the freedom to go where they wanted without feeling repressed and embarrassed by what they wore. Ayesha was in several press articles about the improvement in Lucknow and she always kept her face and her children out of the news. She knew she needed to follow in Harshvardhan's footsteps of helping women but had to do so discreetly.

It had been three years. They hadn't exchanged a word. She had missed him. So many nights she had wondered how she could manage it all. Varun was no help. He often told her, 'Yeh sab kya kar rahi ho? Mummy Papa ko bilkul pasand nahin hai. Don't you have enough work on your hands with two kids?'

Ayesha found strength from somewhere. No matter how tired she was, she would still manage a house, look after her children and be a counsellor for women who were harassed. She had delegated her household duties to Savitri, who looked after the two children, beautifully, like they were her own, leaving Ayesha the time to do other things.

Once Ayesha's parents had come for a Diwali party and had seen Varun gambling. Her father had mentioned to Ayesha that he was upset. For the first time in her life, Ayesha had not defended her husband. She realized that people needed to see each other without the shield of an opinion. Ayesha had been making excuses for Varun all her life. When her parents started seeing how much golf he played or how Ayesha was managing everything by herself, they were shocked. They began to be more supportive of her choices and helped her whenever she needed them to be around for the children.

Ayesha had tears in her eyes as she saw the man she loved

become the prime minister. Her sacrifice had been worth it. It had been terrible for him to shrug off the image that he was having an affair. But he had done so and protected her fiercely. *That* was true love.

Harshvardhan came to the conclusion of his speech, 'Believe in me. Believe in the nation. Believe in every woman around you.'

Ayesha remembered that day at the hospital. She had whispered. 'Yes, I want the baby. Please save her. Please save our baby.'

I'm with you, for you, always. She heard it then. And she knew he said it for her now.

'*Be safe. Be happy. I'm with you, for you, always,*' Harshvardhan said as he looked into camera.

Ayesha had tears rolling down her cheeks. Mia was going to turn three soon. It was time she spoke the truth. She had always been a simple housewife, hiding behind the facade of family and home. She had been the strength for her children. Now she needed to be the strength for the man she loved.

She picked up her phone and sent a message to Harshvardhan: *I'm here.*

He called her an hour later as she slept next to Mia. 'Hello?' He spoke with great trepidation, almost a whisper, 'Ayesha? I'm so happy you sent me a message.'

Ayesha smiled as she looked down at Mia, 'Hello Harsh. Congratulations!'

'Ayesha, my love…'

'I'm so happy to hear your voice, Harsh.'

'And I'm over the moon, Ayesha.'

'I think it's time we met.'

EPILOGUE

3 and a half year back. When it all began…

Pinky could always spot a newcomer at these key chain parties. They were the ones who were dragged by their friends to 'try something new'. They were also the ones who didn't want to mingle too much and stuck to the kitchen, eating something so as not to have the need to make even polite conversation.

She found an extremely attractive older man at the dining table with a plate of food in front of him.

'Hi,' she said, as she offered her hand.

'Hi,' he said, wiping his hand on a napkin and stretching it out to her.

'I'm Pinky.'

'I'm not available.'

Pinky laughed. 'You're not my type.'

He put a hand on his heart and said, 'Thank God. I hate these parties.'

'Why?'

'Because I'm an old-fashioned guy.'

'Then what are you doing here?'

He smiled. 'Oh this is my farmhouse. My brother and his lovely wife wanted to host this party here. But about an hour ago he told me this was going to be a key chain party. And I didn't even know what it meant.'

'Well now do you know?'

He offered her a plate of food and she declined, taking a sip of her vodka with orange juice.

'I know that all the men's car keys are put in a bowl and all the wives pick out a set of keys. Whichever man it belongs to goes home with them. Or if they don't have a place to go, they are allowed to use any of the five bedrooms in this house.'

'You have five bedrooms? That's astonishing!'

'You think that's the astonishing part of this conversation? Did you not hear about the wives going off with different men?'

'Oh come on,' Pinky laughed. 'You'll get used it.'

'Strange people doing it in your bedroom? Or the fact that they're not married to each other?'

'Stop being so old-fashioned,' Pinky said. 'It brings excitement into a relationship. And no one is forcing you to drop your keys into that bowl. And no woman is forced to pick up the keys either. All the couples understand the concept so it's not as if it affects them later.'

He looked at her and knew she had done this before. 'How many times have you picked up another man's keys from a bowl?'

'Oh, a few. It's been interesting. But if someone truly repulses you, you can easily feign a headache and just sleep. Or you can pretend to be so drunk that you slap him or pass out or both!'

He laughed. 'I've never been slapped. I don't think I would like it. I've never done the dating bit. I felt like my brother and his wife had such a healthy relationship. And now I see this happening. I wonder if they're headed for a divorce or if this is the new definition of marriage.'

Pinky took the chair next to him. 'You really are old-

fashioned. Yahan baitho! Main samjhati hoon. Marriages are
tricky. After ten years, you get bored with each other. The
same sex, the same face, the same conversations. There is no
excitement left. But you stay together for the sake of the kids.
Izzat. Society. Families. Yeh sab to chahiye na zindagi mein?
The husband looks after your needs and gives you the dignity
of being a married woman because society is still so regressive
about single women and divorced ones, toh baap re. Divorce
is desh mein toh tauba tauba! The wife gives the husband love
and care but the sparks die. This is a fresh way to ignite that.
Sometimes the sparks come out because of jealousy and
revenge. Sometimes the sparks die altogether and you're just
comfortable with the fact that the spouse is happy. And
sometimes one finds sexual liberation through this. You try
different things. You remain excited, interested and it helps
your creativity! I run a parlour, by the way. Pinky's Parlour.
Best parlour in New Delhi. Ask me why? Because sex fuels
my drive to succeed. Trust me, when your soul and body are
happy, you are a better person in your relationships with
others.'

'And someone else can fulfill that? Why don't you just
have an affair?'

Pinky nodded. 'Affairs are messy. You've given your life
to a spouse. You don't want to have an affair behind his back.
You want to be honest sometimes and you know your spouse
is the one who will always protect you. So why would you let
go of that? It's kinky but it's logical.'

The man shook his head. Pinky could almost see him
shiver with repulsion. 'This is not for me,' he said. 'I'm going
to go for a walk in my lawns. It was nice meeting you. I hope
you find a great key chain tonight.'

Pinky laughed. 'How about I fix you up with someone?
Like a regular date?'

The man shrugged his shoulders. 'Would it be a wife like one of these?' he nodded his head towards the drawing room where the party was in full swing, with a DJ in his element and couples gyrating on the dance floor, half drunk.

Pinky shook her head. 'No not like this. Something simpler. Through a course or something. Hey, do you know how to cook?'

'A little. Why?'

'How about you take some cooking lessons? It's a great way to impress the women.'

He pondered the thought. 'That's a good idea. Your name was…?'

'Pinky. Here's my number.'

'I'm Arjun,' he said, grinning. 'Thank you. For a lovely conversation. Have a great evening. Good night.'

'Good night.'

Arjun shook her hand and walked out into his garden wondering if he would ever find a woman again who was normal. Pinky sat at the counter and finished her drink, watching the man walk out. She looked down at her phone and kept a reminder for what she needed to do the next morning, 'Fix Naina with Arjun!'

She smiled. The plot of this story was already forming in her head.

44

Pinky was sitting at home when she got a phone call from her brother. Very few people knew she had a sibling. It was a secret that she had kept hidden from the world.

'Haan, Bhaiya,' she said as she picked up the phone. 'Kya haal hain?'

'Tum kya kar rahi ho?' Pinky's brother asked.

'Kuch nahin. How are you?'

Her brother sighed. 'I miss spending time with my nieces and nephew. When will you bring them over?'

Pinky smiled. 'You know it becomes difficult. I've always wanted to protect them from the public eye. You come over here when you're free from work this weekend. They'll love to see you. Waisey bhi London toh hum sab ja hi rahein hain this summer?'

'Yes yes. But suno, I need some new fresh perspective about my campaign. Any ideas?'

Pinky thought about it. No one knew that she was behind her brother's success. She had guided him and advised him correctly about his moves so far and he had become the new HRD minister in the cabinet. 'Harsh bhaiya, I think you should throw a party for all the bureaucrats. Call all the wives. Get a new female's perspective and start focusing on how to make women stronger and safer in this country? You'll get many votes and you'll be the most loved politician ever.'

'You're really brilliant, Jaishree!'

'Please! Mujhe woh mat bulao.'

'Tumhara asli naam hai. The one our parents gave.'

'You're the only one who calls me that. And no one even knows that name. I like being Pinky. The silly, stupid beautician with a small parlour and a complicated life.'

'I'm always there for you, Jaishree.'

Pinky smiled. 'I know, Harsh bhaiya.'

'Will you come to the party?'

'No. You know there will be too many reporters and too many questions.'

'I know. I wish I could see you more, though.'

'I would have to have police protection. My children would come under scrutiny. And I would never be able to enjoy the simplicity of the life that I have now. Being a politician was your decision. And I support you. And one day I know you'll become the Prime Minister. And then you'll need me more because the only place you'll be safe will be here in my house, with me. Until then, I would like to go to eat in a restaurant and wear what I want without the media after me.'

'I love you, Pinky,' Harshvardhan said. He understood how protective his sister was of her family.

'One more thing. You must talk to Ayesha Mathur. She's this insipid man, Varun Mathur's, wife. She will give you a new perspective if you ask her for her opinion.'

Harshvardhan knew that his sister had always wanted him to get married and settle down. And she had been recommending women to him for years. However, they had always been too boring or too ambitious for him.

'Married?'

Pinky smiled. 'Things can easily be changed in today's world, Harsh. Speak to her about your political views. Nothing else.'

'What if she doesn't come?'

'Oh, she will.'

Harshvardhan laughed. 'Why do you like doing this, Pinky? These set ups? These games?'

Pinky looked at her perfectly-manicured fingers. 'Because I like to see how ordinary people behave when they're given extraordinary chances.'

She put the phone down and thought about what Harsh had just said. People thought it was destiny and coincidence when things happened in their lives. Little did they know that it was all planned. All it took for people to behave in a certain way was a little push to make them believe whatever they were doing was right. And Pinky knew her friends would thank her later for setting them up and being like their puppet master.

She smiled wickedly. Let the games begin.

The End.